# Wonders
# Never Cease

## Phil Callaway

HARVEST HOUSE PUBLISHERS

EUGENE, OREGON

*Cover by Left Coast Design, Portland, Oregon*

*Cover photo © Stuart McClymont/Taxi/Getty Images*

**WONDERS NEVER CEASE**
Copyright © 2005 by Phil Callaway
Published by Harvest House Publishers
Eugene, Oregon 97402
www.harvesthousepublishers.com

Library of Congress Cataloging-in-Publication Data
 Callaway, Phil, 1961–
 Wonders never cease / Phil Callaway.
     p. cm.
 ISBN–13: 978-0-7369-0777-4
 ISBN–10: 0-7369-0777-7 (pbk.)
 1. Teenage boys—Fiction. 2. Montana—Fiction. I. Title.
 PS3603.A446W66 2005
 813'.54—dc22                                                           2005004957

**Printed in the United States of America**

05  06  07  08  09  10  11  12  13  / BP-CF /  10  9  8  7  6  5  4  3  2  1

## Hear what people are saying
## about *Wonders Never Cease…*

"Stunning and powerful. Callaway has woven an unforgettable mystery, rich in humor and redemption."

Lee Strobel
author of *The Case for Christ*

"Callaway spins a fascinating tale of love and mystery, all in the context of searching for faith. His humor shines through and makes the story come alive with all the humanity and honesty we've come to expect from him. A good read—a fun read. I highly recommend it."

Wayne Holmes
author of *The Heart of a Father* and *Whispering in God's Ear*

"Full of surprises and complex characters, *Wonders Never Cease* will touch your heart and linger on your mind. It traces how faith can survive when prayers don't work, God doesn't show up, and Christ's followers seem to do everything but follow Him. Phil Callaway has a two-fold gift from God, and he is using it. First, this novel is ample evidence that he can write. Second, he has wonderful insights into human nature and what God can do with that nature. Or in spite of it."

Stanley Baldwin
author of *Love, Acceptance, and Forgiveness*
and *A Funny Thing Happened on My Way to Old Age*

"Phil Callaway is one of those rare authors who successfully integrates humor into books that are both significant and worthwhile. In *Wonders Never Cease,* his method is simple, but his message is profound. Read this book and you'll be ambushed by the significant message that happily lurks within. You'll also find yourself laughing at life again—and learning too. A recommended read, not only for those of us who throw a baseball for a living, but for all who laugh too little and worry too much."

Chris Reitsma
pitcher for the Atlanta Braves

"Phil Callaway is one of the funniest Canadians I've ever met, yet his humor comes with a purpose. Few writers can weave such deep truths into so much humor and suspense. The only thing wrong with this page-turning mystery is that it is too short."

Martha Bolton
author of more than 40 books
including *Cooking With Hot Flashes*

# Reader praise for
## *The Edge of the World*

—m—

"I just finished *The Edge of the World*, and it is now my all-time favorite! The way Phil handled hypocrisy and true love absolutely warmed my heart. I have a hard time getting my teenagers to read, and yet every time they heard me laugh out loud, they came running and asked to hear more. I am anxiously waiting to read more about Terry—I love that kid!"

Susie Larson

"Callaway delivers laugh-out-loud humor à la Tom Sawyer through the first-person voice of a young boy caught in a high-stakes moral dilemma."

Romantic Times Book Club

"I laughed and cried all the way through *The Edge of the World*, identifying with so much of this book. More importantly, the message about church and the lessons learned by this little congregation of people is so awesome. This novel shows us that we can admit we have sin in our lives and still be received with open arms."

Becky Schatz

"My wife is normally the great reader of novels in our house, but when Phil Callaway writes a sequel to *The Edge of the World*, I will be among the first to purchase it. This book was filled with his trademark humor, suspense, a variety of characters, and some great life lessons."

Dan Goldsmith

"I absolutely loved this book and I can't wait for the sequel!"

Karen Taylor

"This is one of the best novels I have read in a long time! I was encouraged and found it thoroughly enjoyable."

Martin Whitbread

"Like Terry Anderson, I know what it is like to sit in a hospital room, seeing my Dad hooked up to a variety of machines…I know what it's like to have a praying father, who came to my room every night. *The Edge of the World* brought back memories of the good times and the bad, memories I never want to lose. Reading this book did something for me I do not fully understand, but there is a change in me, a positive, hopeful change."

Neil George

*In memory of my brother-in-law Dennis.*
*Twenty years with Huntington's.*
*An eternity with Jesus.*

# Body Found Near Three Tree Gap

By Jim Haverly
*Grace Chronicle staff writer*

**Grace, MT**—By all accounts the grisly tragedy is one of the worst in the history of this quiet village. Police confirm that a body was discovered Monday night on the outskirts of town. "We believe he was a drifter," said Sheriff Reginald Benson. "He died from a gunshot wound." The male in his mid-to-late fifties is as yet unidentified. Police would not comment further except to say that they are working with possible clues found near the body and have concluded it is likely a suicide. One anonymous source considers the body to be linked to a mystery long buried in this close-knit community. Police say the victim was initially discovered by a local teenager, a senior in high school, Terry Anderson.

# Preface

When I sat down to write my first novel, I had no way of knowing people would read it. My aspirations were meager, my expectations sparse. I remember a bookstore owner in southern Arkansas by the name of Amanda Petrie calling me to see if I would come to a book signing. I hesitated, of course. What would I do if no one showed up? Offer to vacuum carpets? Scrub the restrooms, man the till? The night before the signing, Amanda informed me she had ordered forty-four copies and this before I even knew the publisher had printed that many.

I shuddered.

Expectations aren't so great when they are someone else's.

I thought to myself, *Run for the hills. It's safer.* But the very next day people came by the carload, two of them entire home-school families with seven children each—on assignment, I suppose.

They asked me questions about what it's like to be an author, where I get my ideas, what I do with all the money and the spare time. I told them that writing is like having a good sneeze. You feel better when you're finished. They wrote my every word on slips of paper, so I gave them more. I told them that all writers are optimists, for who else would sit down with this much blank paper and only their minds to fill it? I said, "I write much because I am paid little," and they liked that. They liked contemplating my poverty. I told them that sometimes the garbage can is a writer's best friend, that writing a novel is like driving a car at night. You can't see very far, but you follow the lights.

I enjoyed the attention at first. It was intoxicating, like cheap perfume. People began tapping my shoulder in restaurants and nervously introducing themselves. "Hi, I read your book," they'd stammer. "I can't believe it's you. That book changed my life." What do you say to that? Thanks? It was no problem? My pleasure? They began stopping me on sidewalks to tell me the single most tragic event of their lives. "Hi, I'm Robert, and I just lost my job." "I'm Sarah, and I'm all alone now." I felt like a psychologist, listening to problems night and day but without compensation.

Oh, but there was compensation. Plenty of it.

The publisher began sending me large checks. At first I thought they were fake, like the ones from Reader's Digest Sweepstakes. I stood in line at the bank, trying to act nonchalant, and then I placed the first one on the counter and let out a low cough. It was for $17,143 and some odd cents. The bank cleared it. I waited two weeks before spending a penny, knowing I might be caught and jailed, and then I went out and bought a used Chrysler, a step up for me. I had over fifteen thousand dollars left. What ever would I do with it?

People found my phone number and called it.

I got an unlisted number.

People found my address and began driving long distances to talk with me. They knocked on my door and stood on the steps and told me of their childhoods. Of their failures, their sins—deep secrets they had told no one else. I advised them to share these intimate details with their minister. "He's tired of me," they said.

Fellow writers asked me to review their manuscripts and offer advice, or better yet, write a note of recommendation to a publisher of my choosing. I wrote them back: "This is great stuff; I'm sorry I have no time to read it." They printed the first part of my sentence on the covers of their books.

I stood in line with more checks, and they got bigger. I won't tell you how big. It's embarrassing. Friends who used to like me began to resent me. They saw me driving an even newer Chrysler, and they wanted to pop the tires and shoot out the headlights.

One day a man in a dark suit showed up. It was a slow day, so I invited him in to my living room, expecting to hear his problems. Instead he showed me his IRS card and said he was here to find out about my financial dealings, but that he had read my book and would I sign a first-edition copy before we talked about my taxes?

He glanced through a file with my name on it and shook his head. He said, "We've got a problem sir, a real big problem."

I squinted hard and asked, "What do you mean? I'm clean. I've paid my taxes. Talk to my accountant."

He seemed unconvinced. "I'll have to report this," he said, "unless…well…unless of course, you show me a few chapters of your new book."

I couldn't believe it.

I told him about writer's block. About my study that was littered with broken ideas and false starts. I told him that every time I sit at the keyboard, my fingertips go numb and my heart palpitates and I feel as if I'm suffering a stroke. I said that writing books is the hardest way of earning a living, with the possible exception of feeding alligators. I told him that I have suffered all my life from attention deficit disorder and that for a person with ADD, writing a novel is like trying to drive a golf cart down the interstate without being distracted by honking horns. I told him how my first book was written out of love, out of instinct, out of passion for the subject, but now all that was inciting me to literary labor was the profit, the bottom line, the almighty dollar. I told him that of all the enemies of great literature, success is the most menacing.

He said, "Why don't you tell the publisher you'll do it for free?"

I asked him to leave. I said, "Out!" I said, "Go ahead and slam the door."

He said, "You think about it."

And then he was gone.

I received a notice the next Thursday that I had been audited by the IRS and that I owed more than seventy-two thousand dollars, which just happened to be the exact amount of everything I owned. I wrote out a check the same day, and as I posted it, a tiresome burden lifted from my body. I was free. Unencumbered. Almost weightless.

I sat down that afternoon and began to write. My wife brought dinner to my study—roast chicken with spinach salad and Italian dressing. I didn't even notice. She said, "Honey, come to bed, I'd like to tell you something." I didn't even hear. I wrote through supper, through bedtime, and long into the night. By morning I had the first four chapters of what you are about to read. By mid-afternoon I didn't even need coffee to keep me awake. I was invigorated by the story. My wife sat beside me watching me work.

"Terry Anderson," she said, "you're not going to tell them what really happened, are you?"

I said I was.

She frowned, and then she smiled, and then she laughed out loud.

"You wouldn't," she said.

"Oh yes I would," I countered.

"But they won't believe you."

"That's okay. I'll tell them it's a novel. You can get away with things when it's a novel."

"Will you tell them about me?" She snuggled a little closer.

"Oh yes I will. If not in this book, maybe the next."

"You'll tell them everything?"

"Everything," I said.

And I did.

—◆—

*Home is a place you grow up wanting to leave,*
*and grow old wanting to get back to.*

JOHN ED PIERCE

—◆—

# one

# Greenhouse

The Missouri River drops sharply out of the Little Belt Mountains before snaking its way eastward like a frightened rattler. Five miles west of us, where the land flattens and the plains begin, it slows dramatically, branching off to form Franklin's Creek. The creek is shallow and lazy. Pronghorn antelope and desert reptiles sun themselves along its sandy banks. And by the time it reaches my hometown it has slowed to a crawl, like everything else around here.

To the east and north and south the big sky stoops to caress gently sloping wheat fields, sometimes stroking a wildflower or a grove of poplar trees. The Little Belt Mountains overlook the whole of my childhood, stretching with the horizon like silent sentinels, like friends. Beyond the lesser mountains loom the majestic Rockies, transparent and cloudlike. I sometimes wonder what lies to the west of them. Do they conceal mysteries that may intersect with my life one day?

The sleepy village of Grace rests within a rifle shot of the mountains—though most people here wouldn't know it. We are quiet, law-abiding citizens, minding our own business. If we discover that another's business is worth discussing, we will more than likely share it as a prayer request on Wednesday night at Grace Community Church. People here mean well. They are kind and decent folk who will stop when your tire is flat and drop off casseroles when your mother is sick.

If you spent a day here, or a week, or—heaven help you—a month, you would call us quaint, conservative, backward even. We wouldn't blame you. The town is split in two by the sluggish creek, and most of the Christians live on our side, apparently content to keep it that way. We attend our school, worship at our church, and as much as possible support our businesses. There are the rare exceptions of course, like the few who attend the Catholic church and shop at the Bargain Wearhouse, but we are told not to look down on them. While there's life, there's hope.

Back in the late fifties, when there were more bars than churches here, Pastor Francis Frank arrived from Alabama intent on launching his own sacred colony just a sharp glance away from the pagans. Why he didn't do this in Los Angeles or New York or even Seattle is anyone's guess. But no, Frank had to choose the middle of Nowheresville, Montana, to do the Lord's bidding. Why my parents joined him I'll never fully understand either, for Frank's legacy stands in sharp contrast to theirs. He was an advocate of dressing from twenty-year-old catalogs, and it caught on among his growing band of followers to the point where people began to look like they lived on the edge of the world and subscribed to the *Flat Earth Times* or something.

Not much has changed.

We are still characterized less by what we do than by what we refrain from, less by who we are than by what we look like. Drinking, smoking, and chewing tobacco are taboo, of course. So too are dancing, cards, movies, jazz, makeup, earrings, pool tables, and watching from behind gooseberry bushes as the girls swim.

Pastor Frank defected many years ago amid a rush of rumors, but not before leaving us the only book he ever wrote, *Practicing the Principals,* which despite the typo on the cover, pretty much described the drum he'd been pounding for two decades. The book was hardly a national bestseller. In fact, I think he only mimeographed fifty copies, but to this day those tattered copies have a way of resurfacing during arguments among the faithful.

Thanks a lot, Frank.

Lately there are rumors that our former pastor is back in the vicinity, living in some gated compound in the hills nearby. But rumors are more common than sagebrush around here, so I don't put much stock in them.

When I was a child of ten or twelve, Frank's endless list of prohibitions were more of a challenge than a problem. Truth is, I loved growing up here in the little town of Grace. You didn't need to engage in dangerous activities to be noticed, didn't need to pour gasoline on the school yard and set it ablaze to be a rebel. All it took was the flashing of a gap-toothed grin at the girl with perfect teeth across the eighth-grade classroom, and before you were fully aware of what was happening you were in the principal's office listening to a lengthy lecture on Pastor Frank's social regulations while scanning cheap wall decorations.

But by the time you reach my age, which is eighteen, *Practicing the Principals* is less a book than a millstone hanging about the neck of any able-bodied teenager hoping for just a glimpse of pleasure or laughter or normality.

Administrators at Lone Pine Christian School have designed matching handbooks to address every possible situation, and they are thicker than a liberal theologian's head, says my brother Tony. He should know, him studying to be a minister and all. "We've got more rules than baseball," he says. And we do. We have rules on hair length, sleeve length, appropriate music, and literature. We have rules for dating, dressing, driving, and doodling. It's enough to drive a teenager to drink, and for many of us it has.

The rules are fish bones; they stick deep in my throat.

They aren't easy for parents either. I am the youngest in this family of six, and I've noticed that Dad isn't so strict as he once was, likely because he's tired out from years of enforcing those rules. My older brothers used to ask, "Dad, do you mind if we go to the pool and soak?" and my dad, who lived with constant paranoia that others would see what an awful father he was and would call for his resignation from the church board or perhaps just shoot him, would say, "What? Go to the school and smoke? Are you kidding? You go to your room...now!" By the time I came along however, as my older brothers will tell you, I was able to get away with murder. I'd stroll into the living room and ask, "Dad, can I go to the school and smoke?" My father, who was reading the newspaper and obviously had more confidence in his parenting skills by then, would say, "Don't forget to take your swimsuit."

Although I've experienced more leniency than my brothers, life here is stifling. It's like wearing a parka in church on a hot day in July—you start sweating in places you didn't know you had sweat glands, and you want to run from the building, regardless of what others may think.

—⁓—

My sister, Liz, has been experimenting in the kitchen again. Her latest concoction is something she calls Banana Meat Loaf, a dish that tastes like it came straight out of the compost. She doesn't appreciate my saying so and after taking a swing at me, insists the recipe is from the *Farm Woman Cookbook*. Either she needs glasses or those farm women got a whopping good deal on ripe bananas from Ecuador.

We eat the meat loaf though. It's surprising what you'll swallow when your mother doesn't do the cooking and your sister hauls things from the fridge two weeks after they've been buried there, choosing to ignore that the natural color has drained away or the contents have turned peculiar shades of blue or gray or green. We cast a few knowing glances at one another, but apart from unwelcome comments about the compost, we keep the complaints to ourselves. In fairness to Liz, she doesn't like creating the mess any more than I like cleaning it up. Although she's nineteen, Liz stays at home, taking care of the place.

If only Mother would come do her part.

But that's not likely to happen.

Not anytime soon, at least.

Liz has been trying her hand at growing things other than mold too. The spring's warmth saw her burying tomato roots in a flower bed just like Mom used to do, popping the petunia seeds into holes she'd poked with her bony little fingers. A view to the south is perfect she claims, and the proximity to the house will protect the tomatoes from an early September frost.

Back in April she picked out the plants herself from Werner's Greenhouse, a place that reminds me of our little town, a suffocating spot where they prepare tender shoots for life in flower beds elsewhere.

I once shared these perceptive thoughts with Liz, and she did her best to imitate my mother: "Young plants need these conditions, Tare. And so do you."

"And so do you," I repeated in a pinched-off mimicy little voice, but she just smiled.

To me a greenhouse is a stifling cocoon, a sanctuary from the very things a plant longs for: the sun, the fresh air, and a gentle breeze.

# two

# Saints and Angels

My mother lies on her back in the ten-by-twelve-foot master bedroom, listening to religious programming coming from an old radio and making strange swallowing sounds. I've stopped going in there lately, and I'm a little ashamed to tell you so. When the guilt gets too much for me, I pop my head in the door and exhale, "Hi how are you doing things went well today I'm sure praying for you."

The last part is a lie. I gave up on praying long ago.

When I was a kid, she sang me to sleep at night with the voice of an angel. I close my eyes just right, and I can almost hear her whistling in the kitchen, crushing stale bread with the rolling pin, cracking two eggs, and then mixing it all together with raw hamburger and a diced onion.

Half an hour later she would place a steaming patty before us. New York chefs would kill for her recipe.

She was meticulous with housework, was my mother. Once I watched her clean the outside edges of our bathroom mirror with a toothbrush and taper the ends of a toilet roll like they do in fancy hotels.

I don't know where she got the idea, for although she maintained a passport she never went anywhere. Not to a fancy hotel, not on an airplane, not even on a bus.

She loved to visit the city though, loved to run her fingers over finery we could never afford. Then she would take my father's hand and tell him she didn't need these linens, she just wanted to remember that they existed.

She taught Sunday school to third graders who were even known to listen.

She taught me about Jesus and the Bible and all things spiritual, and for a time I came to believe in them entirely and without question.

She taught me to make my bed and how to hold the pillow with my chin when I slipped on a fresh pillowcase.

She used to knit socks and sweaters and slippers with two needles and a purple ball of yarn. I could never determine if she did this out of necessity or enjoyment, for she rarely smiled while knitting.

She didn't agree with much of Pastor Frank's book and was not reluctant to tell us so. She was rebel enough to snap on earrings whenever we left town, and she loved jazz. Loved dancing around the living room to Duke Ellington's "Concerto for Cootie," playing it over and over until even I had tired of it.

Then came the clumsy gait and the slowness of speech and the doctor's prognosis. More recently the speech has dried up altogether. You can't get a word out of her now as she lies in her linen prison, curled up or stretched out, gazing at us as if she longs to tell us a secret.

It's taken me a while to make any sense of these things, to put them together, and now that I'm a man, I've finally come to terms with the fact that if there's a God at all, He's not on our planet. Even if He were, He has no time on His schedule to visit the likes of the Anderson family. I don't know what else you can conclude when your fervent prayers bounce off the stippled ceilings and echo in your ears night after night, year after year. Oh, I still go to church and nod my head in all the right places. But one thing is sure—when I get through high school I'm out of here like a ham at a Bar Mitzvah, out to see how the other side of the world lives, outside this stifling greenhouse. To me this is a boring little place where nothing much happens and few would notice if it did.

The best place for this town is in my rearview mirror.

---

One thing flies in the face of all my reasonings. It's my mechanic father. If angels walk the earth, surely he is one of them. I have watched his way with my mother, and I have no explanation for his unflinching love.

How does a man care for an invalid without complaint year after awful year, feeding her with a boyish grin on his face, helping her down her cocktail of medications three times a day, carrying her to the bathroom like it's a privilege every husband should enjoy? I can find no mortal answer for his attitude. More and more in recent days the unexplainable has become commonplace around him. It's not only his uncanny ability to predict bad weather, it's his rich tenor voice. When I was twelve he couldn't carry a tune on a stretcher, but after another of his customary miracles he's singing solos at church, the richness of his voice bringing tears to the most hardened among us, sometimes even me.

Dad's ability at predicting storms has me puzzled as to why he doesn't replace old Fifty-Fifty Wiens, the weatherman down at KRUD radio.

It also makes me wonder what he was doing on our mansard roof that particular night. I knew he was bolting an antenna up there so Mom could listen to shortwave radio programs from places like Quito, Equator, but his timing was ridiculous. I asked if he needed my help, but he insisted on going it alone. Still I sneaked out to watch him, becoming alarmed as I watched clouds the color of rotten cantaloupes circle for attack. I've seen my father do some dumb things before, but few ranked higher than this one. He was fiddling with some wires when the rain began to fall, and he was hammering the antenna into place when the rain started bouncing off the rooftop.

Dad suddenly lost his footing. I gaped wide-eyed and helpless as he gripped a thin strand of wire with one hand and tried to steady himself with the other. The wire was not enough of course—a child cannot hope for a miracle every time—but what happened next was unthinkable. Dad skidded completely off the roof only to land with remarkable grace on a twelve-foot scaffold.

At least that's what it sounded like when I heard the clunk of his feet as they touched down upon it.

I decided then and there to tell no one for fear they would laugh at me, but there was no scaffold that night. I checked the next morning for tracks, and they did not exist. Still I clearly saw him hovering there, twelve feet above the ground. I kid you not. Then he began to chuckle. And after looking around to make sure no one was watching, my father started to dance.

I concealed myself lest he see me during this holy moment, for I knew not what to say. As he descended the invisible scaffold, I fully expected feathers to drop from beneath his shirt as the final proof that he was not of this earth.

I later summoned the nerve to tell this to my buddy Michael Swanson, but he just stared at me, wondering when my medication would kick in.

—☓—

Religion is a big thing on our side of the creek. You see it on bumper stickers and sidewalks if you poke your head out a window for half a second on any given Sunday. Whole families saunter hand in hand along our streets, heading for one of three churches, most likely either Our Lady of Sorrows or Grace Community, the latter being ours.

Along about the springtime of my fifteenth year I realized that

I was unable to believe the things the rest of them believed. Don't get me wrong, I respect these people and their faith, but I've come to the realization that there are too many questions, too many inconsistencies that they don't address or even recognize. Too many other religions I'd like to know more about.

Besides, if you were handed a bathing suit or a straitjacket, which would *you* slip on?

I'd prefer no one knows my secret, that no one learns I've turned my back on my parents' God. It would break their hearts, and they've had enough things broken already.

I suppose they've tried their best to insulate us against the world in this little greenhouse. Against evil. Against the unexpected. But surprises lurk here too. Like rocks in a wheat field—they're better left buried. But the big ones have a way of loosening the ground and popping up their heads, or so it seems this summer of my eighteenth year.

# three

# The Forbidden

It is one of the hottest summers I can remember. Late May and the slimy little Greison kids next door have already established a lemonade stand and are turning a slick profit. Early June and ice cream sales are off the charts at the Dairy King—vanilla being the favorite. The heat is a welcome change from a harsh winter that saw Miss Shirley Thomas lose some of her prize perennials and three of her twenty-two cats.

Tonight finds me plugging away at homework, drenched in humidity and dreaming of graduation day a mere twenty-three sleeps away. Thoughts of walking the aisle invite excitement and apprehension all at once, for there are times I know not what to think of a future with me at the wheel. Evenings I study for finals amid heat that would wilt a palm tree, if we had one, and when darkness descends and my homework is done I cruise the streets with Danny Brown, who shifts gears in his Pinto like a butcher grinding meat. Sometimes, on those rare occasions when his father lets him, Michael Swanson joins us.

I wish his sister, Mary Beth, would join us too.

She has grown even lovelier in recent months as she dances

toward nineteen, her blond hair bouncing along with her, causing me heart palpitations. Does she know I love her? Surely she does. What would she say if I told her so? If I walked up to her on the sidewalk in front of the whole town and kissed her lips and took her hand and kept walking? I'm more likely to be squashed by an asteroid, but if I had only one wish, I'm ashamed to tell you I wouldn't know what to choose, my mother's healing or Mary Beth's adoration.

Partly because Danny needs a cigarette and partly because I need a break from all my math assignments, we find ourselves cruising sleepy streets tonight in Danny's Pinto. Lethargic adults lounge on their front porches, gawking at headlines while their energetic spouses move sprinklers. Fifty-Fifty Wiens is calling for rain by the weekend, but you never know. Perhaps I'll ask Dad.

Relief floods me whenever I leave our house, for there are things at home I do not wish to consider. Mother's troubles aren't the half of it. Earlier today my eldest brother, Ben, packed his suitcase and hopped the bus again. I wonder where he goes when he's gone. One thing's for sure, he's too young to be looking so old. I wonder what burdens my brother is carrying.

With the help of a small loan from somewhere, Danny Brown has bought himself this rust-colored Ford Pinto. I've heard a few snickers when he drives past, but it gets us where we're going. Danny would love an orange Dodge Charger like the Dukes of Hazzard drive, one that jumps creeks and rarely needs repair, but we'll settle for the Pinto. Purple lights illuminate the shag carpet, and a small disco ball hangs from the mirror—or at least it did until the night Danny was almost blinded by the thing when an approaching car hit us with its high beams.

Last weekend we managed to escape for a trip to Great Falls, where Danny purchased genuine imitation sheepskin seat covers. They allow us the illusion that we are in the lap of luxury.

We were in the city to see *Conan the Barbarian*, though I am forbidden by both our school and church to do such a thing. Of course Michael Swanson chose to stay at home when we mentioned what we were up to, so it was just the two of us driving down the highway, windows open, smoke belching from our cigarettes. We had parked near the theater and were about to purchase tickets when I noticed the tiny group from Grace Community Church standing at the entrance, smiling and thrusting gospel tracts in front of those who were entering the den of iniquity. The group was led by Eunice Archibald and Walter Solynka, people who know my family well, good people who have sat at our kitchen table numerous times discussing Pastor Davis' wonderful sermons.

Mr. Solynka was busily dabbing the way of salvation on a large mural with wide brushes and bright paints. He was drawing the cross—the bridge between earth and heaven—when I realized who he was and grabbed Danny by the belt loop.

We ducked low near the back of the small crowd that had gathered, plotting how to get past them and into the theater without anyone squealing to the principal and having me expelled or placed on conduct probation. Danny was muffling a laugh, finding humor in these things now that he goes to school on the other side of the creek. Finally he hit on the idea of getting sick and having to use the washroom in the theater, and that's what we did. We asked Miss Archibald if she knew of a place we could go for Danny to throw up. She took us there herself, shielding her face from the "coming soon" posters, proud that two of the youth had come all this way to go street witnessing.

We hurried past the box office with her directing traffic and even offering to stand sentinel outside the washroom door.

"No, that's okay," said Danny, "you go ahead. We'll be a while."

And we were. Two hours and fifteen minutes later when we came out, the crowd had dispersed.

Funny how my conscience still tugged at me though I'd pretty much learned to ignore it. I kept telling myself it was Danny who did all the lying, but still I felt guilt as we pointed the Pinto homeward. Guilt for the dishonesty. Guilt for not paying. Guilt for viewing the contents of the movie.

"I shouldn't have done that," I said, sliding my hands along the fuzzy seat covers.

"Done what?"

"Gone in without paying."

"Oh, that," wheezed Danny. "Forget it. I forgive you."

He laughed, rolled down the window, and tapped two cigarettes from a box he kept in his shirt pocket. We lit them up together.

"Wasn't that about the dumbest movie you ever saw?" he asked.

I was taking a long drag on the cigarette but still managed to nod in agreement. "Probably that actor's last attempt," I said. "So what's your favorite movie ever?"

"*Raiders of the Lost Ark*," said Danny, expelling smoke through his nose. "No doubt about it, not even close. Hey, tell me about the Ark—was it really in the Bible?"

It was a fascinating conversation, with Danny providing the questions and me doing my best to remember things I learned in Sunday school.

It's not easy though, trying to recall how God judged the people who touched the Ark of the Covenant while you're fumbling to light up another cigarette.

—⁓—

Tonight Danny is testing his new auto-reverse cassette deck with badly recorded country tunes he has taped from the radio. "I beg your pardon, I never promised you a rose garden," someone croons, and he joins in with his monotone voice, a duet you would not pay to hear. I roll down the window. "Aooww!" I howl, like I'm trying to attract coyotes, and Danny laughs. He pops in another tape that's even worse.

"What's with that guy? Who told him he should sing?"

"That's Bob Dylan, man," Danny informs me, as if I'd just failed to recognize the moon on a clear evening. Now I remember.

Tony has this album. He's been raving about it. *Slow Train Comin'*. Though the words are forgettable, the tunes are catchy, and I can't believe what Danny is telling me, that Mr. Dylan has embraced Christianity after searching elsewhere and coming up empty. "He's got another one now," he says. "It's called *Saved*."

Bob drones, "Man gave names to all the animals in the beginning, long time ago…" and Danny's fingers are tapping the wheel. I'd prefer he push eject and listen to those country tunes.

Lately our conversations seem to lean toward religion, though I do my part to make sure it doesn't crop up. Danny's father is the town's only self-avowed atheist, so Danny has picked up a few questions I've not heard dropped before. "Where will my dad go when he dies?" he asks, and what am I supposed to say? Straight to hell? Do not pass go, do not collect two hundred dollars?

The questions seldom let up. What was God doing before He created us? Will animals go to heaven? Can God build a lake so big He can't swim across it? I'm never quite sure how to respond, even when I know the answers. It can get quite tiresome really, like a country song that won't end.

It's a strange predicament, being friends with an atheist, one who hangs around the fringes of Christianity, mooching off our girls. I haven't the heart to tell him that I've grown past this thing called faith. Surely he can see the inconsistencies in my life, but still he keeps the questions coming. I wonder if he knows I'm not trying to witness to him, that I don't even believe the fairy tales from the Bible, though I know the main characters from every single one of them.

It's a funny feeling, discussing theology with a pothead who cusses freely and holds his cigarette out the window between his thumb and index finger. There are six air cleaners in the front seat alone. Danny knows he won't get girls to ride in the car if it smells like a giant ashtray. I'm not really sure why I took up smoking, why I started lighting them up, filling my lungs, and learning to blow smoke through my nose. For me cigarettes are a sign of rebellion. For Danny they are one of the four basic food groups.

He goes without a smoke for eight hours and he's not much fun to be around.

"So if God don't want us to smoke, why'd He create the tobacco plant?" Danny has come to a stop sign and leans his head out to take a puff.

I can't help smiling. More often than not his questions make me grin, and sometimes they leave me stumped. If Michael Swanson were here, he'd have a quick response, something about man corrupting the beautiful things God created, but the truth of it is, I'd rather let the questions hang in the air like smoke rings than hear his trite responses.

I've got questions of my own these days. Like why did half the faculty have to show up to approve our songs this afternoon? Surely they had better things to do than hear us strum our guitars. Ever since Michael, Dave Hofer, and I put our little three-piece band together, we've been dreaming of performing before a live audience. When we were asked to play at the graduation ceremonies, we couldn't have been more excited if we'd been invited to Carnegie Hall.

Visions of singing before all those people and pretending Mary Beth was among them were shattered by "You'll have to turn the bass down!" courtesy of Mr. Sprier, who is a math teacher, for Pete's sake. What would he know about music? He stood there in his black suit, the one with the flared pants and pinstripes. "Everything's too loud, so—" His squeaky voice trailed off, a voice I have rarely heard finish a sentence. "The lights will have to go," added Miss Thomas, pointing at the colored floodlights we'd placed on the platform. Miss Thomas is our music instructor and a large woman, large enough to cause an eclipse on three continents if she stands just right, and the poor lady invokes frequent jokes from the students, including me.

She was willing to consider the possibility of our upstart band playing at graduation, but not before she had determined whether we were too loud and whether the audience would be able to hear the words. I wish she hadn't summoned our fathers. Mine has quite enough on his mind these days, and it hurt to watch him standing there like a frightened child, wondering whether or not he should clap his hands and sing along or if his hands were about to be slapped.

The verdict was even more depressing. After three months of practice, we were forbidden to play on account of shallow lyrics and massive amplifiers.

I was stunned. Still am.

One of these days I'll have to admit to my atheist friend just what I think of some of the Christians around here.

# four

# Big Dipper

ranklin's Creek is shoulder deep in June, and it's cooler than the other side of the pillow. Sunday afternoon the pagans lazily ride inner tubes down its spine, drifting along sun-drenched, sucking on cigars and sipping who-knows-what from their little thermoses. Envy them is all we can do from our backyards, as our church forbids such activities on the Sabbath, preferring instead that we teenagers read Danny Orlis books or sing hymns to the elderly in the Golden Years Lodge.

Tonight Danny stops the car beside the creek so we can light up a few more smokes in the great outdoors. He extinguishes the lights and then strikes a match and holds it close to his face. Katydids and crickets duel each other for supremacy. In the distance a dog barks, and to the east the moon rises, a thin sliver of a thing. "God's fingernail," Michael Swanson calls it.

One Sunday each year we hold our church service down by the creek in broad daylight, dunking the willing below the water in the name of the Father, Son, and Holy Ghost and then singing them back to solid ground. A few weeks ago Michael Swanson went under as Danny and I watched. Maybe one day we'll see Danny dipped beneath the water, but for now there's more chance of my mother being healed or of Africans needing block heaters for their car engines.

"What the—" Danny almost stumbles on a tree root as the words escape his lips, words I dare not repeat in polite company. We walk down to the creek bed with Danny muttering to himself and trying not to trip on anything else. Someone has pulled a car under some low-hanging branches, a rare sight this time of night. It must be Mr. Sprier's brand-new Toyota, the only foreign-made car in town. Maybe it ran out of gas.

"Celica GT Sport Coupe," whistles Danny, stopping to admire it. "Ninety-six horsepower, you know. Lucky guy. Brand new. Where does he get the money?"

It seems cooler down here by the creek bank. Pale lilacs hug the bank as if they're cowering from the larger poplar trees. The sun is almost gone behind the west side of the gorge, and we watch the shadow of the bank cross the water, making a quick step from one side to the other. Sitting in the sandy earth, I dig my hands under an inch or so. It's cool enough to make me forget the grains of sand beneath my fingernails. Danny stuffs the cigarette in his mouth and takes off his shoes. He picks up a grocery bag full of old clothes that someone has discarded on the bank, grunting as smoke gets in his eyes.

How I wish my watch would slow down and these nights could drag on forever. Graduation will put a period on so many things. School, for one. Not that I've excelled at it. I just like the security of knowing it's there each weekday morning. School is a place you can go to forget so much. And what about Mary Beth? Michael says her family is leaving, moving to the city. I may never see her again. Just a wedding invitation one day, addressed to the first boy she ever kissed. I am unaware that a smile has crept onto my lips as I think about that sweet and forbidden kiss in the basement of our church, but Danny has noticed it.

"What's up?" he says, tossing a small pebble into the water.

"Not much…I'm just thinking—"

"About what?"

"About graduation, I suppose. About summer. About stupid people."

The ashes on his cigarette must be sticking out half an inch. It's one part of smoking I love—flicking the ashes off.

"Our band played this afternoon. Had quite an audience. Miss Thomas was there, hand in hand with what's his name, you know, the math teacher."

"Mr. Sprier?"

"Yeah. They make quite a pair, don't they? She weighs about three of him. If they get married, I'd like to be around to play practical jokes. She was mad at the three of us. Said we shouldn't be playing that kind of music, lectured us about dragging it into the school. Said it would lead to all sorts of things."

Danny flicks the ashes and lets out a low laugh. "Like what?" he says. "Smiling? Snapping your fingers? Tapping your toes?"

"I don't know. I just wish…" When I'm with Danny, there are some sentences I don't need to finish.

We both lay back until we have sand in our hair from looking straight up into the night sky. It's already pitch black here on the edge of town, and the stars are vibrant, like nothing you'll ever see in the city. We lie in silence for a good five minutes, pointing out the Big and Little Dippers, the North Star.

How honest should you be with a complete pagan? Should you tell him things about your family and your life that have you driving the final nail into the coffin of your faith? Should you tell him details of your day that have you shaking your head and thinking of sweet revenge?

"So do you ever look at the stars and think there's gotta be a Creator?"

Here he goes again.

"I, uh…I guess."

"I think I'm an atheist, like Dad. But sometimes I'm afraid I might be right. I'd really like there to be a God, you know."

It's a surprising admission.

"Did I ever tell you my dad likes it when I'm with you?"

"Huh?"

"Says he knows I won't come home drunk or mad. He'd never tell you that though."

"Next thing I know you'll wanna go to church with me." Danny doesn't catch the sarcasm in my voice.

"I don't know. Probably not."

I withdraw my hands from the cool sand, dust them off, and place them behind my head. "Hey, did you see that? A shooting star."

We watch the skies in silence, me thinking about Danny's words and about my brother Ben, more than anything. Is he lying under these same stars tonight, entertaining any of these same thoughts?

Quiet laughter wafts around a bend in the creek, slowly winding its way toward us. Two voices, I think. Both seem to be female. Danny puts a finger to his lips and we hunker down behind a poplar log. He picks up a rock, hoping to scare them.

The voices are hushed but louder now. One is a lady's for sure. You can see her outlined in the moonlight. It's a huge outline. The two are paddling upstream toward us, like muskrats, only one of them is shaped more like a moose. The closer they get the less I can believe what I am seeing.

"What is it?" whispers Danny, squinting desperately toward the sound, wishing his eyes were better.

"You wouldn't believe it if I told you."

The truth is, I can hardly believe it myself. But it is her. I can barely tell him without breaking into a laugh.

"It's Miss Thomas and what's his name, the math teacher, Mr. Sprier, swimming together, cooling off."

"No way, you're kidding."

But I'm not kidding.

And the funniest part of it all is that they are wearing the exact same outfits they were wearing the day they came into this world. It doesn't take me long to figure this out. Moonlight turns a certain color bouncing off that much exposed flesh.

When Danny finally sees them, he pauses, cups his mouth with his hands, and lets out a soft and mysterious howl, like a distant coyote: *"Hawoooooh."*

The two stop splashing and tread water as silently as possible. Miss Thomas snorts a frightened snort and dives under, staying there as long as she can. Perhaps fearing for her life, Mr. Sprier lifts her up, and she bubbles to the surface with a gasp.

"It's nothing," he whispers to her. "Whatever it is, it's gone, anyway—"

The two of them are hunkered down in the water. All you can see now is the whites of their eyes and some matted hair.

Danny stands to his feet. "Hello there. Are you okay? Do you need some help?" I can't believe it.

There is silence. Then a meek little squeal from Mr. Sprier, "We're okay. Thank you, so, uh—"

"Are you sure? I can swim. I can come out there. I can help."

"No, no, we're fine, we're okay. You go on now, you—"

Danny's laugh starts low and builds from there. "We didn't come to watch you swim," he says when he regains control. "We just came down here to feed the piranhas."

It's my turn to snort. Mr. Sprier gulps some water and sputters. Now that his sins have bubbled to the surface, he doesn't seem as confident as he did this afternoon when he stood in the auditorium, snickering at my music.

"I have a little deal for you," continues Danny. "My friend here would really like to play the guitar at graduation. I think you can make that happen." The two skinny dippers are silent, shocked beyond belief, shivering in the shimmering water.

Mr. Sprier makes a strange hissing sound. He is squinting to be sure of who we are. "You boys go on home now," he says, as if he is talking to third graders.

"Alright," agrees Danny. "But don't forget your clothes."

Danny pulls them from the discarded grocery bag and drapes them neatly over a log. A dress, a shirt, some rather expansive frilly items, and a long pair of black flared pants with pinstripes. We leave the way we came, him laughing softly and me terrified to death of the consequences.

I need to pass math to graduate. Fat chance of that happening now.

Sometimes an atheist from the other side of the creek has a distinct advantage in life.

---

Our ugly green telephone jangles about ten PM, and I'm betting it's the two skinny-dippers calling to apologize. But it's not.

"May I speak with Ben?" asks a male voice, gravelly and mysterious.

"Sorry, he's not here."

"Is he in tomorrow?"

"I hope so."

There is no response, just a gentle click.

An hour later I am dutifully in bed, chuckling about the events of the evening. Dad brushes past the room and then stops. He rarely tucks me in anymore, but tonight he knocks softly, comes in, and sits on the edge of the bed. "You smell like a tobacco plantation," he smiles. "You been with Danny?"

"Yep."

"I know you'll be a blessing to him, Son."

"Yeah," I say, "he sure needs help."

# five

# God Is Good

*I*t is not an easy thing to sit in church on Sunday morning and meditate on the words of hymns like "Shall We Gather at the River" and "There Shall Be Showers of Blessings" when the last time you saw the choir leader she was skinny-dipping in Franklin's Creek.

You try not to think about last night.

You look at the rafters.

You study the attendance chart from the previous Sunday.

But certain images are too powerful to leave you alone. They taunt you loudly during the sermon too, begging you to laugh out loud or at least to snicker. You try not to twirl your head around to locate her skinny accomplice because if you do chances are you'll end up falling off your pew from some gut-wrenching guffaw and looking like a fool.

Everything is funnier when no one else gets the joke.

It's like the time our beloved minister, Pastor Davis, tipped water from the rose in the pulpit down the front of his pin-striped suit without knowing it. The rose was put there in honor of little Ezra, born to Lynn and Dave Graham, weighing six pounds, seven ounces. You try to think of the child or the sermon or anything at all, yet it's tough to listen to a man preach with that much water down the front of his tan pants.

But we did our best then, and I will do my best now.

Every Sunday morning most of the scattered lives of this community come to an intersection at Grace Community Church. And sometimes they come to a crossroads too. Pastor Davis has made it clear that only sinners are welcome here, but self-righteousness dies a slow death. In the front pew sits Blane Wright, my father's first convert. If I lean a little to the right I can see the wrinkles on his bald head. Blane loves to tell of his conversion, how he was in a hurry one day and backed into my father's car. He braced himself for a tongue-lashing or a fistfight but instead got a consoling hug and an invitation to dinner. The two have been friends ever since. But this past year has been a tough one for Blane, to say the least.

Diagnosed with a tumor, he was visited on his deathbed by Murray Nichols, the church custodian, who smuggled a small bottle of schnapps past the nurses "to take the edge off the pain." Murray winked at Blane when he handed it to him. "I thought you'd appreciate this," he said, adding an even more obvious wink to the first one. But Blane frowned. "I haven't touched a drop of the stuff since I was saved, and I'm not about to start now," he said. "You should know that."

Murray was shocked. Rumor had it that Mr. Wright had once been seen emerging from the Draft Choice Bar with an odd-shaped bottle in one hand, and Murray decided to carefully tell him so. The thought that his name had been smeared around town that way was more of a shock to Mr. Wright than the doctor's diagnosis. And the very next week he astounded the doctors by being well enough to get up in front of the congregation and tell them the truth. He had been drinking a bottle of root beer, for goodness sake, "one of those new bottles that looks a little too much like the real thing, I suppose."

Our pianist today is none other than my good friend, Michael

Swanson, who enjoys few things more than disguising popular tunes and playing them during the offertory and announcements. He changes the meter and the tempo, making slight melodic variations to ensure that few pick up on the fact that he is playing hit songs up there, songs our school expressly forbids. This morning's choices include a lively version of "Sometimes When We Touch" by Dan Hill, a slow and moving rendition of Trooper's "The Boys in the Bright White Sports Car," and the theme song from *The Andy Griffith Show*. Only a handful of us seem to notice.

Larry Harper, who plays the piano when Michael doesn't, witnesses solely through the *Grace Chronicle*, our local newspaper. He writes lengthy diatribes against evil, singling out politicians and celebrities, quoting Scripture at length to make his point. A wonderful cast of characters is seated all around me, and they add to the mystique and holiness of this quaint little place. Though I'm steeled in my resolve to turn away, I must admit that I will miss these people, that I cannot sit here without a nostalgic sense of wonder washing over me.

Grace Community Church is peopled with sinners in process, I'm told. "It's not for perfect people," said my father on the day he told me the whole story of Mr. Wright's astounding recovery and restoration. "If it was for perfect people, they wouldn't let me in." Surprising words those, coming from a man who would be a modern-day saint if we were Catholic.

In this place I have heard astounding confessions, made a few myself, and been forgiven beyond my wildest hopes. Here I have fallen in love and been surprised by the sweetest kiss a boy could dream of. And this morning brings another surprise.

Sitting beside me is Danny Brown, whose presence is nearly as shocking to me as the creek-side incident of the previous evening. When I finished my toast and jam this morning and went outside, Danny was standing there on our sidewalk, staring at some marigolds, which I happen to know he has no interest in. It was the earliest part of a Sunday he'd seen in his life, and he was a little bleary-eyed from the shock of it.

"Are you lost?" I asked him.

"Maybe," he grinned. "You got room?"

And that's all he said. And it was all I needed to hear.

Of course this church has room for a lost atheist. People surely notice his presence though. They crane their necks and shift from side to side, hoping to see his response to a hymn, or a verse of Scripture, or the announcement that the youth will meet on Friday night.

Tony sits on the other side of me, one leg crossed above the other, scribbling on the bulletin. My redheaded twenty-year-old brother is all of six feet now. Though he's been at Bible college in California for a year, he hasn't come back weird like I thought he would. He works out regularly when he isn't selling suits at the Men's Store, and he could have any girl in the church on his arm if people didn't frown on you for walking around that way. A few years back his passion was palindromes, backward sentences, words like "Bob" and statements like "Dennis and Edna sinned." But recently he has discovered the anagram, and I am always grateful when he shows me the results of his experiments. They are positively hilarious and a timely distraction from whatever else is going on in the service.

An anagram, says Tony, is a word or phrase you can form from another word or phrase. This morning he uncrosses his legs, sits up straight with a satisfied grin, and pushes the bulletin my way. It feels good to be in the circle of his confidence. Across the front he has scribbled "Clint Eastwood" and then rearranged it to spell "Old West action." I shake my head. Tony whispers, "You fiddle with 'William Shakespeare,' and you'll get 'I am a weakish speller.'" I try it and it works. Amazing. On the back of the bulletin is my favorite thus far. "Monkeys write" is "New York Times." It's something I can't believe Tony has the mind for nor the time to discover. I'm barely able to stifle my surprise before Danny leans in close and asks, "What's that?" at a volume only people who are not churchgoers would use.

Dad leans forward and looks at us, raising one eyebrow as high as it will go.

Today Pastor Davis' sermon title is "God Is Good All the Time." I scan the bulletin for typographical errors because we've had some beauties over the years, like "Tonight: Sin and Share," but I find none.

The text is Psalm 27: "I had fainted, unless I had believed to see the goodness of the LORD in the land of the living." Whenever he says, "God is good," he caps it with a question mark, and we are to respond with the title, "God is good all the time." You have to be careful when Pastor Davis speaks because he asks questions and expects answers. Once when he asked, "What do you think of that?" he was looking straight at me, so I said, "Amen!" a little louder than I intended to and didn't find out until later that he had just passed along a rather alarming statistic on divorce in the church.

Tony hands me a note. It's only taken him a few minutes to figure out an anagram of the sermon title. The note says, "The godliest old amigo." I can't believe it. His notes make memories of Miss Thomas and her boyfriend ancient history, so interesting are they. I've kept a few bulletins from previous weeks in the flap of my Bible, and I whisper Danny into quietness before showing them to him. Anagrams for "Pastor Davis": "Past advisor. Adapts visor. Avoids traps." Anagrams for "Town of Grace": "Cow frontage. Grow fat once" (which reminds me of Miss Thomas, our massive song leader).

As the sermon inches along, I scrawl a few notes of my own. They lack the cleverness of Tony's, but there are things the message has me wondering, things I abbreviate in case someone discovers them later. They reflect my own twisted slant on what life has become:

If God is good, why did He have to create brussels sprouts?

If God is good, why do the wheels on my shopping cart go in different directions?

If God is good, why is Mary Beth sitting with Liz this morning and not with me?

If God is good, why doesn't Ben think so? Why doesn't he darken the door of a church anymore; why does he look for grace elsewhere?

And while we're at it, why is my mother not here? Why does she lie at home leaving me to wonder if she'll still be alive each time I come back through the door? The land of the living? Right. Tell me about it.

If God is good, why is my father holding a toddler on his knee, one who has the congregation wondering what we Andersons will be up to next?

If God is good—

That's as far as I get before Tony hands me two more anagrams of the sermon title: "Gloomiest delight ado," and "Git! Old headiest gloom!" I grin and shake my head. It's hard to believe how fast you can travel from the sublime to the ridiculous, and how ridiculous the sublime can seem when you do so.

With the service over, the foyer is jammed with well-wishers. Dad holds two-year-old Allan, and people ruffle his curly hair—the two-year-old's, not my father's. He is talking with Blane Wright now, who has no hair to ruffle. Perhaps Dad is congratulating him on not being an alcoholic. Two or three of the men stand with Pastor Davis, nodding their heads vigorously. Our dark-haired Italian youth leader, Noah Corzini, spies Danny sticking out from the sea of familiar faces and zigzags our way.

"Glad to see you here," he says, shaking Danny's hand with a little too much enthusiasm. "Why don't you join us Friday night for a hot dog roast?"

Danny shrugs his shoulders, "Oh, thanks…I doubt it though." But the look on his face has me wondering if he just might show up.

Miss Thomas waddles by, and Danny leans toward her and whispers, "I hardly recognized you with your clothes on."

# SIX

# The Envelope, Please

Sunday dinner is visited upon us by my sister, Liz, one year my elder. She was not selected for duties in the kitchen on the merits of her culinary talents, but out of necessity, for the only thing worse than her cooking is the rest of ours. Today we thank the Lord for wilted lettuce, powdered potatoes—that when mixed with milk almost look like mashed ones—and something that, if you close your eyes, plug your nose, and fire up the most active neurons in your imagination, tastes a lot like ham.

The talk is of Danny Brown and his surprise appearance in church. Did I invite him? I suppose I did. Do I know why he came? No, I do not. Dad shakes his head. "Wonders never cease," he says.

Little Allan, our resident toddler, is spewing mashed potatoes all over the floor, and I am designated to scoop them up. Begrudgingly I do so, reminding myself that if you want to enjoy your meal, you sit as far away from a two-year-old as you can possibly get.

Without a doubt, the longest six hours of my week take place each and every Sunday afternoon. I'm told that Jewish texts prohibit thirty-nine specific acts during Sabbath. Pastor Frank's list for Sunday was longer. Until he left, we were not allowed to throw a baseball, toss a Frisbee, yell loudly, read comic books, play prisoner's base, or chew tobacco. Acceptable activities included napping, having devotions, praying, reading stories of the Sugar Creek Gang, or listening to Billy Graham's *Hour of Decision*. When you are a boy of any age, your world does not revolve around these activities.

Though the rules are no longer in vogue, habits die hard, and I find myself lying in the shade of our poplar tree this afternoon, bored and chewing on a long blade of grass. A congregation of sparrows argues over some crumbs Liz tossed out the back door. A robin watches from a nearby nest, disgusted perhaps. The taste of grass reminds me of how many lawns I must mow this week. Since I started the lawn-care business last summer, business has been brisk. I charge three dollars per lawn and people line up. Word travels fast around here. Do a good job of something that wives like to put on their "Honey Do" list, and advertising is a colossal waste of money.

Normally I strum the guitar on a sleepy afternoon, but today, out of sheer boredom, I decide to climb the tree. It's something I haven't done for a very long while and a juvenile act I hope none of the smaller kids will witness. Soon I am squatting quietly on a thick branch, chin in my hands, knees bumping my chest. From here I can peek through the leaves and see straight in the upstairs windows of the house next door, something you have to be careful with now that the most beautiful girl on earth occupies the middle bedroom. Last summer the Swansons moved in, downsizing from their previous house, and it almost made me believe in God again. I wonder what Mary Beth is doing this afternoon. Should I venture farther out on the limb to find out? What would it be like to fall from up here? How would I explain what I'd been doing?

Across the creek, a hundred yards away, Matthew Jennings and his sister Peggy are chipping golf balls at each other, much to the chagrin of Mrs. Jennings, who has better things in mind for her lawn than turning it into a driving range. Peggy is prettier than she was a year ago, something I must point out to Danny Brown when I think of it. She is fashionably pale in complexion and thin in an attractive sort of way, though I have only admired her from afar. Danny needs to find a girlfriend. She would be perfect.

One Sunday afternoon a few years ago, my brothers, Ben and Tony, waited until Mom and Dad were sound asleep and then slipped our old DeSoto sedan into neutral and pushed it up the street. When they were a safe distance from the house, they hopped in and sped away, not knowing I was in the backseat. Just out of town, near Hector's Hollow, they stopped the car, raised the hood, and flipped the air cleaner over.

I watched the whole thing, slouched down low, afraid they'd kill me if I sat up and tapped their shoulders, but I felt like it when they gunned the engine and the air cleaner trick generated extra noise and a rush of power. We sped over dirt roads with the radio full blast, and I was finally so sore from straddling the transmission that I sat up straight and said, "Yahoo," much to their surprise. Very little happened after that, and I'm not sure why I tell it to you now, except to say that I miss those days. I miss Ben's laugh and his mischievous presence around the house. Things get quiet here when everyone's gone, as they are today. Sunday afternoons are great for long walks, and I imagine Liz and Tony are on one, perhaps hand in hand with people they have crushes on or walking Harry the dog.

Next door the Greison kids have found me and are gaping through their fence as if I am in a zoo and they'd like to feed me peanuts. Of course, little kids can only handle gawking at you so long, especially when you're doing nothing, so they wander off somewhere to ogle other things. Disappointed that Mary Beth is absent, I grow tired of the poplar tree too and shimmy down to look for a little spare change to offer Danny Brown in exchange for some cigarettes.

Mother lies motionless on her soft bed, a dark green comforter pulled up to her waist. She always dresses up on Sunday, though she's been to church only once or twice this past year. I tiptoe through her doorway and lean close, something I've been doing more and more lately.

Reading about this disease has helped me understand some things, but it has also set me on edge, wondering. Wondering if the meal my father is feeding her could be her last. Wondering if this night could be her final one. She has not uttered a single word in more than five months. No one knows why. Not even Doc Mason. "There are people you wish wouldn't talk," I overheard him tell Dad one day, "but not your Mrs. She's never been anything but sweet to me. I've never seen the likes of this."

Dad has made brief mention of a healing service that we may be attending. Wouldn't that be something? Seeing my mother dance and smile and cook supper once again?

I tilt my head, lean close to her face, and wait. With relief I feel her breath against my cheek, though I wince at the smell. I guess bad breath is better than no breath at all. There is a little spare change on her dresser, and I briefly consider stealing it. Instead I tiptoe from her room, turn the handle on her door, and close it quietly.

—⁂—

At a small makeshift desk in my dimly lit bedroom, I pull out a pen and some lined paper. I've developed a little hobby lately, something to do when I'm bored. It's surprising what you'll come up with when you have no television. This particular hobby started harmlessly enough last winter when I decided to send a few letters to various Christian leaders, mostly to tick them off but also to poke sticks at them and see if they would jump. The first was addressed to a new kid on the bookshelf, Dr. James C. Dobson, whose book *The Strong-Willed Child* was climbing the charts faster than a five-year-old clambering to hide the spanking spoon. Dad had left a copy on the kitchen counter, and when I flipped through the pages, it got me thinking. So rather than do something profitable, I sat down at the typewriter, and this is what I wrote:

Dear Dr. Dobson,

I am a huge fan of your book because our little Jonathan (whom we named after King David's buddy) has been a problem since he was four months old and I saw the title of your book and knew it was right for us, so I bought two of them just in case they were the last two in existence and boy has it been the perfect medicine, the winning lottery ticket, and now our little Jon Jon is no longer in charge of this house, no sir, I am, but boy is my husband mad, so I was wondering if you would write about that, maybe call it *The Strong-Willed Wife?*

In Grace,
Terry Anderson

I showed the letter to Tony and he actually laughed out loud, which is a great feeling, watching your older brother almost choke on his fake potatoes at something you made up yourself. For years I had considered a career writing poetry, so when Tony took to laughing like he did, I said that perhaps I missed my calling, that I should be a comedian like Bill Cosby or Rodney Dangerfield. He found this even funnier than my letter. Still he couldn't hide his interest in whether or not I would actually mail it, and when I assured him I would, he secured my promise that I would notify him immediately if a response came.

I mailed the letter on a Thursday, licked the stamp myself and dropped it in the slot to Pomona, California. Barely three weeks later a response landed on the kitchen table signed by Mr. Dobson himself. In it, he thanked me for the kind comments and expressed regret that my husband and I were having difficulties. He listed some helpful materials and assured me that he had mentioned my struggle to his staff that very morning and that several had prayed for me.

Tony couldn't quit shaking his head to think that I got a response like this.

I showed the letters to Liz and watched her try to hide her delight. She said, "You shouldn't do that, Tare. That is a great man of God who doesn't have time to answer mischievous boys. He should be spending his time saving souls and helping families with real problems. You should be ashamed of yourself and write an apology."

I said, "There's no way he wrote that himself. He had help."

Liz said, "No, Tare, he's a man of integrity; he would not forge his own signature. You sit down right now and apologize. Here's a pen, hurry up."

I held the letter up to the window there in the kitchen and said, "Look here, it's a fake," but Liz was right. The signature was hand-scrawled in blue ink.

The surprise of receiving a hand-signed letter from a famous author and radio personality, coupled with the sense of importance I felt in showing it to my siblings, caused me to consider that there may be other opportunities out there for people to correspond with me if I wrote them thoughtful things.

So that's what I'm doing today, taking the edge off the boredom by sitting down to compose a letter to another guy my mother listens to on the radio, Charles Swindoll.

—⁓—

A harsh knock from the front door interrupts me. I consider ignoring it, but the tapping is loud, urgent.

Emerging from the hallway, I am startled to find that a tall, large-framed man has pushed open our door and is stooping to fit through the entryway. He holds a crushed Stetson with one hand and is running the other through damp, jet-black hair. His eyes are wide-set and strabismic. A unibrow rides atop them like a frightened caterpillar. His chiseled face seems timeless. He could be twenty-five or fifty.

"Pardon me, is this the Anderson place?"

"Uh yes."

"What's your name?"

"Terry…Terry Anderson."

"Where's your brother?"

"He…I don't know. Out for a walk, I think." I haven't seen Tony since lunch.

I squint upward. Should I know him? There's not a soul I wouldn't recognize in this little town. Is this a new neighbor, a relative I don't know? Strangers don't come often to Grace. We tolerate the occasional drifter and usually discover he wasn't so much a drifter as an old friend someone knew from high school.

This guy's not as rude as my old Uncle Roy, who delights in showing up unannounced and eating our food, but it's not for lack of trying. The stranger takes his eyes off me long enough to move them around the room. He scratches his leathery face, and that's when I notice the ring. It is white gold, encrusted with small diamonds and a blue Yogo sapphire too big to miss. It's incredibly expensive or extremely tacky.

"I'm here to see Ben. He lives here, doesn't he?"

"Yeah."

"I need to talk with him."

"Ben's gone," I state simply, "but he'll be back."

It's tough to know if he is angry or nervous or just naturally gruff. The stranger is sweating profusely and scratching at an ear as if a mosquito beat him to it.

Reaching his ring hand inside his light jacket, he produces a thick envelope, brown, slightly larger than legal size. "Could you make sure he gets this? It's rather important."

He smiles, I think, and steps toward me. I shrink back. He slides the large envelope across the table toward me.

The hat is back on his head now, and without another word he is out the door, leaving me staring at the envelope and wondering. Is it good news or bad? Should I open it or leave it alone? Maybe we won the lottery. I really should find out.

One of my greatest shortcomings in life is that I am passionately curious.

I scoop up the envelope and shake the contents like it's a Christmas present. It has no return address, no strange markings. Just "Ben Anderson" scribbled across the front in red ink. I hold it to the light, but I can't see through it. What shall I do with it? Give it to Dad? Show Tony?

For reasons I'm still unsure of, I tiptoe to my room and bury the envelope in my top drawer.

# seven

# Green Charger

You haven't really lived until you've been greeted by a large and enthusiastic dog first thing in the morning. Slobbery tongue. Whiplash tail. Paws scratching at your bare legs. There is no friend so true, no psychiatrist so helpful. From a dog you can learn so many things: Faithfulness. Patience. Undying devotion. And to turn around three times before lying down.

Harry is the only relative I've been able to choose myself, and though I am not vain enough to believe I am worthy of his affection, he has given me confidence that my companionship is worthwhile, and for a boy of eighteen, that's a gift you don't mind finding on your pillow when you crawl into bed each night. Whenever Harry is asleep on my pillow, I shoo him to the foot of the bed. In fact, he *is* the foot of the bed. His lanky frame envelops it like a rug, and sometimes I have awakened in the dark to find him standing over me, tongue hanging out, one front tooth missing, his ghostly face staring down at me like I am a juicy steak or some Greek god due his homage. Harry's tail wags when I waken as if he is relieved to know I am alive, but his presence gives me such a fright, I feel as if I might not be for long.

"Dogs," says my brother Tony, "can tell when you're dead. You die in your sleep, they'll sit beside you and moan loudly until someone comes and tries to revive you." This has not been a comfort to me, not even once. "Dogs are humble souls," Tony says, "not like cats. Cats won't admit they're sinners, but dogs already know. Just look at 'em."

He should know, him being Mr. Bible Scholar now.

After yesterday's encounter with the stranger, I have never been more happy to have a dog. If only he'd been with me when Mr. Stetson Hat showed up, the stranger might have shown less bravado. When a big dog like Harry is turned the other way you call him Mutt. He looks you in the face and you call him Mister.

Harry was the Swanson's hound until a year ago, Michael Swanson's, really. But for reasons still unclear, they were looking for a new home for the mutt, and I suggested ours. My father wouldn't hear of it at first, but when he saw how neglected Harry looked, how eagerly I poured my affection on him, and how the price tag was nothing at all, Dad could not resist. It didn't hurt that the Swansons threw in a twenty-pound bag of dog chow too. Of course they neglected to tell us it wouldn't last two weeks.

We argued awhile about a new name for him until we settled on leaving it at Harry. Pastor Davis gives all his pets Bible names, so we considered some of them. Presently the Reverend has three cats, Shadrach, Meshach, and Abednego, who were predeceased by their parents, Ahab and Jezebel. You get talking with Pastor Davis about his pets, and you could be a while. Ahab, he's quick to tell you, could have been a celebrity had he known at the time that a feline with twenty-six claws is a polydactyl, and could have held a world record that would have stood unchallenged for years. But the cat had been diagnosed with separation anxiety, a condition that developed each time the minister left home, something so severe that the poor creature would nibble its tail down to the nubbins, offering its poor owner no choice but to take it to Miss Thomas' cat-infested house, where the celebrity was lost in the crowd.

Tony suggested we call the dog Samson. Then he toyed with

combining Moses and Jonah into Mojo because Harry can't speak properly and runs away a lot. But the dog just sat there, disappointed in us perhaps. He only answers to Harry, though we've tried other things.

I've read somewhere that only seven good dogs are alive on the earth at any one time, and undoubtedly Harry is on the list. One thing I love about this dog is that you can tell him things that happen in your world without him sharing it with a soul. You don't take this for granted in a town like ours. I've already told him all about the stranger. About the envelope stuffed in my drawer. Harry watches me pull it out and squint at it again and then wedge it between some poorly folded clothes. He cocks his head to one side as if I am burying a bone or something.

I'm not sure what to do with the envelope. I keep telling myself I'll show it to Dad or save it until Ben shows up, but I have other things in mind. Maybe I'll wait till darkness settles and then rip the thing open myself.

I wonder if dogs keep secrets. Who knows—last night Harry hauled home an old bone and a plaid hunter's hat, as ugly as they get. I wonder where he dug them up and what he's not telling *me*.

—⚏—

They say that every boy who has a dog should also have a mother so the dog can be fed. I understand why. Each and every evening without fail, Harry reminds me that I've forgotten the most important thing in his day. He is well-trained when it comes to the dinner table, sitting in the corner, waiting patiently, making no attempt whatsoever to beg or share my food. I think it may be on account of the awfulness of Liz's cooking, but he never ventures near the table. And he rarely takes his eyes off me, which makes me feel so guilty I could not enjoy the meal even if it was my mother's cooking.

When the table is cleared away and Harry has prepared the

plates for the soapy water, he continues to look at me adoringly, waiting for his favorite word: *walk*. The word enters a conversation and his ears stretch upward and his head bobbles to one side, so eager is he for activity. Most nights we walk along the creek together, me throwing sticks and Harry fetching them. But tonight I am entertaining a wariness of leaving the house on account of a stupid stranger having violated our front door. Is he waiting out there somewhere? I'd rather not see him again. One look at Harry has me feeling fine about it though.

I peek out the window to see who's in the neighbor's yard. I'm in luck. My courage is bolstered.

"Walk?" I say.

Harry's ears unfold and his head flops to one side. I grab the collar and leash.

The Swanson place is a square box two stories high, and it has seen better days. Standing at the end of a short grassy drive, its steeply sloped roof is broken by six or eight dormer windows. The trim is painted a dark brown. Rain-rotted shingles droop over the eaves of the veranda, and two ancient willows keep the sun away like huge umbrellas. Mary Beth is whacking at some weeds in a flower bed, her blond hair pulled tight behind her.

"Hi," I say, ever mindful of my propensity to stutter when she is near.

She stops chopping and leans on the hoe, offering me the most beautiful smile on earth. Harry sprints toward her, his tail wagging in all directions.

"Where'd you get the cap?" she asks, bending over to let Harry lick her face.

"Oh, um, it's Danny's. I forgot it was on my hat…head." You see what I mean about the stuttering.

I pull the Chicago Blackhawks cap from my forehead, conscious that my hair must be a mess. Mary Beth doesn't seem to notice though, with Harry prancing back and forth, begging her to play.

"I'm taking her for a walk. Wanna come?"

"I thought it was a he."

"She is."

Mary Beth laughs.

"Wanna come along?"

"I can't," she says, studying the weed-infested flower bed dejectedly. "I've gotta finish this." My only consolation is that she seems disappointed.

"I'd be glad to help," I offer, putting the cap back on.

She glances up at a nearby window. "No, that's okay. Thanks."

I whistle for Harry to come.

"You whistling at me?" smirks Mary Beth, and I can't think of a witty reply.

"See you...um, later, too."

To get to the creek, Harry and I leave through the backyard, head west toward Hong Kong, then take a right toward Canada. The mutt pulls me across the stone bridge that traverses Franklin's Creek, drags me past the Holy Grill with its weekly special advertised in the window—Bacon and Eggs 99¢—past our broken-down hockey rink, which is used for football come summer, and through the parking lot of the Garden of Eatin' with its delightful smells wafting from a drive-through window. Both restaurants are under new ownership, changing names like we change socks.

It's not hamburgers Harry is on the scent of tonight though. He gets something on his mind and won't stop. A squirrel. A groundhog. Anything alive and moving drives him bananas. Dead stuff too.

Once we're through the parking lot, I unleash him and he's gone like he was shot from a pistol. Along the riverbed he runs, poking his head in every hole and tunnel he can find. Finally he slows down a little but keeps his nose to the ground, allowing me a chance to catch my breath. Stones take three or four skips to reach the other side of the creek, but they'll skim awhile if I throw them north or south. Heave one straight up and it slices the water on impact. Cut the Devil's Throat, Michael Swanson calls it. And that's what it sounds like, I suppose.

It's a good thing I wasn't throwing stones Saturday night. I'm sure Miss Thomas and her boyfriend are mad enough without nursing welts.

I can understand their attraction to the creek this time of year. Few things are lovelier than an evening in June along the banks of Franklin's Creek. The grass is never greener, nor the sky a deeper shade of blue. What a contrast from winter. Here in this very spot I sunk a snowmobile once. I wonder if it will ever surface.

Sitting on the bank, I contemplate the onset of summer and the questions it brings. There is no money for college unless I work for it, and the prospects for a decent job look slim. Three bucks a yard is enough to buy cigarettes and a few other pleasures but not much else. Shall I head for the city to look for work? Or stay here to rot with the rest of these poor souls who prefer life in the greenhouse?

A sense of sadness overtakes me as I realize how swiftly childhood has slipped from my grasp. That mischief and sleepovers and raiding Mr. Greison's pea patch are things of the past, legacies for the next generation.

Harry suspends my thoughts with a sharp but distant bark, something I don't hear from him very often. Before I see him coming, I can hear him panting. "What is it, Boy?" Harry isn't Lassie, not by any stretch of the imagination, but he's not dumb by dog standards. He stands where the riverbank meets Old Man Racher's cornfield, wagging his tail, pacing a little, speaking clearly: "Hurry up, I've got something to show you."

Hindsight is 20/20, of course. Looking back, I wish I had taken off in the other direction, but I didn't. In fact I'm convinced to this day I wouldn't have seen it had Harry not shown it to me.

I follow him up over a rise and along the neat rows of corn, some of the plants already approaching four feet in height. A hundred yards from the riverbank, in a small grove of firs the locals call Three Tree Gap, Harry stops his running and says, "There, see? I told you so." Or something like that.

I have to look carefully at first because I can't really see anything.

The sunlight is beginning to wane, and thick shrubs must be pushed aside to see what Harry is seeing.

It is a Dodge Charger, medium green. Slightly dinged up on the driver's side but none the worse for wear. I'm not the sharpest tool in the shed, but I know better than to approach a parked car and open the driver's door. I'd done it once with Danny Brown, only to discover a couple inside in a reclining position, their lips mashed together. When Danny tapped on the window for a joke, it was like someone had sounded a couple fire alarms inches from their heads. And so I stand still for a moment, studying the car. Strange. Why would Harry care about a car? Did it remind him of something? Was it the smell? The color? I've heard dogs are color blind, so that's impossible. It could be Old Man Racher's car, abandoned here when it gave up the ghost. But this one hasn't given up anything. It's a car most teenagers would kill for. Chrome wheels, fat tires on the back. No sir, something doesn't fit.

I move a little closer, wishing Danny were here with me. What he wouldn't give to see this thing.

His favorite show is *Dukes of Hazzard,* which features a car like this. It makes his Pinto look like an oxcart. I can't wait to show it to him. Perhaps tomorrow night.

If Harry weren't here, I wouldn't go near the thing. But a boy with a dog hears fewer noises, so I tiptoe forward and look in one of the windows.

The car is unlocked, but then again, most things are in this town.

The driver's door opens easily enough, and the interior looks clean as a hospital except for a backseat cluttered with blankets. I step back and scan the trees for anything suspicious. Harry wants in, but my leg won't let him. He makes the worst messes, and I'd prefer the owner not show up one day and brain me with a tire iron.

Supposing someone stole the thing and left it here while they try to sell it? I've heard of such things. In Great Falls thieves can strip a car bare—like desert ants in a western—and sell the parts before the car engine has cooled. I doubt it happens here in the little town of Grace though. Not much of anything happens here.

I climb in. The interior is in mint condition, and I expel my breath slowly as I run my hands over the black upholstery. Mary Beth wouldn't mind being seen with me in this. I grip the steering wheel, tap some gauges, and feel beneath the front seat for a key.

Wouldn't it be fun to pull into our driveway with this? I remove the Blackhawks hat from my head and hang it on the stick shift. Wouldn't Danny love to spray it orange and paint a confederate flag and *General Lee* on the roof?

The sheepskin seat covers from the Pinto would fit just fine. We could pop in the auto-reverse cassette deck.

Harry is outside the car, pouting and whining. I roll down the window. He barks and wags his tail.

I check the side-view mirror and fiddle with the rearview, smiling into it, like I see my dad and Tony do.

Twice in my young life has something happened that caused every hair on my neck to rise and spiders to crawl all over my body.

This is the second time.

A guttural cry escapes my lips, but I cannot move my body. Completely frozen, I tear my eyes from the mirror and stare straight ahead at the chrome decal on the steering wheel. No words will come. My throat will not scream. I try to let out a garbled cry, but the fear pinches it off.

Once again I glance in the rearview.

There is no doubt about what I see.

I turn my body only slightly just to make sure.

With one swift motion, I kick the door outward and jump from the car. I backpedal away from it, horror on my face. All I can think to do is run. A fast and horrified run. I can't recall moving this quickly in my entire life. My arms are flailing, my legs are reaching farther with each stride. Harry bounds along behind me, yapping his fool head off.

When we reach the sandy bank of Franklin's Creek, I am

wheezing a little, feeling every single cigarette I've ever smoked. I bend over to rest, hands on my knees, sucking for air.

And here I am once again.

Finding things I'm not supposed to find.

Things that will change my summer.

And maybe even the course of my life.

# eight

# Letters

**F**unny how life can go along so smoothly for a while and then change course all of a sudden as if you're in a fiberglass canoe with no idea the rapids ahead are Niagara Falls. I had been down this creek before.

In the winter of my twelfth year, I found myself paddling along happily until I bumped into a secret. A secret I should have declared to others immediately. But the growing realization, as I stick close to Harry and steer him straight home, is that for very different reasons I can tell no one this latest discovery, not even my brother Tony. The thought terrifies me, the prospect of carrying something as weighty as this on my own once again. I find myself racing for home, barely noticing that Mary Beth has left her flower bed, missing out on the shades of a glorious sunset reflecting off the quaint little houses.

Of all the towns and cities of the world, Grace is the most unlikely place for a murder. This is not Miami or Washington. This is a town of fewer than a thousand, where you couldn't get lost if your brother told you to, where you know exactly who wears which pair of pants when you see them hanging on the clothesline.

But happen here it did. I saw it myself.

I never wanted to find a body. Not a dead one, that's for sure. Not one that was lying half under a blanket, half out, looking pale and silent and void of breath. It was covered in blankets, but they were not enough to conceal an arm and part of the chest. The moment I saw that arm I knew I needn't pull back the blanket to see the rest. I knew exactly who it was. I also knew it would haunt the corners of my mind until I grew old and forgetful.

When I was much younger, two of the Hanson kids discovered the frozen corpse of Mr. Mercer in the middle of winter, and I never quite looked at those kids the same. They were on another plane altogether. They had glimpsed eternity and survived to tell about it. How could they ever be the same as the rest of us?

Mr. Mercer was an old bachelor who had gone out to feed his chickens in the middle of a blinding snowstorm and was still looking for them two miles north of his old farmhouse when they found his body, his right hand still clutching kernels of wheat.

I wanted to ask the Hanson boys exactly what it was like to hop off your snowmobile and find a man frozen upright in a cold bank of snow, but I never had the nerve. Instead I was left to gaze admiringly at them, and to imagine how *I* would respond. Would my own body be paralyzed? Would my brain freeze up? Would I be scarred for life?

I need wonder no longer.

The numbness is worse than when I first glanced in the rearview. I try to think of other things, of summer camping trips, of songs I like, anything at all to take the dull thudding from my chest. But an icy sensation has taken hold of me, and it's positively paralyzing.

Sneaking through our squeaky backdoor undetected would be a tough enough task for the most seasoned burglar, but it doesn't stop me from trying. I'd rather not see anyone right now.

Harry takes off the moment we're inside, skidding around the corner, looking for a warm body to pounce upon. I am left alone, standing in mute bewilderment over the cold body I have just seen. I place my shoes on the newspaper in the entry, taking unusual care to line them up right. The entertainment section boasts current box office hits. *Gandhi* looks like a yawner. *Porky's* and *Chariots of Fire* are an unlikely pair. I'm sure Danny will want to see *Rambo: First Blood,* but I have no desire to see more bodies right now.

A film of my own is playing around my mind. How I wish I could ban these startling images from my life as easily as the movies in the newspaper have been banned by the authorities around here.

"Hey, Terry. Come here."

Tony is laughing out loud in the kitchen, so I poke my curious head around the corner to see why.

There is little enough laughter in this house lately, and I am hoping he can jar me from the shocking world I have just entered.

Tony is pulling a letter from the typewriter and putting his signature to the bottom with a huge lasso on the *y.* Leaning back, he folds his hands behind his head and smiles the satisfied smile you use on Christmas Day after you're finished with the fruitcake.

"You thought your letters were funny," he says, turning his head, obviously delighted to see me. I can tell he wants me to share in the smile, and though I am still stunned at the events of the past hour, I must shuffle forward and peer over his shoulder.

I have always felt a sense of pride when Tony shows me something, for I have looked up to my anagram brother all my life. We've had the odd scuffle, to be sure, but Tony has been everything you could dream of in a sibling: protective, kind, and downright flattering at times. I'm so glad that he is home. I find myself standing behind him now, my mind tugging a dozen directions. Surely I can tell him my secret, can't I? But what if? No. It is impossible. Unthinkable.

I search for something else to contemplate. Anything.

Lately I've noticed that Tony's hair is beginning to lose its redness and that he suffers from dandruff. It almost makes him seem human. Perhaps he's not getting enough vegetables there at the Bible college, where he's been studying things like strange religions and how to be a minister. Perhaps it has something to do with all the time he spends indoors at the typewriter, poking out words, crafting letters and articles, sending them to editors and newspapers and journals and anyone he thinks might say yes.

Already he's had a letter to the editor published in the *Minneapolis Star,* so he's well on his way. Tony will either be an author or a preacher one day, maybe both. I suppose if I had my choice, I'd want him to be a big-time author because I've heard they make wads of cash, and that's something we could use a little more of in this family. I've heard him say he wants to communicate God's truth to the masses using comedy. Humor is a gift he's been given, a gift that wasn't always appreciated by his elementary school teachers, but he insists they'll be proud once his first hardback is published.

"You gonna just stand there like a stiff, or will you read it?"

"Sorry, I was...let me see."

I am two sentences into the letter when it dawns on me. Tony is showing me the ultimate form of flattery: plagiarism.

"Where'd you get this idea?" I ask him, knowing the answer already.

"From you. But I've decided to send these letters out with a purpose. I want to use them as a witnessing tool. I'll expose some falsehood, help some people. Your letters have given me the impetus to write a new genre called humorous apologetics. Anyhoo, I'd like to put these letters and the responses in a book called *Notes from a Religious Nut.*"

"Those are big words. Where did you learn them?"

"Listen, I've already sent a few query letters out to publishers. Haven't heard back from any, but you never know. 'Ye have not, because ye ask not.' Here, read this." He is looking at me sideways because my heart doesn't appear to be in it.

"Come on. Read it. See what you think."

The letter was written a few months ago and addressed to the famous Pastor Pedro. I've heard of him, of course. Who hasn't? He's one of those big television and radio personalities. A faith healer from Texas or some other place far from here.

"He's coming to Great Falls in a few weeks, you know," says Tony eagerly. "Go ahead. Read it."

And so I do.

# nine

# Blue Sapphire

*T*ony's letters are without a doubt funnier than mine. You can have corn fritters for brains and know this. The way he twists his words around, cleverly luring the recipient to respond. I sit down across from him and prop my elbows on the table, hoping the letter can pull me out of this fog I find myself in.

Dear Rev. Pedro,

I just love your show! I never miss it except when I fall asleep (it comes on at 11 p.m. here so I hope you'll forgive me!). I tape all the radio shows and sometimes people steal the tapes. That's okay, as long as they get the message.

A friend of mine sent me your vial of oil from the Jordan River! He poured it on my head and I had a headache go completely away just the next day. Just like that! Almost right away! What I'm wondering is if you have any small statues of yourself that I can get. I would certainly want to send a pretty large donation to get one of those. Don't worry, I wouldn't worship it or anything,

I would just have it by my bed to remind me to watch your show and also to send money when my monthly check comes and also the one from the inheritance and also my Marine pension. I'm not sure what I should do with all this money. I don't think my children should have it (they've made fun of your program) and I don't really go to church (you are enough). Let me know what you think.

I like it when your wife is on the program, because she is so genuine and also pretty. I like it too when you heal people or know someone in the audience has a problem. (How do you do that? I heard your wife helps you! That's naughty but I'm sure it's not true.) Well, don't forget about the statue. I can't wait to see you when you come our way.

In Grace,<br>Mr. Anderson

I hand the letter back to Tony, hoping he won't notice that my hands are shaking, not with laughter, but from the shock of earlier events. Tony seems disappointed.

"You don't like it?"

"Sure I do. You gonna send it?"

"Yep."

"Think he'll write you?"

"No doubt about it."

"How do you know?"

"I mentioned money."

"What will you do when he writes?"

"Get a conversation going. Level with him. He obviously needs help, and who will do it if it isn't me? Most of the letters will deal with people who don't call themselves Christians though. They have souls too, you know. Anyhoo, I'm hoping to help."

He fishes around a fat file on the table, hoping to find another letter. I perch myself on the edge of a chair and take a look. The diversion is a pleasant one, I must admit. Momentary visions fill my head, visions of my brother as a big sensation on the bestseller lists. I'll be able to say I helped him, offered him some advice, gave him the idea. Maybe he'll write a murder mystery. The way things are going, I may be able to help him with that too.

"Here, try this one."

The letter is shorter, and it's addressed to the First Church of Christ, Scientist in Boston, Massachusetts.

"Is that their real address?"

"Yep."

"Where'd you get it?"

"The library. Come on, just read the thing."

And so I do, pausing often to smile and shake my head at my brilliant brother.

Dear person in charge,

I am doing an assignment for our Religion Clas (I keep flunking). It counts for 20 percent of my final marc. I am sapposed to write a papor on Christian Science (The Way to helth and Happeness?), so I am stedying your discoverer and founder Mrs. Eddy and I was supposed to put it in my papor her real name, but the book in the liberry said she is name Mary Baker Eddy, but I'm not sure if that is really her name because she was married quite a few times.

Her name was first of all Mary Ann Morse Baker. I think that was when she was borne. But then she married Mr. George Glover when she was 22 but he died sadly. Then she married the dentist Dr. Daniel Patterson, and they had a divorce. Then she married Asa Eddy I think it was in 1877. So alls I need to know is shold her name be Mary Baker Eddy or shold it be Mary Glover Patterson Eddy. Or shood I put the Ann and the Morse in there too. It's maybe not a very big deal but I am hoaping you will write and tell me and it will help my marcs. I hoap it might help my grade to have a letter from you too.

Bye for now,
Tony Anderson

The note is just the ticket to get my mind off the trouble at hand, but I still have to work at it.

"They responded," he says, proudly.

"You've got to be kidding."

But he isn't. The letter he hands me is living proof. It has an embossed seal at the top, and the contents read, "Thank you for your interest, Mr. Anderson. You sure are one for getting all the facts straight. We are comfortable referring to our founder as Mary Baker Eddy. We wish you well on your paper."

The letters provide temporary relief, but I can't keep the questions from circling. Once again Tony seems disappointed at my lack of response.

"What's the matter? Do they need improvement?"

"No. I just…can't believe you're doing this." I pause, hoping he won't find the leap too abrupt: "What's the deal with Ben?"

"What do you mean?"

"Well, he's in trouble, isn't he?"

Tony hangs his head a little, pretending to look at the letter. "He's always been in trouble," he says.

I try to laugh.

"But…it's different now, isn't it? What kind of trouble is he in?"

Tony clears his throat and searches my face, hoping to find out how much I know already.

"I'm not really sure either. I know we should be praying for him, that's about all."

"You knew about him being adopted, right, him and Liz?" I don't know what this has to do with anything, but I do know I'd rather the conversation not come to an end.

"Yeah."

"Tony, if you knew things about Ben, you'd tell me, wouldn't you?"

"I suppose so. Why?"

"Because…I worry about him sometimes."

"Well, why pray when you can worry?"

He doesn't say any more; he just turns to face the typewriter once again and begins rolling in white sheets with carbon paper between them.

Harry wanders into the room and sits beside me, looking back and forth from Tony to me, measuring the situation. Never before have I envied a dog, but now I do. Wouldn't it be nice if the biggest problem in your life was how to get comfortable on a carpet? Or which tree to sniff next?

What if dogs could speak? This furry creature would tell Tony about the body, that's for sure. And I should too. Tell him all about the film playing around in my head. I could describe the whole thing in living Technicolor. The mysterious car. The blankets in the backseat. The hardened blood, the bullet wounds in the chest.

But I cannot bring myself to do so.

And the reason is simple.

I close my eyes and I see the body in the backseat, clear as day. The large forearm hanging crooked. And the craziest thing of all is that I knew instinctively that it was his right hand.

I had seen that hand all too close before.

Just yesterday.

A ring had fallen from a cold and rigid finger. It lay on the floor of the Charger. The band was gold encrusted with small diamonds and a blue sapphire.

—∭—

There are two places to look if you would learn of one's character, says my father: behind his ears and on his nightstand. The first will inform you of cleanliness, the other of character. One look at the books by my bed and you will be impressed with my moral fiber.

There is the usual array of the spiritual: *The Screwtape Letters* by C.S. Lewis, *Pilgrim's Progress* courtesy of John Bunyan, and *The Late Great Planet Earth,* though Tony insists Hal Lindsey's chronology is dubious. Atop them all is the Holy Bible, King James Version, "Presented to Terry Anderson upon the event of his eleventh birthday. You'd better read this or else, with love from Liz."

My mother instructed me to keep that Bible atop all other books, for it is a book like no other. To this day I cannot set a cup of juice on it—or my watch, or so much as a pencil—not without remembering the challenge she inscribed inside the front cover once I'd opened the gift: "Sin will keep you from this book; this book will keep you from sin."

It is the last steady handwriting I have on record from my mother.

Many things have kept me from this book. Life, in general, I suppose. School. Girls. In fact, this Bible is merely a dustcover for the other books. Not the ones by Lewis or Bunyan, but the books beneath them, the ones that are just as thick but a little thin on message. Three times I have read *101 Crooked Little Crime Stories.* I have placed little asterisks beside my favorite tales in *Alfred Hitchcock Presents,* and though the old English boggles my mind sometimes, I am nearing the final pages of *The Complete Works of Sherlock Holmes* for the second time.

I love few things more than a good mystery. But it's a quantum leap from lying on your back reading one to jumping onto the pages themselves. I suppose I've always preferred to be a spectator, to let those who are more cunning and audacious enter the game. I'd rather applaud their every move from a padded chair, sipping a drink, crunching some popcorn.

Tonight I planned on finishing Sherlock's final tale, "The Sign of Four," but a greater mystery has me transfixed. I still cannot hold my hand level with my face without it trembling. How I wish I'd been blessed with the mind to figure this one out. If Sherlock were here he would say, "Elementary, my dear Terry," but the only mystery I can solve right now is the one in my top drawer. Somehow I know that if I open the envelope, I will enter the game.

But passionate curiosity lures me onward, making me fear a missed opportunity more than the consequences of seizing it.

Harry stands guard as I quietly open my top drawer.

The dresser is a hand-me-down from Ben himself, and each drawer could tell you a story. Of stolen money and forbidden magazines. Now it speaks to me of a mysterious package that has become the focus of my entire attention. Carefully I peel back the fold of the envelope, knowing all the while that I'm an intrusive little voyeur.

Inside are eight to ten sheets of financial figures, boring receipts, things I have no interest in reading. In the midst of them all are black-and-white photographs bearing raunchy and unfocused images. I'm ashamed to say these interest me a little more. I've always known Ben kept forbidden paperbacks, but seeing them delivered in this format is unusual. They're rather graphic. What could Ben be up to?

A handwritten note falls from the envelope:

> Ben,
>
> You thought I couldn't get them. Told you so. Meet me same as last time. Someone will kill for these.
>
> CB

Quickly I push the sheets back into the envelope and bury it deeper in my drawer.

— ᴍ —

I suppose I have dreams just about every night, but rarely have they been so vivid. In this one, I answer the pounding at the door only to encounter a dozen people on our front step, all of them draped in plaid blankets. They are angry, exceedingly angry. Each is bearing one of Tony's letters, and though I don't recognize anyone, they appear to be from various cults. In the midst of them all is the dead stranger, holding his right hand up as if swearing an oath. The hand is trembling and bearing a shiny sapphire ring.

"Where's your brother?" they ask in unison.

And I can't remember which brother they're looking for, nor which brother is in the deepest trouble.

# ten

# Open Secrets

*E*very family has its secrets, and I'm not talking about muffin recipes. I'm talking about news we'd rather not have plastered on the front page of the *Grace Chronicle*. Things we don't hang on the clothesline, not in broad daylight. Keeping secrets allows you to smile easier when you walk down the street, to sit up straighter in church, knowing the rest of the congregation isn't staring at the back of your head, shaking their own.

But some secrets are easier kept than others.

The whole town knows about Ben's smoking, about my mother's illness, about my temporary kleptomania that winter of my youth. Even a blind rooster finds the occasional kernel of grain, they say, and few are blind in this town. But still there are some juicy kernels we've managed to keep from them. Kernels I intend to keep stored away, right where they are.

Secrets are nothing new to this family. "You shake a family tree too much," jokes my father, "you'll find some squirrels up there. Maybe a few nuts too."

He and my mother were married on a New Jersey Saturday, June 7, 1941, six months to the day before the Japanese bombed

Pearl Harbor. Or so I was always told. But one of the benefits of having a sick mother is that sometimes—especially when doctors are switching her medications—she'll tell you things you're not supposed to hear, things you would not learn otherwise. That's how I discovered that she and my father were really married twice—once on that Saturday in June, and a second time a few months later in New York City. "We eloped," she told me, a pleasant smile on her face and a faraway look in her eyes. "Didn't tell a soul except for my late sister Terry. Remember? She's the one you're named after. Our parents thought we were working at Bible camp." My mother chuckled softly and her eyes lit up with mischief.

The secret was safe for those two months until somehow my Uncle Roy found out, and though he has taken a lot of vows in his life, a vow of silence wasn't one of them. My mother's father, a short but fiery man whose parents emigrated from Scotland, was furious. Though he waged a daily battle with Huntington's disease, the betrayal rallied him for a time, and he reverted to pacing the house, speaking with a deep brogue for most of a week. Grandpa, a staunch Scottish Presbyterian, demanded that the couple be married properly in a Scottish church and took it upon himself to schedule the wedding. He selected the music. Bagpipes, of course. He arranged for a Scottish minister, ordered invitations printed on thick tartan-style paper, and even chose the flowers himself: Scotch thistles. Believe me, the wedding took place on schedule.

Until that time, my mother believed she was her father's favorite child. After all, she had given up dreams of a college education to stay home and nurse him. But he considered her eloping a terrible violation of trust and never treated her the same again. Sadly, a family rift developed that never healed, and Grandpa was buried in 1956 not having seen his daughter in fourteen years. As a result, the grandparents on my father's side were the only ancestors I ever knew. Mother's smile turned to tears as she told me this story, and I sat beside her, not knowing what I could add that would possibly help matters.

It seemed scandalous at the time, but the years have a way of rendering such secrets harmless. Though it seems unlikely, perhaps they will do the same with the secrets we are now concealing. I think about them as I dream my way through another day of school, wondering if there are even more secrets waiting to be revealed.

—⚬⚬⚬—

When I was fifteen, my eldest brother, Ben, left home. I asked where he went, and Tony answered, "To Seattle."

I said, "Who's Attle?" and he laughed a glorious laugh that pleased me even more than it pleased him. Two weeks later Ben showed up unannounced and knocked on our front door, something he'd never done in his life before. The knock came in the middle of dinnertime, and I was elected to answer it. There stood Ben, arm in arm with the happiest girl you ever set eyes on. Her name was Jennifer, and she was grinning from ear to ear as if she'd just won something she was dying to tell you about. Jennifer was wearing high-heeled boots, which she needed just to reach Ben's elbow, and a dress that, as Tony later put it, was hiked higher than the price of oil. But you could tell she adored my brother, and that was enough for me. Petite and dark-skinned, she had something Indian in her cheekbones, and she was so young she still smelled of high school. But the surprise on our doorstep was quickly surpassed when Ben coaxed Liz and Tony and Dad and me back to the kitchen table and then produced two wedding rings and the documents to prove the pair had been married a week, courtesy of a justice of the peace in Clackamas, Oregon.

Rarely are we Andersons speechless, but this was enough to render us so. My father was nibbling on a scone at the time, and as he stared at the rings and the marriage license, crumbs tumbled slowly from his open mouth as if he were a toddler who had fallen asleep in his high chair. I couldn't know what was going through his mind, but I'm sure he considered taking the same road my grandfather took, of calling Pastor Davis and ordering up some bulletins and bagpipes and Scotch thistles, but perhaps he began to reflect on his own sins because soon the shock gave way to a wonderful smile. The next thing I knew Dad was cradling Ben and his new daughter-in-law in his arms, rocking them back and forth on the squeaky kitchen floor and loudly praising the Lord.

"Mother," he thundered, hoping she could hear him in the bedroom, "we're gonna be grandparents."

Dad meant it as a joke, of course.

Ben didn't laugh at all.

He quietly left the house, slammed a car door, returned through the front door, and stood there holding a laundry hamper jammed with blue blankets. Setting the basket on the table, he carefully pulled away the covers, cooing softly.

And there he was.

My nephew, three weeks old.

If I hadn't been leaning on the table for support, you could have knocked me over with a chicken feather.

Suddenly, and without anyone asking permission, I was Uncle Terry. Either this was a miracle of mathematics, or these two had been living in sin.

I wish to this day I'd had the nerve to grab Ben and hug him like my father did. But I couldn't move. I just stared at the baby and said, "Boy, he's sure a big one," which was really dumb, almost as dumb as something I'd say around a beautiful girl. But no one seemed to care. I couldn't stop gaping at the little guy, at his feeble attempts to kick his socks off, at his little energetic fingers, always grabbing, always on the move. And I couldn't stop looking up at Ben, my adopted brother, all grown up. The one who used to doodle gruesome images of Old Testament battle scenes in church, the one who once hosted an imaginary talk show late at night as we tried to sleep. Ben, my hero for a time, all wise in the ways of the world.

The newlyweds stayed long enough to know it was time to find a place of their own and long enough for all of us to notice that without some serious help and maybe a miracle or two, they wouldn't be married long.

Unfortunately we were right.

By my seventeenth birthday Ben was single again. Jennifer vanished, leaving the child behind, and suddenly I found myself with a younger brother named Allan and a part-time babysitting position. Every one in town thinks we've adopted this little guy, and though they cast glances at us, wondering if we're crazy for doing so, we don't feel the need to clarify things.

Once little Allan got settled, Ben was back to his old ways, showing up the odd weekend, then leaving for who knows where. Going to see Attle, I supposed.

# eleven

# Coming Clean

*A*t the equator the days are divided equally, twelve hours of sunlight, twelve hours of dark. Water goes straight down the drain, I'm told. But up north where we live, water vanishes clockwise and a June evening holds fast to the daylight even after some of us are asleep. Tonight sleep won't show its elusive face but not on account of the daylight. It's all these secrets flying through my head. I strip the blanket off my bed, much to Harry's surprise, and throw a lone sheet across my knees. I have turned the pillow over a dozen times, finished two glasses of water, which could come back to haunt me in the night, and still nothing can cool me down. Harry is licking his paws, an irritating little slurpy sound, but it can't stop the secrets from swirling.

The one I am battling now is the worst I have ever imagined. Skeletons in other people's closets are frightening enough. Imagine one in your own.

My mind searches out every conceivable possibility. Perhaps the stranger at my door was running from someone as a marked man. Maybe he was in some other kind of trouble and was being followed. Could he be involved with some illegal substances or magazines or drugs? It could be a suicide, couldn't it? Or how about this? Perhaps the body beneath the blanket wasn't the stranger at all. Just a random body with a sapphire ring on it. There are dozens of those rings around, aren't there? This could be any body. Or a fake torso someone put there as a macabre trick. Not a real one at all. Tony has been known to concoct his share of impractical jokes. What if he picked up some pieces of a mannequin at the Bargain Wearhouse?

But try as I might, everything within screams that the body was as real as the arm in my sweaty sleeve and the stranger in the car was the stranger at my door. Yes, the terrifying reality is this: Mysterious Ben is not only father to my nephew brother—he is a cold-blooded murderer, plain and simple. You can have sawdust in your head and know this. My only consolation comes from remembering that he's adopted. That though this secret is almost too great for me to bear, murder doesn't really run in the Anderson bloodstream. It just runs in our family.

Harry stops licking and looks at me as if he knows something he's not telling.

"What is it, Boy?" I whisper. He goes back to licking.

And that's when it dawns on me: Danny Brown's hat is missing. I left it in the car. The shock of remembering jolts me with a cold shiver. Surely they'll know whose it is in a town this small. I am left no other option than to tell the truth. Yet wouldn't I be the lead suspect right now if I reported it? Surely not. There's nothing linking the two of us, is there?

The last time I was faced with a surprising discovery, I hung onto it myself. Buried it like Harry buries a bone. But I am older and wiser, I suppose. I will not make the same mistake twice. This burden must be shared with someone else. But who? My father, that's who. But doesn't he have enough trouble on his plate? Doesn't he have a sick wife and an extra mouth to feed and a dead-end job as the town's most honest mechanic? No, I'll wait on that one. How about my sister, Liz? Or better yet, Mary Beth Swanson? Perhaps the common quest to solve this mystery will knit us together. One day we'll be able to discuss it on our honeymoon.

No, that's impossible. How am I to solve a murder looking into those big green eyes of hers? I can't think straight when I'm around her or even talk straight for that matter.

Tony's room is at the other end of the house, a room I helped insulate one not-so-memorable Saturday many years ago when shards of fiberglass insulation threatened to drive me insane. Tony is awake, strumming his Gibson and listening to the radio. He turns it down when I tap the door just below the sign that says, "Tony's room. Trespassers will be shot. Survivors will be shot again." The sign was funny until last night.

"Yup?" Tony swings the door wide. His pajamas are a little immodest by anyone's standards, and he stands there wearing little more than a frown. "Come on in," he motions, holding a guitar pick in his teeth. "What is it?"

*Where do I begin?* "I think Ben's in trouble."

"What else is new?"

"I mean major trouble. I mean, well, let me tell you about it."

Amusement registers at first and then skepticism as I start with the stranger, watching Tony's face all the while. He picks at the guitar as I begin, then muffles the strings abruptly as I get to the part about my backseat discovery.

"Tell me you're kidding," he says, but he's smart enough to know I'm not. Boys with graduation on their mind don't concoct murder mysteries.

"Have you told anyone?"

"No one."

"Why?"

"I was scared for Ben. What if he's the murderer?"

He gazes at the floor when I'm through and doesn't say a single word for a full two minutes.

I know what he's thinking though. All our lives Ben has been a mysterious sheep, if not a black one. Late at night we'd awake to find him sneaking in the window, smelling like a tobacco plantation. There were unexplained absences, flashes of anger, and the constant propensity to choose the crooked path. His likeable character could turn ugly if something set him off. Lately I've been asked by classmates if it's true that Ben is up to his ears in gambling debts. I can tell Tony has heard the rumors too. We both know that Ben is involved in something beyond his control.

Harry has followed me into the room. He stretches his back legs out behind him like he's trying to be human, jumps up on Tony, and gives his tail a lazy wag or two.

"Was he here on the weekend?" I ask.

Tony doesn't know.

"Where is he now?"

"I…I'm not quite sure."

"What do you mean?"

"I told him I wouldn't let anyone know. I promised."

"Well—" This is a new wrinkle, and I need a moment to iron it out.

Tony puts the guitar aside. "You know what happens to people who bury evidence? You wanna hang out in jail? Ask Matt Jennings what that's like. Come on, we've got work to do."

My brother gets something in his mind and he moves like the fast-forward button on those new VCRs I've heard about. He tugs on some pants and a matching shirt. The hour is late and the night is hot, but still I am shivering. We're off to see the police.

The realization that a crime of this magnitude could have occurred in his jurisdiction with two people as young as us knowing about it before he did is almost too much for Sheriff Benson. He sits at his desk, scratching flakes of dandruff from what little hair he has left, and you can tell he is not just embarrassed, he is unsure of how to proceed. He nonchalantly roots through every drawer in his desk, hoping to disguise the fact that he's coming up empty. He turns to a file cabinet and flips through dozens of files folders before finding the right papers. In fairness to him, it's not a report he has to file every day.

As the sheriff scratches some notes, Tony tells him as much as he knows. Then it is my turn. I am unusually honest, strikingly clear with the details. A sense of freedom washes over me. For once in my life, I can tell the story exactly the way it happened, for I did nothing wrong. I don't even fear the questions: Exactly what time did you find the body? Are you sure you were alone? Are you sure you didn't do it? Are you guys making this up? This is not funny, you know, we don't joke about these things.

"The body's there," I tell him. "I saw it. I'm still shaking and can hardly sleep." I must explain for the third time why I didn't come yesterday, that I've been wandering around in a daze, stunned, in shock, unsure of who to tell.

"We'll be in touch," he says, trying to regain some sense of control. "You two fellas don't go anywhere now. We might need to question you further."

The walk home with Tony is unusually quiet. Is he wondering what I'm wondering? Could we have spent our childhoods oblivious to the fact that we were sharing our bedroom with a cold-blooded murderer?

—m—

I am proud of my honesty. Of my careful attention to detail.

I have even told Dad and Liz all about it. The four of us are scattered about my room now. They are talking softly, consoling me. Dad even bows his head and commits this tragedy to the Lord. They leave my door open and the hall light on when they say goodnight. I don't get up to change things.

It's good to have Harry here.

I have gone over the details three times tonight. The only thing I didn't tell them about was the ring. And why should I? No one needs to know that I reached back and picked it off the floor. That I buried it deep in a bottom drawer in my room. What would a dead guy want with a beautiful ring?

I guess I've done a lot of foolish things in my life. At least I've done them with enthusiasm.

# twelve

# Aunt Shirley

There are things I love about my hometown. The quietness of an evening. The brilliance of the stars at night. The fact that the sheriff here doesn't throw you in jail for waiting twenty-four hours to report a crime. But small towns have their shortcomings too. As sure as tiny puddles are breeding grounds for mosquito larvae, small towns give birth to rumors. There is little to see or do in this little village, but what we hear makes up for it. I am wondering what the word is on the street today. Thankfully, the news came too late for the Wednesday paper, but that won't stop the murder from becoming public knowledge anytime today. By next week this time, the pressman at the *Grace Chronicle* will be working overtime, cranking out extra copies, and I'll be a celebrity—unless they neglect to mention who reported the crime. Surly they'll say something about me. But no one has shown up to take my picture yet, and the phone hasn't been ringing.

It's just as well. Being the target of a small-town rumor is about as much fun as being in an outhouse during a hailstorm. Just ask Mr. Greison, who lives to the north of us.

A few weeks ago, someone noticed he was making his wife, Annabelle, lug boxes of groceries in from the car while he held the door for her and barked orders. The rumor hadn't a leg to stand on, but it got around other ways. In fact, the story made its rounds within hours, complete with a sidebar about their marital problems. "I always wondered about those two," folks whispered as they gathered around to dissect their food at the Holy Grill. Sadly, few seemed to offer apologies when they discovered that poor Mr. Greison had cracked three ribs in a softball game.

The worst rumors are those that touch our own lives, of course. And when the subject is your very own mother, you are positively furious and often embittered.

Somewhere along the line, my mother inherited this cruel disease that has rendered her unable to walk straight or eat solid foods or make it to the bathroom on time. My father wears a weary smile about all this and though the smile seems genuine, it is beginning to fade as time does its work. Sometimes at night when I should be asleep I hear him talking to God, and his sentences are punctuated with sobs and whys and what ifs. Who can blame him? The woman who once bathed me behind the ears and taught me to ride a bike and fold my shirts just right is a skeleton lying on a bed she cannot change in a darkened room she cannot leave on her own steam.

To make matters worse, someone has concocted some vicious tales about her. Someone working in the rumor mill claims my mother's problem is not so much genetic as it is alcoholic. If ever you've seen her walk, you'd think the rumormonger has a point. It is more of a stumble, really, a lurching gait you wouldn't wish upon your worst enemy. Of course no one has seen that gait in a while, so the rumors have fallen silent, but I haven't forgotten them, nor their source.

The rumor headquarters of the universe is two houses down from us on our side of the street. I learned most of what I know about the middle-aged spinster who lives there back when we had a party line. Eavesdropping was a favored activity of my childhood, and ancient technology made it easy. In those days each house on our block shared a common phone line with the three others on its side of the street, and each phone had a different ring. Who needed television with this kind of entertainment at your fingertips? I would quietly lift the receiver and learn the exact time Mrs. MacDonald was to come to the hospital and have her corns removed, or when Bob Greison's mother-in-law was arriving from Florida and on which airline and just what Bob thought of her last-minute decision to come. Mr. Greison got wise to us after my brother Ben started mimicking his mother-in-law right in the midst of a call, and that's when Bob began using the dog whistle to clear the lines. We learned to listen closely for signs of that whistle and pull the phone from our ears fast.

The party lines are gone, but the rumors keep coming. Saturdays you'll see the spinster striding like royalty down Main Street, waving happily as if she is on a heavily flowered float and can't wait to get to the end of the parade and the awards ceremony. Her confident gait belies her age and stands in sharp contradiction to the crowfoot wrinkles on her puffy countenance, wrinkles embedded by diets that have pulled her face back tight and let it go a few times too many. She knows everyone in town, and she greets them all with good cheer and best wishes. Aunt Shirley, as my mother insisted we children call her, has not missed a Sunday service since she suffered from the whooping cough as a small child. It's a long walk from her house to Grace Community and an even longer one to the shops on our one and only main street.

If our town had postcards, her house would adorn them all. Painted white and accented in green, the two-bedroom bungalow deserves a nicer street. It is framed by a decorative flower garden meticulously interspersed with flat rocks and bursting forth with her legendary marigolds. The house is home to a few dozen cats who stay in the yard except at night.

Most townsfolk don't give more than half a Saturday to their flower beds, what with our short growing season, but our neighbor once-removed is not most people. Her house stands out like a pearl in a pawnshop. Delicate window trim is underlined by flower-boxed marigolds. Overflowing flowerpots stand like sentinels guarding her front steps in case the cats neglect their jobs. Vases within her domain burst with the hardy flowers, and a vine-covered pergola rises from elaborate iron lattice-work where a thousand more of the golden orange flowers open faithfully each summer day from nine until three. This regular expansion and contraction of the flowers gives rhyme and reason to Aunt Shirley's changing world, a world where she prefers to have everything neatly on a shelf, timed, charted, and accounted for.

All summer she dries the flowers for broth, prescribing it freely should you confide that you're experiencing an ailment such as headache, jaundice, toothache, or the common cold. Culpepper's immortal words are taped to her fridge: "A plaster made with dry marigolds in powder, hog's grease, turpentine, and rosin, applied to the breast, strengthens and succors the heart infinitely in fevers, whether pestilential or not."

Strange that someone so adept at curing other people's ills has such an insatiable appetite for spreading their problems.

If you meet Aunt Shirley for the first time, chances are she will pull from her purse pictures of her beloved flowers and display them for you in lieu of grandchildren. But while her yard is busting at the seams with these bright treasures and she has been known to lend some broth to help others in their ailments, she guards her flowers as she would an old family secret.

Once my father requested her permission to cut some of them for an Easter flower arrangement, and he may as well have asked if he could cut a few of the dear lady's cats open and borrow their livers. So surprised was she that the words would not come, and she relied on shaking her head and scowling to provide the unmistakable answer.

Those who know her well know that quaintness does not end on her property. No, Aunt Shirley believes she is the self-appointed watchdog of morality, ethics, and theology for the entire town of Grace. In a word, she is a gossip, one who feels it her duty to confess the sins of others. First thing each morning she brushes her teeth, smiles broadly, has her devotions, and then sharpens her tongue and goes out to remedy the town's ills.

My father once told me that when we gobble down gossip, we are never nourished by the feast, but Aunt Shirley seems nourished in every way.

I suppose it won't do any harm to tell you who she is.

She is Miss Shirley Thomas, our intrepid music instructor, and more recently the massive skinny-dipper of Franklin's Creek.

# thirteen

# Prayer Rug

*T*wo letters arrive Wednesday afternoon. Thankfully, neither is from the police or the FBI. The thicker envelope was post-marked in Minneapolis, Minnesota and shipped west by U.S. Postal Service employees to the Andersons, Grace, Montana—address enough for a town the size of ours. Mr. Hewett, our postmaster, who knows everyone's license plate by heart, the names of our pets, and enough personal information to make some of the faithful a little queasy, delivers them himself.

He normally drops letters in our mailbox, but today he rings our doorbell, hand delivers them to my father, and just stands there as if we ordered pizza and he is waiting for a tip.

"So what do you suppose this one's about?" he asks nervously, standing tiptoed and staring earnestly at the return address.

Dad smiles and pats Mr. Hewett's shoulder. "Probably won another lottery, Tom. Whatever will I do with all the money? You run along now, you've got quite a bundle there."

Mr. Hewett laughs and then looks at my dad with uncertainty as he closes the door.

The letter is in a gray brown envelope, and I can tell my father is puzzled by it. He squints at the return address up there in the top left corner and then studies the hand-scrawled ink across the bottom. "YOU are about to be BLESSED!" is underlined in blotchy red ink.

"What is it?" I ask.

"I'm not quite sure. Looks like it's advertising something."

"What's the other one?" I am tugging on his white-starched shirtsleeve.

"Oh," he says, clearly distracted, "it's for you. Here."

I try to act as if it is no big deal to receive such a treasure, but a squeal of delight pries my lips apart as he pushes the letter my way. Letters don't come often. Not with my name on them. I sprint for the kitchen, slide across the linoleum in my socks, and rattle through a drawer for a dull butter knife with which to slit the envelope's throat.

For some reason my father has taken his letter to the bedroom and closed the door. I stand in the kitchen with mine, the color draining from my face as I read it again and again. The envelope is plain, white, and wrinkled, and it bears no return address. The paper within is tattered a little and the handwriting is hasty. You could knock me over with a Q-tip as I read it:

> Terry,
>
> We know where you were and we know where you live. We think you should just remember that nothing happened. Everything will be just fine that way.

The words jolt me hard at first. How could they know my name? Nothing happened? It's too late. I've already told the cops. I'm dead meat.

Then it hits me. The creek. Why, of course. This has nothing to do with the murder and everything to do with two naked teachers who are frightened for their jobs.

A wicked grin spreads quickly across my face. I can't believe it. Why on earth would two skinny-dippers write a threatening letter? Don't they realize I might show it to my dad? Or the principal? The answer is obvious. Who would believe the twisted story of two troubled teens, one of them an atheist? Liars are seldom believed, especially when they tell the truth.

Grabbing the receiver, I dial Danny Brown's number. His father answers with all the warmth of a wounded porcupine. "Brown here. What's up?"

"Um…may I speak to Danny, please?"

He grunts and drops the phone without a word.

I read the letter again while I wait. It is written by Miss Thomas. At least that could be her handwriting. She used to write my name on the blackboard rather frequently when she taught us music class.

"Hi, I'm Danny. What's up?" The apple doesn't fall far from the tree.

"Hey, you won't believe this. We just got some fan mail. Listen."

I read him the words, slowly, dramatically.

"Sounds just like 'em," he says, swearing loudly enough for me to clap my hand about the earpiece and look around.

"You know what this means?"

No, I confess, I don't know.

"It means war. We need to think of something fast."

He hangs up without a goodbye. I guess manners run in the family.

—⁊⁊—

Seems I'm not the only one obsessed by the contents of a letter tonight. Dad is seated at the kitchen table, waiting for Liz to bring us some mediocre morsels and poring over the contents of the letter he has received. I set some plates and utensils on the table and take a seat nearby him without saying a word. I've discovered this is a good way of getting him to talk.

He looks up from the letter with a weary smile. The lines on his face seem more pronounced in recent weeks, his hair is dipped in silver. The square chin has retreated a little, though his face offers no external hint of weakness.

I don't know if it's possible to admire someone more than I admire my father. Yet I must disappoint him so. For years he has dreamed that one of his sons would try on his shoes and his coveralls and become a mechanic. Ben and Tony haven't, and it's down to me. From the time I was knee high to a Tonka truck, I knew of his dream, caught the subtle hints: the wrenches and screwdrivers, the pliers and hammers beneath the tree at Christmastime. I showed promise at first, spending Saturday mornings with him at the shop, but soon I grew disinterested, much to his chagrin. Lately, with the start-up of my lawn care business, he has brightened, but it's no use. I can start a mower, but I couldn't tell you what to do if one stopped.

My father is straining his eyes for the hundredth time at the tiny return address up there in the top left corner. I lean over and have a look. Pastor Pedro, Minneapolis, Minnesota. He shakes his head as he passes it to me and grins like he's known Pedro for years, the old swindler.

The envelope contains a black-and-white picture of a lady about my mother's age. Her name is Amanda Martin, and she is borderline pretty. "BLESSED WITH $32,000 AFTER KNEELING ON THE PRAYER RUG," boasts the caption. "HEALED TOO!"

Amanda is married, has four children—all of them boys—and suffers from mononucleosis, an ailment that includes largeness of the spleen. One Thursday evening in March, a friend brought her a letter identical to ours and containing a "Glory Power Prayer Rug." The "rug" is a piece of paper that when unfolded reveals a painting of Jesus with His eyes closed. I look at it carefully. It's a little creepy, to be honest. But Amanda didn't find it creepy. She followed the instructions obediently. She stared at the picture on the rug until she was quite sure she could see His eyes begin to open. Listing seven things she needed God to do for her, she anointed the prayer rug with vegetable oil, as instructed, opened her Bible, and put her right hand in the air and her left on Matthew 9:29, "According to your faith be it unto you." Prostrating herself there in the living room, Amanda squeezed both of her not so tiny knees onto the tiny rug and prayed, going over the needs again in case God had trouble reading her handwriting. Finally, Amanda placed the prayer rug inside her Bible, nudged it up against Philippians 4:19, and there she left it overnight.

First thing in the morning, she sprang from her bed, pulled the prayer rug from her Bible, and wedged it into the enclosed postage-paid envelope. A brisk walk later, her task was complete. The letter was in the mail headed back to Minneapolis.

But not before she sowed a seed gift to Pastor Pedro.

A seed gift of $77.77.

Exactly one week later, Amanda received the news that she was with child. She just knew it would be a girl. The very same day, Amanda's great aunt died, leaving her $13,000, mostly in jewelry. She didn't even know she had an aunt. And the mono had not been a problem. In fact, she had begun to feel better the moment she knelt on that prayer rug. She was sure she could feel her spleen shrink.

"You too can experience God's holy blessing power," says the letter. "It is in the enclosed anointed prayer rug we are loaning you! Don't forget to send it back tomorrow morning with your seed gift!"

Dad points at what appears to be a genuine hand-signed note from Pastor Pedro. "I'm coming to Great Falls in a few weeks. Would love to see you there."

"I wonder how I got on his mailing list," ponders Dad.

Liz arrives with supper. It couldn't be more fitting. It's a tray bearing baloney sandwiches.

—◇◇—

It's eleven o'clock at night and the doorbell is ringing. I've almost forgotten we have one because most people knock. I hesitate to answer, wondering who could possibly want something at this ridiculous hour. Could it be the sender of the ominous note? Shall I grab a baseball bat? Opening the door slowly, I find no one there. Harry slips past me and into the house, but no one else is around. Probably someone's idea of a joke.

# fourteen

# The Devil's Mailbag

anny Brown is like anyone else. Perhaps more so. He loves a choice morsel, especially when it relates to his favorite enemies of late, the brazen blackmailing letter writers. As we come up with our plan to settle accounts with them, I delight in egging him on, telling him everything he wants to know about the skinny-dippers.

We are standing on the creek bank, a stone's throw from our place of discovery a few nights ago. I brought him here to tell him of the murder, but he won't believe me. Thinks I'm making it up. It doesn't help when we sneak through the fir trees of Three Tree Gap and find nothing. No body. No hot car like the one I described. "You'll see soon enough," I assure him. "You watch the front page of the local rag."

"The Chronicle?"

"Yep."

He's not closing the door on the idea that I may be telling the truth, but he's more interested in Miss Thomas and Mr. Sprier. He wants to see the threatening note again. "What do you know about them?" he keeps asking. "They go to your church, right?"

The trouble is, I know lots about them. More than I should say. But a juicy story or two won't hurt. One or two I've experienced myself. And a few I've heard from my father when he didn't know I was listening.

In one of my earliest childhood memories I am standing in Solynka's Grocery, wondering how many grapes it is legal to sample before you have to buy some for yourself. The chimes on the front door jangle and in steps Aunt Shirley Thomas, who is not hefty yet by anyone's description, but she is showing definite potential.

"Good morning," she says to Mrs. Green, the one and only cashier. "You know Alvin Thomas, don't you? He's a new member of the church."

I hide behind some shelves and listen carefully.

Yes, Mrs. Green is quite sure she knows Alvin.

"Why, did you know that he left his blue Ford pickup outside the bar all afternoon last Saturday? Sad, isn't it? First the man takes a drink, then the drink takes the man."

Mrs. Green is busy sticking price tags on cans of tomato soup, but she can listen at the same time.

I follow Aunt Shirley out of the store and down the street, sucking on a grape and wondering what else I can learn from our neighbor. She bumps into Janice Silver, and I squat on the sidewalk, pretending I've found some ants.

"Isn't it a sad thing to watch Mrs. Green neglect herself so?" says Miss Thomas quietly, fussing with a bun in her hair. "She's working way too hard at the grocery store, and her child doesn't look quite right. You have to wonder if they're paying attention to nutrition at all. Of course her own eating habits aren't so healthy, you know. We really should pray for her."

Her next victim is Olive Sanders, whom she gently accosts in front of the barbershop. Mrs. Sanders listens as Aunt Shirley informs her of the tragedy it is that Janice Silver's husband can't hold a job. "No wonder she's a basket case. I could see it in her eyes a minute ago. We really must pray for her."

It is a terrible thing to hear her talk, but *ah,* how I love to listen.

Danny loves to listen too. He sits on the creek bank, blowing tight little smoke rings into the night air. The rings remind me of the smoke Danny's Pinto has been belching lately. The car smells awful inside and out, so he's put it to rest for now. I'll get my father to fix it one day. I suppose the walking has been good for us, but we feel the smoke in our lungs a little more acutely by the time we get to the creek.

As we skip stones across the placid water, I tell him of the invention of the Barnabas Cards a few short years ago and how they sparked the first case of church discipline I'd ever heard about.

Danny listens, a satisfied grin creasing his face.

My dad was the one who first suggested the cards at an elder's meeting. "It's an opportunity to write a short note of encouragement to others in the congregation and lift them up," he explained. "We'll call them Barnabas Cards after the apostle of encouragement. We could use a few bouquets around here." The word picture wasn't lost on those who knew the reputation of Aunt Shirley, I suppose.

"They're already using those cards over at the Catholic church," another elder argued, drumming his pen on a notepad.

"But that's no reason for us to abstain," insisted my father.

And so it was that the next day our church secretary Emily Gamble found herself printing them six to a sheet, with 1 Thessalonians 4:18 underlined at the top: "Wherefore comfort one another with these words." Harold Leno trimmed them neatly in the EBA Multicut at Harry's Printing, and the youth helped stuff them into the backs of the pews beside the hymnals that Friday night.

Pastor Davis couldn't have been happier. The very first one he found tucked behind his nameplate on his study door. "Great message, Brother," he read. "I needed that more than you can know."

Members of the congregation began pulling the light green three-by-five cards from their postal slots in the foyer, and some brought tears to their eyes.

"I'm praying for you, Sister. You'll get through this."

"Loved your new dress!"

One even had a twenty-dollar bill paper clipped to it, and the recipient never knew who it was from. Anonymity is a noble thing when the subject is positive, for it reflects well on everyone. But anonymity was where the trouble began.

Mrs. Roberts' mouth dropped open as she stood before her postal box the Sunday after Easter. "Your hat will certainly never go out of style," said the note. "It will continue to look ugly year after year. And what's with your hair? Do you comb it with an egg beater or what?" Signed, Leviticus 21:10.

Though Mondays were normally his Sabbath, Pastor Davis made the mistake of coming in on his day off and rooting through a pile of mail. He tossed a Reader's Digest Sweepstakes envelope into file thirteen, briefly glanced at a magazine from his alma mater, and then spied an encouragement card and smiled. But as he began to read, the smile faded fast.

> Dear Pastor,
>
> Fine message, but it's getting tougher to listen to you lately with the way you've been dressing. A sweater and tie are certainly no substitute for a nice suit coat. But I suppose they do distract us from your irrelevant sermons. The only thing good about them is that I don't have to think. I take the opposite position you do and I'm always right.
>
> Signed,
> Zechariah 3:3

Pastor Davis didn't quite know the Bible by heart, so he had to look up the verse to see what he was missing: "Now Joshua was clothed with filthy garments, and stood before the angel. And he answered and spake unto those that stood before him, saying, Take away the filthy garments from him."

"Emily," he hollered, hoping his secretary hadn't left her post, "Please tell me you wrote this. Please tell me it's a joke."

But Emily hadn't written it, and it certainly was no joke. In fact, she had received one too. It said, "Do you realize how many typos you put in each bulletin? By my count ten. What's with the Wednesday night *meating?* What's next? A suppository sermon? Signed, 1 Corinthians 10:31." Pastor Frank laughed out loud, then buttoned his lips fast.

"What's this verse?" asked Emily.

"That's 'Whatsoever ye do, do all to the glory of God.'"

"Maybe we should call the youth group and have the cards removed," Emily suggested.

"Ah, she's had her little fling," said the pastor.

"How do you know it's a she?" asked Emily.

The pastor just grinned. "I'm sure it's over," he said.

# fifteen

# Enragement Cards

It wasn't over, of course. In fact, it had just begun. The notes kept coming with increased regularity and hostility. My father was so upset he mentioned it at the dinner table one night.

Dave Philips, who leads the singing once a month, handed in his resignation the day this one arrived: "Do you really think anyone besides you likes your song leading? You look like you're directing airplanes up there. Signed, 1 Corinthians 12:31."

Pastor Davis refused to accept the resignation and instead began planning next Sunday's sermon a little earlier than usual. Though he was in the midst of a lengthy series on the book of Mark, he departed from it and spent the next two Sundays on the "Whatsoever things" of Philippians 4. He even printed the words, handed a copy to each of us when we got there, and had us stand and read it together as a warm-up for his message. "Finally, brethren, whatsoever things are true, whatsoever things are honest, whatsoever things are just, whatsoever things are pure, whatsoever things are lovely, whatsoever things are of good report; if there be any virtue, and if there be any praise, think on these things."

When he looked up from the text, he was not necessarily thinking of good things himself. "Take these Barnabas Cards as an example," said Reverend Davis, strolling away from the pulpit, holding one of them high. "They provide the perfect opportunity to do something good, to build others up, as our Lord commanded. There is so much to thank God for, so much to praise in our congregation. But," and here he paused for added effect, "someone in our midst is using them to tear others down. Someone has taken the 'c-o-u' out of encouragement and changed them to *enragement* cards." Tony liked him playing with the letters like that.

I didn't hear much of the rest of the sermon because I was too busy looking around at the suspects. Pastor Davis continued until well past twelve-thirty, and I did hear something about a gossip's mouth being the devil's mailbag, but mostly I heard the beckon of the great outdoors and wished we could play softball on Sunday afternoon like the kids on the other side of town.

The service ended with us singing, "May the mind of Christ my Savior live in me from day to day, by His love and power controlling all I do and say." I scrambled to the back of the auditorium as the organ died, but I slowed a little as I remembered that we Andersons were rarely the first ones to leave.

I strolled through the foyer, waiting for my dad, running my hands along the top of the faded wainscoting, scratching my fingernails over the mailboxes, impatient and not minding if I looked it. By the time I discovered a fly on the windowsill and rendered him wingless, Mr. Sprier was about all that was left of the congregation. He strode past me without saying a thing, and I watched his Adam's apple bounce around like a yoyo on his skinny little neck. He glanced around briefly, and then pushed three or four green cards into the appropriate slots. I was more interested in the way the fly was buzzing circles on the windowsill now, but I did notice that one of the cards fluttered to the carpet behind him as he left.

"Mr. Sprier," I called, as I bent to pick it up. "You—" but he was gone.

The card was addressed to Alvin Thomas.

I'd seen him just a minute ago. He was stacking chairs and rearranging the bulletin board. But he was gone now.

I looked around and since no one was there, I read it, of course. It said,

> Dear Alvin,
>
> What's wrong with you anyway, you big drunk? You're part Scotch and part ginger ale.

When my father came out of the sanctuary, I handed him the Barnabas Card and watched the blood drain from his face.

"Where'd you get this?" he asked, studying the card with a deep crease in his brow.

"Oh, it was on the floor over there."

"Did you see who dropped it?"

"Yep."

"Well, who?"

"Mr. Sprier."

"Norman Sprier?" he asked, with growing interest.

"Yep."

It was the first time I squealed on anyone in my life.

—⁓—

One of the benefits of a small town—which include an easy-going pace of life, a sleepy police force, and people who will call in the location of your dog should it get lost—is the fact that no one locks their car doors at night.

It is an unfortunate truth for our math teacher, Mr. Sprier, this warm June evening.

The scrawny little skinny-dipper has even left the driver's door window on his Toyota Celica down without considering the possibility of bad weather. Yes, after scratching our heads and pooling our mischief, Danny and I have landed on a plan that has us laughing for a full fifteen minutes and me almost forgetting the troubles in my life.

And so it is that we find ourselves sitting nervously in the white car as darkness drops its mantle on Grace. There are no keys beneath the seat nor above the visor, but it's just as well. We'd like to keep the noise level to a minimum. I slide the Celica into neutral, hop out, and steer through the open window, glancing over my shoulder to see if any lights are coming on in Mr. Sprier's place.

Danny pushes from behind, and though we are sweating by the time we get there, it is a short push down the gravel road and around the corner to our block. We glide to a silent halt in front of Miss Thomas' pristine house.

A big black tabby cat stares at us suspiciously and then lopes off to hunt for mice, but as far as we can tell, no one else is the wiser.

We will leave the car here for the night, something that should get chins wagging in this community. As if that isn't enough, Danny stuffs his little note above the visor. I said no, but he insists.

> To the perfect couple,
>
> There's more where this came frum. Unless we call a troose. You know what we want. Let him play and we won't say a word.
>
> > Most sincerely,
> > You know who

Unlike the water of Franklin's Creek, sometimes gossip flows both ways.

—⁓—

It's eleven PM and the doorbell is ringing again. Must be some neighbor kids pushing it and running. It's a trick I've played myself a dozen times or more, and it's always more rewarding if someone chases you. I tap on Tony's door and ask him to join me. Slowly we open the door. Sure enough, no one is there. Harry slips past us again, and we take off running around the house in opposite directions, hoping to trap one of the neighbor kids and threaten to call the police. But there are no neighbor kids.

It's a little spooky, I'll admit.

# sixteen

# Doorbell

*B*y Wednesday noon each and every week the *Grace Chronicle* hits the counters of most stores in town, and by evening those who haven't purchased a copy or found one protruding from their mailbox have managed to borrow the charming paper and are poring over its contents. Some hunt for tiny pictures of themselves in the second row of the championship softball team, or the background of a ribbon-cutting ceremony, or as a tiny dot at the rodeo or track meet. Others scan the "Grace Happenings" section, which provides a comprehensive listing of relatives who are spending the summer here. If the gleanings are sparse, people flip to the editor's "My Musings," which reminds us just how lucky we are to live in a smog-free town where our children can spend an evening outdoors playing hide-and-seek without their parents worrying if they'll ever be found.

But those reading the paper tonight have cause to question that long-held assumption.

Front and center is an out-of-focus picture captioned "Car found at crime scene. Police ask help for clues." The photo is so bad you can't tell whether the car is a Ford or a Dodge, or the trees are fir or poplar. But the headline is unmistakable: "Body Found in Three Tree Gap."

The two columns omit almost anything of real substance, calling it a possible suicide, downplaying the event as if we were a tourist destination and bad news might frighten folks away. It does mention me by name though, and I have to read it twice just to make sure. The only other time my name has appeared in the *Chronicle* was eighteen years ago, under birth announcements. This is a far cry from that. "Police say the victim was initially discovered by a local teenager, a senior in high school, Terry Anderson. Anderson discovered the body more than a week ago while out walking his dog and was unavailable for comment."

Unavailable for comment? No one ever called.

I inspect the columns for Ben's name and am relieved to find it missing. But people here like to talk. They've undoubtedly been discussing things over coffee, around grocery carts, and as the main dish at the Holy Grill all day. News spreads as fast as wasps at a family picnic there, and I wonder if my brother's name is being whispered yet or not.

I was a bit of a celebrity after school today as my comrades gathered to poke questions at me. And the phone has been ringing off its ugly green cradle as others probe for further details. I take it all in stride, of course, like I'm a private detective and finding a body is an everyday occurrence for me.

Tony has just washed his hands because the ink from the paper spreads, and my father is sitting down to look the *Chronicle* over when a timid knock hits our front door. Sheriff Benson and Officer Hodges are standing there, fumbling with their hats, and they seem genuinely sorry when they say so. The two are aware that townspeople compare them to Andy Griffith and his bumbling sidekick, Don Knotts, and the officers go out of their way to avoid dressing like the TV stars. Though I'd rather my father shut the door and bolt it, he invites them in.

"Have a seat, gentlemen," says Dad. "I'll put on some coffee."

After ample small talk and eager sips from Grain Growers mugs, the officers clear their throats and get down to business.

"Where was your family last Sunday night?" asks Sheriff Benson apologetically, his eyes shifting about the house.

"Here at home. Are we suspects?" My father seems surprised.

"Well, no," stutters the sheriff. "But your sons here have told us about the...well, the body...and well, we've heard some things, some rumors really, and we need—"

"You're going on rumor, on hearsay?" Dad's voice rarely betrays anger.

"Just doing my duty here John, that's all."

"What do you know of this car in Three Tree Gap?" asks Don Knotts, who has not yet had a chance to interrogate me. "Anything?"

"Just that I found it," I say. "The body too."

Everyone turns to look at me. And though I try not to, I cannot stop answering their questions, and everything I say seems to come as a new revelation. Before long they have fixed their entire attention on me and my big mouth, and I am spilling every little detail for them, details I can't believe I'm sharing. The stranger's knock. His exact words. Things about Ben too, things he wouldn't want them to hear.

"Now, see this, Barry," says Officer Hodges, though he has scratched my proper name at least twice on his little pad, "we've dusted this car for fingerprints, and they're all over it. Maybe they're your prints."

"I'm sure they are," I say, meaning no disrespect. "I was in there like I told you. Mine are on the steering wheel. Maybe other places too."

The sheriff leans in suspiciously. "Weren't you involved in something a few years back? Something to do with, what was it, stolen money?"

"Yes." I hang my head.

The officer is scratching more notes on his pad. I wonder what he's writing and wish I could back up a few minutes or find some words to defend myself.

"Well—" is all the sheriff can manage.

"You've got quite a reputation," adds his skinny little sidekick confidently. I'm surprised to realize that I don't blame him. Who wouldn't accuse me when you come to think of it? I've been in trouble before. Surely murder isn't too far a stretch for a kid like me.

"I told you the truth," I say.

Andy Griffith seems satisfied, but not Don Knotts. He twitches his nose and leans in for the kill. "We think you know more about that car than you're tellin' us." He points his crooked little pinky at me. "We think you're hidin' something. We think you're protectin' that scoundrel brother of yours."

"Now just you wait one solitary minute," interrupts my father. "I won't have you talking about my son that way. Are you accusing him of something? Because if you are, I want you to know that you are way outside your boundaries, Hank."

I'm not sure I've heard my father talk this way before, and it has the effect of snapping both of them to attention, turning their advance to a retreat. People here may have questions about our family, but they never question my father's character.

Officer Hodges fumbles for an explanation. He has been under a lot of stress lately. He hasn't slept so well. Things with the Missus aren't that great right now, and the timing chain on his engine needs adjusting, would Mr. Anderson be able to tune it up?

Tony is smirking and Liz is in the kitchen making faces at us both. I am unaware that my mouth is hanging open. Why do I choose all the wrong times to say too much?

"Have you seen Ben?" I'm thankful the sheriff is not looking at Tony when he asks this.

"No," says my father, quite adamantly. Liz shakes her head. Tony is staring at Dad and pretending to be deaf.

"I will need you to call me the moment you do."

No one says anything. Dad is noncommittal.

"It's for his own good, John. Will you do that?" asks Sheriff Benson.

There is silence. Too much of it.

"I sure will," I say.

Tony raises another eyebrow at me.

"He was shot in the chest," says the sheriff, eyeing each of us for a reaction. "Murdered in cold blood. We'll be watching the house."

The two officers ask to talk with my father alone, and we are shooed from the room. Tony disappears into the pantry and returns chewing on an apple. "Ever heard of silence?" he asks, or at least that's what it sounds like past the apple.

"I'm sorry," I say. "I don't know what happened to me."

"Nerves," offers Tony.

"You told me once that if we tell the truth, we've nothing to hide."

"I think I'll go out and stuff this apple in their exhaust pipe," he whispers. "Cover for me."

"You can't be serious," whispers Liz. Tony laughs.

When the officers have said their goodbyes, Liz summons me to the kitchen, where she is scrubbing sticky stuff from the counter—hard.

"Tare," she says, "Would you really turn in your very own brother?"

It's not something I've given much thought to, and I don't know what to say. I'm trying to dodge the image of our family standing on main street watching him swing from makeshift gallows like we're in an old Western movie.

"I don't think so," I say.

—⁓—

As I pull back the covers on my bed tonight I find a note on my pillow. Tony has left it there. I half expect it to be a letter of scorn and derision or at least one reprimanding me for my loose lips. Instead he has scrawled these words at the top: "Terry, thought I'd write one for you. Keep your head up."

The letter is a welcome companion. As I read it, I cannot help the smile on my face.

June 11

The Holy Spirit Association for the Unification of World Christianity
1365 Connecticut Ave.
Washington DC

Dear Sir or Madam,

I am writing to apologize for a rather sad incident in an airport recently. I can't believe it. I am so terribly sorry. Last week we were going through New York and we were walking past some of your people (the Moonies, I think they were called, or is that someone else? I get them mixed up). Anyhoo, they sure looked nice in their orange outfits and they do preach a nonjudgmental, accepting kind of love, a vision for world unity and peace. I used to study about it. But your founder claimed to be greater than Jesus himself, plus he had four wives, so that put me off a little.

But that doesn't matter. What happened this afternoon was this. I was rolling along my new carry-on luggage cart (black) and was in a huge hurry. We were almost late for a flight when one of the wheels got caught in the folds of the suit of one of your nice young men. I thought someone was grabbing my luggage to steal from me (I'm always conscious of this in airports) and so I pulled with excessive force. What happened next still makes me cringe and it is the reason for this note of apology. I pulled quite a bit of his robe off!

He was left standing there and I probably shouldn't describe him because it was quite humiliating I am sure. I still have a good-sized strip of orange cloth with me.

How should I send it back to him? Would you send it to him if I send it to you? Have any of your followers complained about a missing piece of robe? Do you think he still wants it? The young man was quite upset and used some very bad words and shook his fist at me.

The others gathered around to shield him. I am sorry. What should I do? Would money help?

With apologies,
Tony Anderson

—⚊—

Tonight when the doorbell rings, I am ready.

Flipping off the light, I inch the curtain to one side and press my face against the glass. No one is out there. I wait. Sure enough, Harry is standing on his back legs. The mutt has figured out how to get into the house whenever he wants by ringing the doorbell.

I thought so.

I pray it's not the only mystery I'll solve this summer.

# seventeen

# Mary Beth

As if things aren't strange enough around here, household items are beginning to disappear. Small things mostly. Tools from Dad's toolbox. A set of kitchen utensils. The ketchup bottle. Father is alarmed. He says we're being robbed blind, that we need to start locking our doors and maybe loading the gun. He's joking when he says this, I think, but the mysterious disappearances have us all a little jittery. My brother Tony's favorite Bee Gees album has vanished, and he's not happy about it. He looks at me with an accusing glance, and I tell him that if ever I steal a Bee Gees album I deserve to be shot. That if I hear them sing "New York Mining Disaster 1941" again fifty thousand years from now, it will be too soon. He looks around for someone else to blame, but who is there? Liz? Dad? Little Allan?

Though no one says much, all fingers seem to point my way. After all, I've stolen things before. The sins of my youth are beginning to haunt me. "A good name is more desirable than great riches," is an oft-quoted Proverb around here. Ecclesiastes 7:1 hangs in plain sight on a plaque in our hallway: "A good name is better than precious ointment," it says. Tonight Tony is missing another album: *John Denver's Greatest Hits.* He corners me in the hallway. "Come on, Terry. What's going on?"

I laugh. "Ask Liz. She likes that stuff. You know, 'Life ain't nothin' but a funny funny riddle.'"

Tony just shakes his head.

Could it be that Ben is in need of things and is sneaking into our house late at night? I wonder. He's always liked ketchup. Got four bottles on his birthday once. But what would he want with Tony's albums? He's never cared for John Denver. Could he be pawning them off to pay for his habits? I'm new to this detective business, but none of the clues make sense.

As long as no one searches my drawers, I'll be fine.

—⁓—

Two years ago, when I received news that the Swansons were moving in next door, it was better than having my name on the front page of the *Grace Chronicle.* I got down on my knees and thanked God every night for a month. I'm not saying I believed in Him, I'm just saying that when good things happen you have to thank somebody. I even considered pasting a Scripture verse to the wall beside my bed: "Love thy neighbor as thyself."

Mary Beth's presence next door brings a measured comfort to me in these dark times, even allowing me the illusion that I have a better chance of winning her heart than if she resided a few blocks away. Whether she likes me or not is hard to tell, but she can ignore me no longer. Each day when she leaves for her job at the Dairy King I find an excuse to be outside. I find myself doing odd jobs around our yard with increased regularity lately, even if I have to make up the jobs myself.

I read in a magazine once—a magazine I shouldn't have been reading—that the top things women want in a man are a handsome face, a hairy chest, confidence, a great sense of humor, independence, sensitivity, and a long memory. Or something like that.

I wrote these things down on a sheet and promptly misplaced it. But I am working on each item, on the confidence issue in particular. I am also learning jokes, keeping our yard neat, and cutting the grass in symmetrical lines, careful not to miss a blade. And when I till or hoe the garden, I go sleeveless and am mindful to flex at all times in case she happens to glance out her upstairs window.

Having Michael Swanson as a friend doesn't hurt my chances of earning her affection. I am particularly kind to Mary Beth's little brother, and if I call the Swanson house secretly wishing to speak with her and Mr. Swanson picks up the phone, I am looking for Michael. If it's Mary Beth I say, "Oh, I was going to talk to Michael, but…um…how do you feel like about doing something…um…around…you know?" Here I am eighteen years old and I still haven't learned how to talk around beautiful women. I guess the confidence issue is a big one for me.

Tonight when I call, Mary Beth is smiling. I can hear it in her voice. "What did you have in mind?"

"Oh…um…just to be out going on a bike ride or something." I can't see her face, but still I stumble over my words.

"Sure," she says, and I can't believe it. I pump my fist in the air like it's game seven of the World Series and I'm rounding second base after smacking a fastball out of Yankee Stadium. Imagine a girl wanting to be seen with a boy who is almost an inch shorter than she is. "How about I meet you somewhere?" she offers. "Like in front of the Five and Dime?" She'd rather I didn't show up and knock at the front door I guess.

Dad is stooped over paperwork in the kitchen with Harry lying motionless at his feet. "Have you seen my favorite pen?" he asks, clearly frustrated. "I haven't," I tell him a little too adamantly, and point at Allan, my nephew brother. "Maybe he took it." I'm tired of being accused of such things. Yesterday it was a wrench; what's next?

Dad shakes his head and insists that if I'm going anywhere I take little Allan along and be careful because rain is on the way.

The truth of it is, my nephew is turning out to be an adorable little guy, mostly when he's sleeping but sometimes while he's awake too. Besides, he'll make a great conversation piece if I run short on things to say. I'll tell Mary Beth he's been stealing things, trying to frame his uncle Terry, trying to have me jailed as a thief.

Out in the shed, I rummage around, pulling cobwebs from Dad's red Schwinn—the one with the child seat on behind—and then locate an old hockey helmet for Allan's protection. The seat is a little small for a two-year-old of his size, but the pudgy little guy doesn't complain. He just sits there wedged in like a cork in a bottle, watching the trees fly by, a wide and endearing grin on his face.

I turn to see the grin just as a bug smacks him right between the eyes. He is stunned for a moment but releases nary a whimper, still grinning like he had been hoping it would happen. Allan is my kind of kid. An endearing little turnip with dark beady eyes and black hair.

It's a short ride to the Five and Dime, across the bridge, between the potholes, under the red, white, and blue lamppost of the barbershop, and soon I am off the bike, shouldering Allan and bending to let him loose. Most kids my age are picking up their sweethearts in fancy cars, not rickety old bicycles, and few of them are bringing along their nephews. But what's a boy to do? Sometimes it seems I have too much baggage to pursue life at normal speed. I lean the bike against the storefront and sit patiently on a hard stone bench, waiting for Mary Beth. Allan is teetering around the sidewalk, putting disgusting things in his mouth. He is particularly drawn to cigarette butts these days, so I'm not able to sit still for long. He's talking pretty well, and sometimes I can even understand him. "Bubs," he says. He hasn't learned to say Terry yet.

—◊—

Our main street is neglected this time of night and the stores are closed, save for the Draft Choice Bar. A middle-aged couple strolls past me hand in hand, trying to stay in shape, the man avoiding his wife's tug to look in store windows.

Allan is on all fours trying to chew secondhand gum off the sidewalk. The couple notices and laughs. I shake my head. "Hey! Stop it." I pull him away and scold him softly just as Mary Beth arrives.

She halts her orange bicycle in front of me, places her elbows on the handlebar and her chin on her hands. "Hi, Allan," she says. Allan looks up with gum all over his gap-toothed grin.

"Haoo," he says.

"Hi to you too," she smiles, looking my way. "So is the child yours?" The joke is a reference to the times I've been asked this question by a dozen others who were trying to be funny, but this time I laugh.

"Yes," I say. "He's our third."

I am happy to report that this marks the first time in our relationship that I have completed a single sentence properly instead of wiping out on my words. Could this be a sign of things to come? Ah, if only Allan *were* our child. What I wouldn't give for that.

"So you're a bit of a celebrity around here," she says. "Is it true what's in the paper?"

"Pretty much."

"What was that like? You saw the body?" There is admiration in her face, she cannot hide it.

"Oh, it was nothing," I lie. "Just a body. It was dead."

She laughs, thinking I intended to be funny.

Mary Beth is wearing her denim coveralls tonight, the new ones with the slight flare above her tennis shoes. Her narrow face is partly hidden by wispy blond ringlets that fall down over a turtleneck sweater too warm for the evening. Her eyes are bright and excited, though there is a certain sadness there that I am strangely happy about. Perhaps I can change it one day. I have a hard time looking at her without staring, for when she smiles all wrongs are made right, things at home seem manageable, and world peace an achievable goal. When I was twelve she blessed me with my very first real kiss, and I have scarcely washed my lips since. There has been no hint that she remembers it though, no hint that I should linger on the hope of it being repeated.

The benefit of lugging a child like Allan around with you is that it adds three or four years to your life. Girls seem to look up to you even if you're shorter than they are.

I hand Allan to Mary Beth and she coos softly, stroking his multiple chins, uttering kind words about his cuteness.

How I envy the child.

I turn my head to watch her place chubby little Allan into the child seat and pull the belt snug about his waist.

The only problem with having him along is that we look like a genuine couple, and in our town this spells trouble. People looking at you are thinking, *That's sweet, they look good together. I think I'll report them. Turn them in.* And they do. They report you to the principal or your parents or the pastor and tell them they are concerned that the relationship is progressing too fast and that they saw you holding hands by the hardware store, which is perfectly ludicrous. You weren't even near the hardware store. But how do you argue with the words of people who have sat in church since before you were born, people who live in terror that on one of our streets or in one of our homes someone somewhere is having fun? It's one of the things that has driven me far from their ideology.

To retreat from prying eyes, we point our bikes westward and climb aboard.

The gravel road is rough, abounding in deep potholes, and our bikes rattle over the rippling washboard corrugations with creaks and groans. Thick clouds hide the sun, and the humidity is heavy for a June evening. Everything has a gray hue to it except the green grass that sparkles in contrast.

I sometimes wish we could ride along the ocean together or sit beside it, watching the sun hang over the sea and the waves tumble over the shallows. But the wheat fields give you a similar sensation if your imagination is working at all. Besides, it is enough that Mary Beth rides behind me, playing games with Allan, whose grin has turned to a giggle. How much better things seem when she is near.

It's a good thing she isn't in front of me. Last time we did this, I got to admiring her pullovers so much that I veered off the road and hit the ditch. It hurt more than I let on to narrowly avoid a culvert by smacking a tree, and the scabs on my knees are enough to keep me from wearing shorts tonight.

Shall I tell her about Ben?

Shall I follow through on my plans and give her the ring that's almost rubbing a hole in my pocket?

# eighteen

# Sweet Rain

We ascend a small hill on the outskirts of town and then stop to look back at the miniature houses and trees and cars. For some reason Grace looks larger from here, like it has possibilities of becoming a small city one day. Now though, it almost appears abandoned, the quiet whine of a competing lawnmower the only sign of life. I wonder where I will be should it ever shed its small town image, should people discover its magic and move here from the city. Will I be far away in a high-rise somewhere? Or still at home taking care of my mother, unable to attend college, a lifetime bachelor procrastinating on some correspondence course?

Allan is restless, kicking me with his bare feet, making engine noises with his mouth. He's right. It's time to move along.

One mile west is Hector's Hollow, a favorite haunt for picnickers and small-horizoned explorers. The lake is more of a slough, not the sort you'd choose to swim in unless you enjoy sharing a swimming hole with a herd of cattle. We lean our bikes against a worn-out picnic table and sit on its creaky bench before the ashes of an exhausted campfire. I pull from my pocket three lollipops, and Allan eagerly reaches for his.

"So," I say, popping the sucker into my mouth and offering a red one to Mary Beth, "what are, um, you doing this summer?" Allan has handfuls of gravel and is heaving them into the cold fire pit.

"Working," she says, as if I don't already know.

"Right. Any…uh…thing too?" I am trying to herd the conversation along, trying to make it look like the lollipop is responsible for my speech impediment, that I could talk properly if I just took it out.

"I promised my father I'd take a year off to work before college," she says. "I've done that now. Looks like I'll head for Minnesota pretty soon."

My stomach turns uneasily at this, and I can't think of a rejoinder. Shall I say what I'm thinking? Shall I get on one knee and beg her, "Please don't go. Stay here and marry me. We'll adopt Allan and live happily in your parents' basement. Here's the engagement ring"? Thankfully I think better of it.

Allan stands before us holding the sucker in a filthy hand. "Bub," he says, out of the blue. He is looking from me to her. "Bub," he says again. Mary Beth plops him on her lap with a hug, not seeming to mind the stickiness of him. She kisses his cheek, the lucky little guy.

"He's not my brother, you know."

"He's not?"

"He's Ben's boy."

Mary Beth is silent, smiling at Allan, as if it's not such a big surprise. "Uncle Terry," she says, still smiling at him.

Allan hops down to pick up more stones.

"Danny and I come here sometimes," I say. "We tried fishing here once until the worms drowned."

"You hang around him a lot, don't you?"

"He's a good friend."

"He was in church Sunday."

"Yeah, I was as surprised as anyone."

A week ago I asked if she'd go out with me on graduation night, but she still hasn't given me an answer. No news is good news, they say. Besides, I haven't a clue where I'll take her if she says yes. I'm half thinking of getting my father to fix Danny's Pinto and taking her to Great Falls in it. But I'd need to get my license first and that hasn't been a priority for me lately. Maybe Danny would take the two of us or we could find a nice little pagan girl for him and make it a double. How about Peggy Jennings? She's had more boyfriends than Montana has trees, so maybe he has a chance.

The conversation is waning, and I must try to bring it to life.

"So is a handsome guy in the...um...picture?" It's a question I've been wondering about awhile but never dreamed I'd ask.

She laughs at my boldness.

"Come on, tell me."

"Oh...I don't know." I sense she is smiling, but I dare not look at her. I look instead at Allan. He has lollipop all over his chins, and I have brought nothing to wipe it off.

"How do you don't know?" I can't believe my grammar. Where did I go to school? "I mean, you don't know?"

She laughs. "You seem nervous."

I remove the lollipop. "I guess I've never been much for good around...um...girls like you."

"Girls like me?"

"Yeah," I stammer. "The pretty ones."

There is a promising pause. "That's sweet," is all she says.

"I've...um...wanted to ask you something for...well...five years."

She turns to me expectantly. "You have?"

"Do you remember the church in the basement kiss? I mean the time you and me, oh man—" There are two things a man cannot hide: that he is drunk and that he is in love.

"Yes I do," she says happily, without a trace of remorse or regret.

"Well…uh…I didn't wash my weeks for a lip."

She squeezes Allan and almost doubles over laughing. "Me neither." The smile is there again. This time I can't keep my eyes off it.

Thunder rumbles on the far hills and Allan turns to me with concern, as if I'll know what to do. "Bang," he says, clapping his hands together.

I don't want the thunder to steal mine. "Why did you?" I ask.

"Why did I *what?*"

"Kiss me?"

She smiles. "Because it seemed like the last thing on earth my father would want me to do."

"That's it?" I can't hide my disappointment.

"And because I wanted to." The smile is wider. Much wider.

Moments ago the gray clouds were as innocuous as lilacs in a kitchen vase, but they are trimmed in ragged edges of black now. Dark clouds circle, growling at us, carried along in a rush of wind. The drops are tiny at first, shifting from west to north, then back again, uncertain how much damage they can do. I take Allan from Mary Beth, hoping he won't panic. The drops grow heavier, angrier, slamming into us with unusual force.

The recess in the rock is more of an overhang than a cave, but it will do. We hunch our way under it until we reach dry ground.

Thunder crashes and the rain pelts down, drenching our bicycles and washing the lollipop Allan has left on the table. He spies it through the rain and points to it with a whine. Before I can stop her, Mary Beth is sprinting to the picnic table, returning in a flash, drenched but holding the candy. Allan pops it in his mouth with a grateful smile.

The wall behind us is warm enough to lean against, so we sit on the dusty ground, our backs against it, silent at first. There's a lingering smell here like woodsmoke. Allan's eyes are wide as he searches the ceiling over our heads.

"Terry," Mary Beth wants to say something but seems unsure. "Your parents always seemed so happy."

"They were—are." I am smiling now. "Speaking of kissing, they used to kiss too much of the time."

She smiles at this, then her eyes seem sad again. "When I was a little girl, I thought my parents were brother and sister. I never saw them kiss."

Suddenly she seems embarrassed by the intimacy of the discussion, and tries to change topics. "Do you ever wonder why God would let this happen to your mama?" I like the word when she uses it. *Mama.* And I'm ashamed to say that all I can think of is how the possibility of a kiss has vanished. "Don't you ask yourself why awful things happen?" She is staring out at the rain, not really seeing it. Allan has settled up against her, surprisingly quiet.

I've thought of these things often but have yet to come up with viable answers. "I don't know. What made you think of it?"

"There are things in my family too. Things I haven't told anyone."

I'm not sure whether to ask for more, or leave it there.

"Terry, if my father knew I was with you, I'd be in trouble."

"Why?"

"It's not just you, it's any boy."

"How come?"

"I don't know. He's...I—" She doesn't finish the sentence, just leaves it hanging there.

Darkness comes quickly in the gray of the evening. The rocky overhang hastens it along, of course. Though the thunder has stopped, the rain is steady, unflinching in its resolve. Both of us are afraid to voice the obvious: That we will have to spend the night in this place before descending to town to face scandalous rumors, the disapproval of parents, and the discipline of the school board. I will be refused graduation, maybe expelled from town after a lengthy and humiliating ceremony.

Then why can't I stop smiling? The truth is, I can't believe my luck. Who wouldn't smile at being stuck here with a girl like this one? I hope the rain continues for years. I hope it washes half the town of Grace and its tiny incompetent police force away. We'll forage for squirrels up here, live off the land. "It was too wet to send smoke signals," we'll tell our parents.

Allan has fallen into a fitful sleep against Mary Beth, and I wish I had a camera. He is curled up, relishing the tenderness of her voice, the gentle pat of her hand against his curly black head.

"Terry," Mary Beth is whispering now, "if...if it came to believing someone else's word against mine, what would you do?"

"Yours," I say, without hesitation. I'm relieved at the relative clarity of my sentence but more confused than ever by her question. I thought Danny asked some strange ones.

She smiles at me. "Thanks."

It seems like the most natural thing in all the world, to move closer to her and cuddle up and maybe sneak a kiss. But I can't bring myself to do it. It's like my legs are paralyzed or sound asleep.

"I'm cold," she says. "Come here." The magnificent invitation comes without warning and, despite my rubbery legs, I wriggle over to her and lean close.

"You...I...um...well..."

"Shut up and kiss me," she laughs, pulling me to her.

Allan opens his eyes and blinks at me.

"Don't mind him," she says, pulling me even closer.

Never in all my imaginings could I have predicted that a kiss could be this gratifying, but it is. We savor it, both of us, until Allan pushes his sticky fingers between our lips and pries us apart, the little weasel. We laugh together and I embrace the two of them.

Sadly the rain has stopped more suddenly than it started.

"I won't wash my weeks for a lip," she jokes as I stand nervously to my feet.

We will head for town now, taking separate paths for the last few hundred yards, avoiding suspicious glances and wagging tongues. I wonder why I couldn't summon the nerve to give her the ring. And I wonder why a beautiful girl like her would kiss a clumsy guy like me.

It's a good thing we haven't called the police to inform them of the thief in our house. I solve the mystery myself. The big break comes when I catch her with a jar of mayonnaise tucked beneath her arm. Tracking her to the bedroom, I watch her wiggle the closet door open and stash the mayo behind some Sunday shoes. She climbs shakily into bed then, a satisfied grin on her face.

The Bee Gees album is at the bottom of the laundry hamper. John Denver is hiding behind a pothos plant next to the living room sofa.

Perhaps she had grown tired of the music, I do not know.

We still haven't found the ketchup bottle nor the set of kitchen utensils, though I'm confident we will one of these days. I gently ask her why she did it, but she doesn't answer. In fact, she seems confused by the question, as if I am asking her something in Swahili.

There are times this disease makes you want to cry. Times when you look in on your sleeping mother and wonder how a loving God could allow such a curse to visit someone so lovely. And there are times you break out laughing because giving way to despair is a greater evil than anything else. I will never be able to pick up a wrench or hear a Bee Gees song or splatter ketchup on a hamburger without thinking of this glorious day.

I smile to think of that bike ride, of that sweet and forbidden kiss.

And I smile to think of the thief who was my mother.

# nineteen

# Prowler

F ear can be a good thing. It can keep you from licking frozen doorknobs or climbing into the wolverine's cage at the zoo. But it can also wake you in the middle of the night, choking you hard in its grip. Tonight the rain hits our roof loudly enough to waken Harry, and for some reason he decides to stand over me with his drooling face inches from mine, thinking I can do something about it.

"Big baby," I whisper once my heart begins to beat again. Harry scurries beneath the sheets.

The wind is howling through a narrow gap beneath the window. I reach for a blanket and pull it high. *Was that kiss a dream?* I lie awake long enough to smile at the answer, hoping to drift off with thoughts of the sweetness of it floating round my head. But Harry is too large a dog for so tight a spot. He stretches out with parts of him tangling with parts of me. I try to move him, but there's no use. The mutt is convinced thunder and lightning are terrifying enemies intent on doing him in. My gentle words and soft pats to the head do little to change his mind. I can feel his rhythmic trembling whenever the thunder rolls. It's crazy, this fear over something so explainable. I roll and toss, wrestling Harry for space, refusing to give in to the big hound.

Concerns of the day are multiplied in the middle of the night, and I am wide awake. Suppose the threatening note from the skinny-dippers wasn't from them at all. Suppose Ben isn't the murderer after all, and the killer knows my name. It's a chilling and wonderful thought that Ben could be innocent.

A branch scrapes the window and I jump, kicking myself for not shutting the darn thing. "It's okay," I tell Harry again, but this time I am comforting myself more than my dog.

The truth is, the darkness brings out the jitters in me too, and memories of the note amplify the problem. A thousand-piece murder puzzle is unscrambling in my head, which may be normal for kids from New York, but growing up in a town like Grace leaves you unprepared for such things. In all the years I've been alive, there's not been a hint of a murder here, at least none that I'm aware of. It's tough to find a record of a decent robbery for that matter. You read "Police Beat" complete with its grammatical errors in the *Grace Chronicle,* and it's better than reading the funny papers. I smile to recall a few of them, hoping their memory will put me to sleep.

> Thursday, October 30: Suspects caught launching rotten pumpkins and other spoiled produce onto street from Miss Merryweather's garden. Juveniles apprehended. Warning issued. Police later called to help dog bite victim.

> Monday, March 17: Constable summoned on St. Patrick's Day to eradicate skunk from front porch on fourth street. Four separate complaints regarding potent odor coming from fourth street residents. A purple ladies bike was found missing.

> Saturday, May 9: Auto theft reported by Mrs. Jennings.

Upon further investigation, it was discovered vehicle had been taken by Mr. Jennings to run errands.

Tuesday, May 12: Suspicious character seen near Greison home. Suspect detained and questioned. "Was out sleep-walking," Mr. Greison said.

Have the police made any further discoveries? Are they finally earning their keep? I imagine them out in the rain now, searching for more clues. Or they could be sound asleep at home.

This much I know, everyone in town can tell you who found the body. Until now I've been relatively unconcerned about the fact. But what if the wrong people come looking for me? Like the Great Falls Mafia? The middle of a dark and rainy night is no time to be conjuring such horrors.

The tree scrapes the window again, louder this time.

I toy with pulling the covers over my head but manage a brief glance at the window first. It is a mistake. A shadow sweeps the windowpane briefly, and my heart begins to pound. The shadow reaches for the window and hoists it upward. Please tell me it's Mr. Greison out sleepwalking.

I'd like to scream, but my jaw is locked up tight with the rest of me—frozen stiff, paralyzed. Harry crawls higher. I can feel his ears stretch upward, and he is shaking too. How I wish I had a gun or a baseball bat or a tough enough bone in my body to do something brave. I've yet to experience a heart attack, but this can't be far off.

The prowler plunges in headfirst, toppling softly and landing on his back.

He stands up, wet and shivering. A low growl escapes Harry's rigid body as he squirms from the blanket to face the foe.

"It's okay, Pork Chop," says the prowler in a soft voice that sounds a lot like Ben's.

Harry lets out a relieved yipe and hops to the floor. The two of them have never been the best of friends, but Ben kneels down, enjoying the warmth of Harry's attention. "Hey there, you little pot-licker."

"B-Ben…it's y-you." My heart is beginning to slow down, though I could still die of fright. "What on earth are you doing?"

"Tony called. I came back because I need a few things."

Ben flips on my bedside light and roots quickly through a drawer of his old dresser. I expect him to pull out clothing, but he is searching for something else.

"Bingo," he says, shuffling my way and holding something to the light. I crane my neck to see what it is, but no such luck. It is a small scrapbook with an old newspaper clipping of some sort, that much I can see. Ben leans closer to the light and carefully pulls the clipping away from the book. I manage to catch the date in the top right corner, but that's about all.

Folding the paper into his pocket, Ben kneels beside my bed like my father used to do, almost like he wants to pray with me. Maybe he'll confess the whole thing in a tearful outburst. There's enough light in the room to tell me that he is tired, frazzled, and plenty worried.

"Ben, I found the body, you know."

"Yeah…thanks." He pats my head and lets out a low laugh. "So I've been told."

"Did…did you do it?" I can't look at him when I say this.

"Do what?"

"Murder him?"

He smiles down at me and shakes his head. I'm not sure if it's from denial or guilt or the disbelief that I could ever consider him capable of such a horrible thing.

"Were you scared, finding the body?"

I shrug. "Where have you been all this time?"

Ben is gazing out the window he's just come in. He is likely wondering how much to tell me. "I've been working in a restaurant not far from Seattle. I'm involved in some things. Maybe I'll tell you about them one day." How I wish he would trust me with his secrets. "At night I...I go looking for her." He is still staring out the window.

"Do you think she'll ever come back?"

"Come back?"

"Yeah."

"Who do you mean?"

"Jennie? Your wife."

He smiles. "No, it's not Jennie I'm looking for. It's...it's my mother."

"Your mother?"

"My birth mother. All my life I've wanted to find her. Every Mother's Day, every Christmas, I think about what she's doing, what she looks like, what she would say if I walked through her door. I think about things in my life I can't explain. Thoughts. Feelings." His voice trails off for a moment, and he chuckles softly. "It's funny to miss someone you don't even know and haven't even met, isn't it?"

"No, I guess not."

"Well, it's become an obsession. When I was eighteen, I spent most of the summer searching for her. Mom and Dad thought I was counseling at a Bible camp." He shakes his head shamefully. "I didn't know what else to tell them. I felt guilty about wanting to find her—as if it was a betrayal of them. I couldn't bear the thought of hurting their feelings. Mom told me the name of the adoption agency. But the people there said I had to be twenty-one before they released information and that all the paperwork would take months once we started. Three years seems like forever when you're eighteen, so I got as much out of Mom as I could and went looking."

He runs his fingers through Harry's dark coat as he talks. It's the first time I remember him paying the dog much attention.

"I didn't know if she'd be glad to see me once I found her. But all my life I dreamed of looking for her. I was pretty small when they told me I was adopted. It was a shock, you know. I remember wandering around Solynka's Grocery once, looking for my mom.

I used to think she was following me, so I'd check around the school or the church looking for women who looked like me. Sounds dumb, doesn't it?"

"Women?" Ben hardly takes a breath. It's like he hasn't talked to a soul in weeks.

"I was nine or ten, and someone brought me to Mom, saying I'd been asking ladies in the church nursery, 'Are you my mother?' In my imagination she was out there somewhere, keeping tabs on me, playing some peripheral role in my life. Family friends, Aunt Agnes, the school nurse—they all became suspects. I played out these elaborate dramas in my mind, imagining shocking reunions and chance meetings. I pretended my mother was an international celebrity, living abroad in some exotic location. I collected pictures of Jane Fonda and Raquel Welch. They were suspects." He laughs. "It became a fixation for me. I know it sounds dumb, but I attributed all sorts of positive qualities to her. I believed she could somehow fill a gap in my teenage world if I could only find her. Whenever I argued with Mom or Dad about staying out late or smoking or not doing the dishes, I was convinced my birth mother would understand me, that she'd let me do whatever I wanted."

The wind is moaning through the gap in the window, louder than before. Harry hops up on the bed, looking to climb under the covers again. Getting up, Ben quietly slides the window shut.

"What about your dad?" I ask, when he has knelt once again beside me. "Don't you want to find him?"

Ben doesn't answer at first. "I've wondered what I'd do if I found him," he says finally. "Probably wring his neck."

"Why?"

"Kids used to tease me about being adopted. I said I didn't care, but I did. At least they had a dad who stuck around. I told them they were fleabags and their parents were stuck with them. At least I got picked. I told them they grew in their mother's bellies, I grew in my mother's heart. Sounds silly now. Anyway, Mom finally told me as much as she knew just last year. She gave me some details that are helping me track her down. I work in the day and spend the evenings searching whenever I can."

"Are you close?"

He shakes his head. "To tell you the truth, I'm a little afraid of finding her. What if she doesn't want me in her life?"

He pulls the covers up for me.

"Listen, I need to go, but I'd like to see Allan first."

He didn't order me to stay in bed, so I follow him.

The door opens without a creak, and soon he is down the hall, stopping at an open doorway, the last one on the left.

The moon in the room is full, and the breeze from the window touches us both. At the foot of the bed is an old cedar chest, made by my father's father, a twin to the one in the attic. In the bed Allan sleeps beneath a down comforter, the black sheen of his wispy hair barely visible, his breathing soft and steady. Ben doesn't move. He just stands under the door frame, looking in as if he's an Old Testament priest, afraid to tread on sacred ground. The moonlight is an angel, enveloping the child in its arms, whispering peace, promising sleep. Quietly my brother crosses the room and stands over his child. He tugs the comforter a little higher and studies the line of his son's cheek, the lids of his eyes, the dark hair curling over the tiny ears. I wonder what he is thinking, looking down at this form so perfect, so new. He smooths Allan's hair and bends down to kiss the child, this mirror of himself.

"I'll always love you," I hear him whisper. "I'm so sorry." The words are choked with emotion, and I can only imagine the regret Ben feels for what he's done, for the legacy he's leaving. He turns from the bed with a sigh and brushes past me. "I need to go," he says.

The click of Harry's claws is all I can hear as I follow Ben back down the hallway to the room of our youth.

Ben stands beside me as I climb into bed, hoping he can't see the tears that have come as a surprise, sliding down my cheeks and onto the pillow. Ah, I had almost forgotten how much I love my eldest brother.

The loud thumping of my heart is gone now, and I lie there wondering if Ben has more to say. Is this all a dream?

I lived with Ben long enough to know that he didn't intend to get lost. He was like the cow who nibbles on a tuft of grass on the far side of the pasture, moving slowly from one delicious clump to the next, and soon he's broken through the fence on the near side, nibbling away at the tufts he knows will satisfy his hunger. And before you know it he finds himself out on the road stopping traffic.

I don't think Ben ever wanted to wander from the green pastures. He just nibbled his way to lostness. First came the bundle of bad habits, then money and marijuana, then a young sprout of a girl who promised what the last bundle lacked, and one day he woke up with some rather formidable headlights bearing down on him.

"Goodnight, Terry." He pushes the sliding wooden frame upward.

"Be careful," I say. "They're looking for you, you know."

"Who?"

"The cops."

"It'll be alright," he says. And much quieter than he came in, my eldest brother wriggles through the window and into the night.

—⟋⟍—

There are things I must know about my brother.

An apprehensive smile spreads across my face as I realize where they may be found.

# twenty

# The Cedar Chest

The attic door swings downward with barely a squeak, releasing dust and heat and musty odors. It's been months since I've seen the ladder slide toward me, bidding me clamor upward. Tonight butterflies are flapping around my stomach on account of the fear and the anticipation.

I yank a strand of coiled rope to secure the door behind me and then look around. Who said detective work was easy?

Filtered moonlight struggles through the shuttered window, illuminating the dusty floorboards and my somber face. I've had adventures here before, plenty of them, but never in the middle of the night. If I'm caught, I'll try to think up another excuse, one I haven't used before.

It's a shameful thing I do, but the truth is, curiosity has lured me here as surely as if it had sent out a gold-embossed invitation.

The heat and stuffiness are almost unbearable, and I stifle a dry cough, remembering stories I have read where the entire plotline rests on a sneeze, or a sniffle, or a hiccup.

The first time ever I swigged beer was up here with Danny Brown. My entire family was gone for the evening, so we stood by

the south window, our heads turned awkwardly to watch the setting sun. It appeared to be round when we started drinking, but
it began doing funny things. I was pretty sure after I peeled open
the fourth can of beer that the sun was actually *rising* in the west
and that the country songs on the transistor radio we'd dragged
up here were being sung by none other than Jimmy Stewart in a
slow, annoying drawl.

The only thing worse than the music was the warm beer,
though I didn't point this out to Danny. He had stolen seven or
eight cans from his father, who had had enough of them himself
that evening to make counting impossible. It was a joke we began
to play on Mr. Brown with increased regularity, bringing our emp-
ties and piling them around him so that when he woke up he had
not only a hangover but also a deep sense of shame for finishing
fifteen cans of beer all by himself.

I suppose I drink not for love of alcohol but because I am forbidden to do so. It is like I have a list of don'ts and am crossing
them off one at a time, hoping I can throw the list away by graduation.

At the time I winced at the thought of my drinking or smoking
being discovered, mostly because of the shame it would heap
upon my father but also from the knowledge that I would be
kicked out of school. Though I am not the smartest kid to ever
occupy a desk at Lone Pine Christian, I know that expulsion
during your senior year looks a little out of place when underlined
on your job application.

So it was that Danny introduced me to carrot leaves as the
proven remedy for erasing pungent and forbidden odors from my
breath. Deodorant took care of the rest. Unfortunately the cure was
just about as bad as the disease, but still we would stagger into Mr.
Swanson's carrot patch late at night and eat those leaves by the
fistful unless we were too drunk to tell the carrots from the thistles.

Tonight I am glad my faculties have not been dulled by alcohol
as I grope for the bare lightbulb and twist it clockwise. A huge spiderweb frames the window, but the spider has scurried from sight.

The screen on the south window has been pried away by the years, providing a clear and inviting view of the north side of Mary Beth's house, a view I've enjoyed a few times before. It's well past midnight, and the house next door is in darkness, of course, the upstairs lights off, everyone asleep. I am partially disappointed to know this because I must tell you that I've been lured by the view over there as if I were King David looking for Bathsheba. Turning from the window, I scan the room.

The large cedar chest on the westward side is filled with memorabilia and historical news clippings. I should know, being the snoop I am. I saunter over and open it like I've done a dozen times before. On top of the pile sit a foldout hat and a baton from Dad's war years. They rest on Mom's satiny white wedding dress, folded neatly so many years ago. Reverently, I nudge it aside. Buried beneath the dress is a large folder, barely visible in the dim light. I turn it toward the bare bulb. "Will" is stamped across the front. It is unsealed, so I slip it open. Two envelopes with elegant crests are first. They are sealed with red wax, and though I may be curious, I'm not curious enough to break them. Behind the sealed envelopes I find four more. They are addressed to Ben, Liz, Tony, and me. Many years ago I perused the one bearing my name and discovered that there is a mysterious inheritance awaiting us, though I know not how or when.

Today I shall examine Ben's, the thickest of them all.

Sweat is forming on my face and neck, and I am careful to keep it from dripping on the envelope. The last time water ran from my face I was being lifted from Franklin's Creek in baptism, immersed in joy, glowing with newfound resolve. That was two years ago. How times change. There are greater things than faith I need to know about. Things this letter may reveal. Secrets that could help me solve the greatest mystery I've encountered in my short life.

The envelope consists of translucent yellow paper, older than the others. It is crisp, almost brittle, and I take my time unfolding it lest it crumble like a dry soda cracker. With a small neat hand—clearly a woman's—someone has inscribed "Benjamin" on the front. I only dared call my brother this name once, and he punched me hard for it. "It's Ben to you," he said, keeping his fist clenched and raised above me. "I kinda like Benjamin," I told him, backing away toward the door. "But suit yourself, Benjamin," I said. Then I ran like the wind.

Lowering the lid on the cedar chest, I carry the thick envelope closer to the light. There are two letters within and several formal documents titled "Adoption Papers." I must admit I've always had a passionate curiosity for things forbidden. I can remember tip-toeing into my sister's room when she was gone and rifling through her closet for no good reason, or rooting through my mother's purse or Ben's record collection. Mom and Dad would often write things on the jackets, like "Rotten" on the Who's album *Who's Next*, and I would listen carefully to see if they had a point. This insatiable curiosity has been my undoing in times past, but it will not be tonight.

I listen for the sounds of Tony or Liz or Dad. Nothing.

The adoption file holds neatly arranged documents about Ben and Liz, each of them adopted from different families, it appears. I smile to think of the first time I realized that my sister Liz was adopted, for the strangest thought hit me: I could marry her. I wondered what the laws are on such things, but more than that I wondered which I'd die of first if I married her: food poisoning or fatigue from her constant herding. "Man Weds Older Sister in Surprise Ceremony." It would make for the best headline since our editor Edwin Ward's ill-advised slipup: "Father of Twelve Fined $100 for Failing to Stop."

Among the buried papers is a data sheet with lines for birth parents' ethnicity, ages, physical attributes, and the social worker's assessment of their intelligence. I'm relieved that such an assessment has not been done on me.

Has Ben seen this file yet? I wonder. It holds the secrets of the universe for him. His birth mother was 18 when she had him, it says. Graced with brown hair and brown eyes, she weighed 115 pounds, and stood five feet, four inches tall. The most worthwhile information is found in the address section: "1045 Mountain View Crescent, Seattle, Washington." But what about his dad? Under "Birth father" is the answer: "Unknown," a word I have to stare at for a moment. Could he have died tragically? Is he still out there somewhere?

Tucking the files back in place, I wipe the sweat from my face with my upper arms. With surprising reluctance I pull two sheets of paper from an envelope tucked inside Ben's larger one. They are framed by a floral border and worn around the edges, and the handwriting is delicate, feminine. Clearly Ben has read it before, but why would he return it to the chest? I hold the letter reverently, convincing myself that it is a noble task to which I aspire, that I am reading this for everyone's good.

Dear Benjamin,

I am your birth mother, and you are my first child. Today I have made the most difficult decision of my life. I have given you to those I consider more capable than myself. I have wept more tears than I thought possible. I have such happy memories of you. I loved watching your hands and feet move across my stomach when you were in my tummy. Sometimes if I tickled your feet, you'd kick back at me. Three times you woke me in the middle of the night with all your squirming and kicking. Each time I was glad you did. I'd turn on the light and sing to you and pat you until you quieted down again. It was like an angel had wakened me to tell me things would be alright.

Some think I must have been upset and unhappy when I found out I was pregnant. I was angry at myself but never at you. I worried about what to do and what would happen to you and me. But I was awed and pleased and a little proud to think of you inside me. You cannot imagine the things I went through when my sins became known in this little community. Giving you up is the only option that makes any sense. You do not want to go where I am going, and I am ill-equipped to be your mother. Often I think of what it would be like to keep you. I think of how happy I was on the second day of your life, when you first smiled at me. But deep down I wouldn't have been satisfied knowing I wasn't giving you the best I could. Today I did the hardest thing I will ever do. We had a little ceremony, your new parents and I. They are deeply religious, and I hope I have done the right thing by giving you to them. It seemed only right that I gave you up to the one couple in the church who showed me they cared.

I wish for you a full and happy life, and I can only pray that you approve of my decision and don't think too badly of me. The thing I most want you to know is that I love you.

> Yours forever,
> Marguerite

I am sweating profusely as I arrange the envelopes in their rightful spot and close the lid on the chest. I cannot imagine learning so much of my past in one short letter. Has my brother found the house on Mountain View Crescent? Apparently not. Does it still exist? Where is he off to tonight? *Marguerite*. Have I heard that name before? I'm surprised to find small tears in my eyes; perhaps it is the lateness of the hour.

Suddenly I feel exhausted from an evening of discoveries. A light catches my eye. It comes from Mary Beth's house. My pulse quickens as I tiptoe toward the spiderweb and crane my neck for a better view. A thin curtain veils her room from view, but it cannot hide the faint sound of voices wafting out the partially opened window.

"No." It is Mary Beth's voice. "No," she repeats.

From the corner of my eye, I see something move. It is the largest, furriest spider I have ever seen. It has been waiting just inches from my head. The eight-legged creature wriggles toward me aggressively, as if I've stolen one of its babies. Reaching to my right, I grab a dusty old rag and squish it.

A door slams, and Mary Beth's light is extinguished.

I watch through the window, but there is no further movement, only the moon filtering through the willow trees onto the Swanson house.

In the years to come, I would think back often on this night. On that bike ride along the gravel road, that talk in the rain. I would think of the richness of the evening, the fading sky, the reddish dusk. I would remember Mary Beth's smooth skin, the smell of her perfume—Gentle Mist, I think they call it. And I would recall the unforgettable letter and that open window next door.

So many mysteries, this summer of my youth.

# twenty-one

# Album Covers

*I* have read somewhere that there is a drug one can take to aid in concentration during school hours. Never have I needed it more than today. The physical fatigue of being up half the night, combined with the sheer exhaustion of the events of the last few days, have caused me to drift off in the midst of one of Mr. Sprier's boring and nasal lectures on permutations, binomial theorem, and the derivative of a function. He may as well be speaking Mandarin with an Irish accent.

Mr. Sprier's physical characteristics are usually enough to keep me awake. He is a walking cartoon character and the only man I have ever met who displays a gold tooth on those rare occasions when he smiles. Though I've never had the nerve to ask him, rumors persist that the tooth grew that way at a miracle crusade. "Miracle, my eye," laughed my dad when he heard about it. "God is no cosmic dentist, no celestial tooth fairy who fills teeth and sprinkles a little gold dust around."

Whenever I sit in one of his classes or see him drive by in his fancy sports car, I am reminded of what we did to that car, and I wonder why he doesn't call me in or haul me to the principal's office or just tell me outright that I've flunked his math class. Perhaps the most irritating response to a practical joke is to say nothing at all, to act as if it didn't happen, or even worse, to show that it didn't bother you.

I have never fallen asleep in a classroom before, and Michael Swanson stabs me with a compass the moment I do. It is unfortunate. I need my rest.

The clock above our heads inches toward ten o'clock, and in my listless state I am half expecting the police to poke their heads through the classroom door and interrogate me about the ring. By noon, I'm wondering if Tony will come to tell me Ben has been arrested, and by three I am imagining they'll send my father to break the awful news. But instead I hear the constant drone of our instructors, trying to explain more concepts I will never fully understand.

There is no squad car in front of our house after school, no snipers on the roof. It's a good thing. I have three lawns to cut today, and I'd like to finish them before dinner. I have formulated a plan for this evening. Hauling out our rickety old mower, I fill it with fuel, careful to flex my muscles all the while. But Mary Beth is nowhere to be seen. In fact, Michael seems to be the only one watching. Bummer. He leans over the fence and laughs at who knows what. "Hey, come over for a drink," he beckons.

"What do you have? Vodka?"

"Very funny," says Michael. "Come, I've got something to show you."

From the outside, the Swanson place looks dark and secretive, but inside, it is a thing of beauty. Shag carpets have been peeled from aging hardwoods, and the walls on the main floor have been brightened with fresh paint, the color of watered-down mustard. Mary Beth stands in the kitchen leaning over the sink. "Hey!" I say as I pass. Her mouth is too full of something to respond, but she manages an embarrassed snicker. It's a good sign, I think. The glance we exchange is filled with memories of last night. At least I hope she finds as much in the glance as I do.

Michael's bedroom is at the bottom of a narrow and rickety set of basement stairs where we come often in the summer months, retreating from the heat to listen to music through headphones.

It's funny how my relationship with Michael has cooled lately. Danny Brown and I have more in common it seems, but I'm doing my best to keep Michael as a friend. Is it on account of him being the younger brother to the girl of my dreams? Perhaps. Somehow he has always been able to earn more money than I have, which is not necessarily the basis for a good friendship, but it is a start. He spends his money freely, buying the latest top-forty albums and letting me record them. Once he threatened to bill me for them, but I got to reading carefully selected portions of the copyright infringement laws on the back cover, and he changed his mind.

He too wants to know about the body, so I indulge him a little, embellishing the details, recounting the puffy face, the thick tongue hanging out, the one eye that wouldn't quite close.

Michael takes the stairs two at a time to bring us some weak lemonade. "Look at this," he says, pointing at some gizmo he's just pulled fresh from a box.

In recent months he has graduated from his cheap Phillips tape recorder to Sony equipment that I am guilty of coveting as I sip the lemonade. Today he wants to show me something called a mixer, which allows him to plug in two record players and a microphone and then filter the sound to a tape player, doing voice-overs and dubs that would make a radio station proud. I once entertained hopes of being a DJ one day, of hosting a weekly show called Terry's Top Ten or something like that. I would start each broadcast with a tribute to my brothers Tony and Ben, of course, as they gave me my start during those imaginary radio shows we had when we could not sleep.

Most of Michael's record albums don't have jackets because they are in the trash. If his father found a Rolling Stones record, that would be the end of his world, so Michael is careful. I once asked him about possible punishment were he caught, and all he did was shudder. "I don't even want to think about it," he said, sliding some forbidden vinyl LP into a Sunday Singers jacket.

In no time at all we have plugged the cords into the system, and I have plunked myself before a microphone. Scattered about me on the bed are record albums. Pink Floyd. Steve Miller. The Eagles. Linda Ronstadt. They have been concealed in jackets bearing pictures of George Beverley Shea and the Bill Gaither Trio.

Michael fiddles with levers and buttons as I start practicing for the big time: "We're comin' at you from radio station KBIZ playin' the hits you love to hear." Michael smiles and fades in the first song, with a catchy keyboard and bass riff. "I'm sending this first one out to one of our loyal listeners, a girl who makes heads turn and hearts beat faster wherever she goes, Mary Beth Swanson."

"One of these nights," sing the Eagles, and I peel the headphones off and sink back in the chair. Michael, the technician, is watching the needles bob around, and he seems content with his part. "I'm taping it," he says. "You can give it to my sister. She'll love it."

My DJ voice needs some work, so I try various styles: soft and low, the voice of a crooner; excited, like Wolfman Jack, whom I caught Tony listening to once. "Baby, this is one of the greats, one that makes you want to get down and boogie, boogie, boogie." Michael is trying not to laugh as he fades my voice out and the song up: "Jungle love, it's making me mad, it's making me crazy."

I dedicate most of the songs to Mary Beth, especially ones by Olivia Newton-John, breathy songs like "I Honestly Love You."

When we are through, Michael scratches my initials on the tape and adds it to a private stash.

I'll finish it tomorrow and then summon the courage to give it to Mary Beth.

I am only able to complete two yards before dinner, one for Pastor Davis, whose wife, Irene, pays cash, and the other for the Hodges, who have been promising to pay for two weeks now.

Three bucks later, I'm home, poking my nose in the refrigerator, optimistic that a snack is waiting. Liz is kneading bread nearby. She shoos me from the fridge and makes me put on an apron to help. "I'm building my very first loaf," she says. "Didn't rise a bit. Flat as a sidewalk. Must be the yeast. Or maybe the kneading. Here, you smack it awhile." Liz wants nothing more than to be a mother one day, but she may have to order meals in.

"If it won't rise, smacking it won't help," I say. "I remember watching Mom doing this."

"Just hit the thing," she orders.

"We can use it for a boat anchor," I say, causing her to smile and pummel me between the shoulder blades.

The flour-covered book she has open before her is *Western Cookin' Made Easy* by Idella Martz. She reads it to me: "Always keep the work area clean. Keep a damp cloth nearby and a knife to level off the measuring spoons." Liz sprinkles a dash of caraway rye into the dough and then pinches some off to sample it. "Not bad," she says rather proudly. "A little crispy though."

It feels good, punching the bread with my fists, watching it give way to my energetic smacks. I find myself imagining it being the faces of the two homely police officers as they cross-examined us.

Dad has told me to respect the jerks, that the Bible urges us to pray for those in authority, but suddenly we're not playing on the same team, are we? Suddenly they are the Yankees and we're the Dodgers. I wonder where they're surveying the house from and what they see.

"Tare," Liz interrupts my violent thoughts. "Do you like Mary Beth?" Her voice sounds like she's been thinking about it awhile and finally has the nerve to ask it. Now what do you do with a question like that? You try to answer it nonchalantly, as if it's no big deal, but the very mention of Mary Beth's name causes me to smile.

"What do you mean *like?*" I say belligerently.

"You know what I mean."

"Who wants to know?"

"Me. I've been over there quite a bit." Liz is spreading a towel on the dough as I continue punching it.

"Yeah. So?"

"I just don't know that it's a great idea, that's all."

Of all the harebrained things I've heard today, this tops the list.

"I don't understand. You sometimes hang out together."

"I know. It's just that—"

The phone interrupts our ridiculous conversation. Liz slaps the flour off on an apron before answering it and handing it to me. I cradle the phone between my shoulders and neck while continuing to slam the dough with my fists.

"Terry," Michael Swanson is out of breath and whispering. "My dad found your tape."

"What tape?"

"The one you made for Mary Beth."

"Oh, *that* tape."

"You're in trouble."

"*I'm* in trouble? What about *you?* They're your albums. You made the tape."

"What will we do?" Michael is making strange clicking sounds on the line, like he's scratching the receiver with nervous fingers.

"I don't know. What's your dad gonna do? Shoot me? Hang me?" I am imagining Mr. Swanson's face in the bread now.

Michael pauses, then laughs, a fake and nervous laugh.

"He wants to see you Sunday night. After the evening service."

"You're kidding."

"I wish I were."

"Why does he have to drag it out so long?"

"Who knows. Just don't be late."

I shake my head. "I'll be there."

# twenty-two

# Circle of Six

My first task after dinner is to brush my teeth, something that almost removes the taste of the Spam sandwiches dear Liz concocted. Then I'm off to finish another yard for a nonpaying customer before dodging light raindrops to the Franklin Library, which is open one evening a week.

Named after Ryan Franklin, founder of our quaint little town, the library is brains in cold storage according to Tony. He used to play a joke on the librarian by slipping Ryan Franklin III's book *A Brief History of Grace* into the fiction section, for though it claims to tell the story of our roots, the book is riddled with dubious details, placing Cherokees where they weren't and heaping undue praise upon Franklin for feats he could not possibly have achieved. The joke was never funny to Miss Hudson—few things are—but she was not hired for her sense of humor, nor her ability to sport the latest fashions. Today she is wearing thick spectacles, a blue blouse with pink stripes, and a plaid skirt that almost reaches her ankles. She pulls a pencil from behind an ear and points me left, past the fiction section and over to the archives.

The annals of the Franklin Library are sparse, save for neglected piles of our weekly newspaper that date back to the 1940s. With few exceptions they are stacked by year, and I flip through the waist-high mountains of yellowing papers until the date on the front parallels the date of the clipping Ben pulled from his dresser drawer, September 11, 1957.

Sitting down at a dusty table, I thumb my way to page seven. Bingo. The fuzzy photo on the far right bears a brief caption: *Men of Franklin Baptist to start ministry.* Five smiling faces are in the photo. Three heads are crowned by cowboy hats.

A familiar face grins at me from the far left. Though the years have added wrinkles and stolen some hair, I'd know those kind eyes anywhere. But who is that beside my father? I'm unsure at first. It's hard to believe he ever weighed this little, yet a promising little paunch pokes out before him, and it's undeniable. The man is Mary Beth's dad, Mr. Swanson. Smack in the middle of the frame is Francis Frank. I have to look at the tiny story beside the photo to know this. He is proudly lapping up the attention, clearly the center of it all. His arms rest on the two on either side of him, and his head is bald as a cue ball. I was just a kid when he left town, and I cannot remember his face. Next up is a beady-eyed bullfrog of a man. I'd know those squinty little eyes anywhere. He is Danny Brown's atheist father. It's one of the only times I've seen him smile.

I strain to see the fifth man, the guy on the right. He is taller than the rest, his face shaded a little from the Stetson on his head. I don't think I've seen him before, though I cannot be sure. According to the story his name is Clive Barker; nothing further is written about him.

In the background, I see part of a vaguely familiar face, but I can't quite tell who it is. He must have been moving when the photographer clicked the shutter. I can see a hole in his grin where a tooth should be. Was he upset at not being included?

The accompanying article explains how the men are set to begin a traveling ministry, evangelizing the western states.

Strange my father never spoke of it.

—⁓—

Tony is on a roll in the irritating letters department. He received another response today—though not from Pastor Pedro—and is anxious to show it to me. His outgoing file is growing as well. He is holding two of them when I enter the house.

"Hey, check it out," he says, grinning. "This is the original."

It is dated about a month ago and addressed to The Watchtower Society, Columbia Heights, Brooklyn, New York.

"What do they believe?" I ask.

"Read it, you'll see. Then I'll show you the response."

And so I do.

> Hello,
>
> I am 12 years old and I am to do a paper for our seven grade religion class and it is counts for 50% of my farnal mark and that meeks me mad! But I am hoping for you. The papor is on The Last Times (are we there yet I think I might call it), so I am stedying The Jehovah's Witnessers.
>
> I am saying when the end of the times would be and my dad said that you perple no. My dad gave me some of yours books that he had downstairs. There really old and beg. One is called The Battle of Armageddon, and I think that was a cool kuver, but it weren't what I thought. Dad showed me were it say the coming of Jesus (second one) happened in 1874. I didn't know that be for now.
>
> Then he shown me that the Watch Tower papor said the world would end in 1914. Then God or someone changed it to 1918 and 1920 and other times like 1925, and 1941 and 1975. I just need to no when it will end now. Do you no? Also is it true that Michael Jackson is

the really Arkangel Michael? I heard that. Mom was reeding a novel about it saying the end was near so she is interested to.

Please write,

Tony Anderson

PS: Did you know that Watchtower Society can be rearranged to spell "Wow! Try a choice test"? I thank that scool.

All I can do is shake my head.

"Look. This came today," he says, holding up an envelope like he's about to announce a lottery winner. "Pretty impressive that they'd turn it around in a month." He pulls out the letter and lets it flutter to the kitchen table.

Dear Tony,

What a treat to hear from you! Your questions are good ones, and we are happy that you included your street address. We will be sending a representative of our faith out to see you and to answer them.

Sincerely,

John Namp,
The Watchtower Society

—⁓—

As I hold the ring in my hand tonight, I wish for all the world that I hadn't taken it for myself. I found it irresistible at the time, sitting there on the floor, calling my name. What could a dead man possibly want with the thing? It wouldn't hurt anyone to take it. Besides, I had learned how valuable they were when we studied Yogo sapphires in social studies class.

For some reason I was paying enough attention that day to

learn that a hundred years ago a gold miner by the name of Jake Hoover sent a cigar box full of them to Tiffany's in New York to see what they were worth. According to our social studies teacher, the regal blue rock has been America's most precious native stone ever since. When I showed the ring to old Mr. Penny at Penny's Jewelry, he didn't say a word. He just took it from me and examined it with his magnifying loop. He was shaking badly at the time, something I took as a good sign, but my hopes were soon dashed. He placed the value of the fake stones at three dollars—what I make from a paying customer cutting their grass.

I am examining it closely when I notice a small engraving on the inside of the ring. It's a tiny circle with the number six in it. Or it could be nine. I push the ring back in my drawer, wondering again why I picked it up in the first place.

# twenty-three

# Backyard Witness

What's it like having a Christian for a dad?"

We are flat on our backs, hands cradling our heads, gazing straight up at the Friday night sky from the semi-privacy of my backyard. It's been quite an evening already. Danny showed up unannounced at youth group, for the second week in a row he tells me, and was surprised at how much fun he had. He has peeled off his socks, rolled up his pant legs, and stretched out in the uncut grass beside me, with more questions than an annoying three-year-old. For the past few months his blasted inquiries about things spiritual have been unrelenting, and I have grown weary of the endless and escalating string of them.

"If there's a God, why doesn't He do something? Why doesn't He fix the world, end all the hunger, the sickness? And how could He send people to hell? These aren't real bad people we're talking about here. And what about the hypocrites? Your church has tons of them."

The truth of it is, I couldn't agree more. These same questions began haunting me a few years back when Ben started asking them. He liked to stand with me at an open refrigerator late at night, destroying my fragile faith while building himself a pickle sandwich. He had usually been drinking—his breath smelled like someone spilled the rubbing alcohol—as he asked me deep questions I was unqualified to answer. How I wished Tony were there. Tony, my blood brother, who always had more answers than Heinz had pickles. But he was away at Bible college, deepening his beliefs while I lost mine.

I wonder why I'm unwilling to tell this to Danny. Perhaps an admission that I've been wrong all these years is a slight against my intelligence, against my family. And why'd he have to pick me as Mr. Answer Man? Why not Michael Swanson? He's questioning the one guy on our side of the creek least likely to care about the answers.

"What if the devil repents? Would God forgive him?"

I can't help laughing. "I guess so. Why not?"

"But then what happens to the Book of Revelation? All that Bible prophecy?"

"Do you remember when Mr. Baumgartner used to witness to us?" I am trying my best to divert him. Danny snickers as I remind him of a favorite activity of our childhood.

Ned Baumgartner was the church Sunday school superintendent back then and a walking Bible encyclopedia. But with all his knowledge of Christendom, he could not for the life of him recall our names and faces, which side of the creek we lived on, or whether or not we were in his Sunday school class the past weekend. When Danny and I discovered this we decided to have a little fun with it. We would pass him on the sidewalk, purposely sporting miserable expressions. Ned would stop us, of course, and ask with genuine concern in his voice, "How you doing, boys?"

"Not very good," came the answer.

"What is it?"

"I can't find any cigarettes. Do you have any?" Danny was bold enough to say this.

"No, but I have something much better."

"What is it? Drugs? Alcohol?"

"It won't cost you a thing, boys."

"Good. Because I spent all my money on gambling. Do you have any chewing tobacco? I'm so hungover from that party last night, I couldn't handle another drink."

I couldn't believe Danny's words, and the sheer implausibility of it all put me in mind of chiming in. "You shoulda seen him," I added. "I didn't think a guy could throw up that much."

We both stared at Mr. Baumgartner, bleary-eyed.

Gingerly climbing off his one-speed bicycle, the old man selected a couple of tracts from a wicker basket taped to the handlebars and handed them to us. They were entitled *This Was Your Life* and showed a man who lived for wickedness, for wine, women, and song, until the angel of death came for his soul.

"Wow, this is really cool," I said. "We'll look them over." And we were on our way, waving at the kind old man, me chuckling softly, hoping the laughter would hide the terrible guilt I was feeling inside.

But tonight the guilt is gone. Tonight I am wearing Mr. Baumgartner's shoes, wondering which of Danny's questions are serious and which ones I should laugh at. I'd hoped Danny's foray into church would cure him of all these questions so he would leave me alone. But it's only served to double them. I wish he'd just keep quiet or talk about something else. Girls preferably.

"So, if God created us, why did He do it?"

"So He could love us, I guess. So we could love Him."

"And where is He? Is He up there?" Danny points at a constellation. Orion, I think.

I don't wish to look ignorant, so I do my best to parrot the answers I've been given through the years. Tonight I wish I had some electronic apparatus like they use in the movies, with Tony prompting me on the other end. It would be fun. Maybe he could hide in the bushes with thick Bible commentaries and feed answers through an earphone, answers that would astound my friend, causing him to marvel at my brilliant responses.

"He's in heaven, I guess. He's everywhere, actually. He's omnipresent." I roll my head a few degrees to look at Danny. He seems impressed by my use of Tony's word. "And omnipotent," I add.

*"Gesundheit."*

"It means all-powerful, you know? Omniscient is all-knowing."

The more definitions I add, the less impressed he seems. "Terry, you don't talk about God much anymore." He states it as a fact; it's not up for debate.

"Oh?"

"Does growing up around God make it easier to believe?"

"I don't know. I think it makes it harder sometimes."

"Dad says some people believe in unicorns, but that doesn't make them true." Danny's jumps in logic are hard to follow.

"But what if you had pictures of a unicorn? What if you found one and you fed him some hay?"

He laughs. "I don't see what that has to do with anything."

"Me neither."

"The Irish Rovers believed in 'em."

"What?"

"Unicorns. You haven't heard their song?"

"Nope."

Danny plucks a piece of grass and wedges it between his teeth. He starts to sing "Green alligators and long-necked geese" without changing notes once.

"How can you know there isn't a God?" I ask just for the fun of it. "Aren't you a little scared there might be?" I'm mimicking Tony really, and I'm sarcastic if I'm anything.

Danny stops fidgeting and grows quiet. "Know what really freaks me out? I've been listening to Supertramp—you know, *Breakfast in America*." He starts to sing in his monotone voice, "There are times when all the world's asleep, the questions run too deep for such a simple man."

"That's me," Danny continues. "I lie awake at night thinking about eternity, wondering how everything can just go on and on for millions of years without end. It's got me spooked. I have these deep desires inside me that I don't understand. I once heard your brother Tony ask my dad if he was walking down a dark alley late at night and he saw six men coming toward him, would he be glad to know that they had just been at a Bible study? It's one of the few times I've heard Dad laugh. I know some of these things, but I'd just like to see some proof that God exists."

"Maybe you haven't looked everywhere. Maybe you're looking in the wrong places."

"I suppose. Have *you* seen Him?"

"Who?"

"God."

"No. I guess not."

"Well then."

I know what Tony would say. "Have you ever seen the wind?"

"Nope."

"But you've seen trees blown over, right? You can see what it does."

"I guess so. I just don't see God knocking people over, that's all. I don't see Him doing much with you." Ouch. Why'd he have to add that?

"You'll find stories in the Bible where He knocks people over. Knocks 'em out." Tony would like that response.

"See, that's another thing. My dad says the Bible is full of holes. Lies. Inconsistencies. You can't believe any of it."

"Do you read it?"

"A little bit. Dad finds out, he'll murder me. How about you? Do you?"

"Well, not much anymore. But that's no—"

"You don't read it much?"

"Well—"

"Okay, here's something I've wondered awhile. How can you

believe in God when, well, when your mother has gone through all this…stuff? I mean, don't you ever get doubts in your mind?"

The pause is so long Danny probably thinks I've taken offense at his asking. "My dad won't talk about my mother," he says, trying to fill the silence. "Says it's gone. In the past. But it's not. It's with him all the time."

"What do you mean?"

"Something happened when I was just a baby. I don't know what it was. I just know that she died. My dad was a minister, you know."

"A what? A minister? Your dad?" Of all the people I've met, he would be the most unlikely. I've never heard a man cuss a blue streak quite as eloquently as Mr. Brown. He would make comedians like Richard Pryor blush. I've heard him rant against the church, shaking his fist at God until I was amazed God didn't knock him dead. He's a man who needs a dustpan to go with his sweeping generalizations. And I admire him for it.

"What kind of minister?"

"Baptist, I think. I know it's hard to believe, but I found boxes of books once—three or four of them—in our basement. God stuff. And there was a plaque. He was an ordained minister."

"When?"

"I don't know. Before I was born, I guess."

"Do you ever talk about it?"

"No. I tried once. Didn't get far."

Suddenly I'm glad he's asking these questions. They've unsettled me, to be sure, but they've provided comfort too. It's good to refresh my reasons for not believing, good to have a friend who feels the way I do, who believes life is for living, not contemplating.

I wonder when I'll summon the courage to tell him exactly what I think.

I wonder how blind he is to the inconsistencies in my life.

# twenty-four

# Orphan

*D*anny yawns and stretches his arms. Then he settles back and looks at the stars. His silence is a relief for me. All this hypocrisy is hard work.

I've been watching Mary Beth's window, wondering where she is and when she'll come home. She usually arrives about nine, a little early for a girl her age. It's nice having her there though, seeing the light come on. I wonder what she'd do if I tossed pebbles at her window to say hi. I wonder how much longer she'll be occupying that room.

"Do you mind me asking about your mom?" Danny follows my gaze and looks at the window too.

"Nope. Fire away."

"Don't you get angry at God sometimes?"

"Yeah. There are things I don't understand. Important things." I'd prefer he not hear how angry I've been. It's one thing to try to explain faith. Maybe it's harder to explain a lack of it.

"Like God is supposed to be good, right? Why does He let such awful stuff happen?"

"I've tried to answer that. I don't think I can. Maybe God has a reason. Dad says we're tested. Maybe this is a test. But it's a long one. She's been sick for years. Tony says the world is full of sin and that's what happens. Says God doesn't owe us anything."

"But isn't God supposed to be a father? Would you let your kid suffer if you could help it?"

"Nope."

"Then I just don't get it."

"Me neither. I guess the one thing I can see is that it's changed my dad and Liz and Tony. Made them better people."

"What about you?"

"It's—" I cannot finish the sentence.

"You know, the thing that keeps me wondering about these things is watching your family. I've never been able to understand how your dad can smile and joke around with me. It's—well, not what I'm used to."

How can I disagree? The truth of it is, I can explain my way out of most things, but I cannot explain my father's life.

"Hell," says Danny. It's not unusual for him to start a sentence that way. But that's not what he means. "What about it? Dad always quotes some guy named Ingersoll. Roger or something. He says only a God who loves revenge would invent such a horrible thing."

How can I tell him that I totally agree?

"Tony says that Jesus believed in it and that's good enough for him. He says that's why Jesus came and died, so we don't have to go there. Everyone gets to choose. That's how God made us. We get a free will." It's an explanation I've tried to argue against myself.

Danny is quiet awhile, and then he's back at it. "Dad says Jesus was a good man, a great teacher, and that's the end of it."

I'm surprised to be remembering all these arguments Tony has used. "'Anyone who claimed to be God can't just be a great teacher,' my brother says. 'Either he's lying, or he's loony tunes, or he's Lord.' That's what Tony thinks."

There is more silence. "I know the answer." Danny's voice is barely above a whisper. "I know which one."

The stars overhead are dimmed as someone turns a light on at the Swanson home. It is Mary Beth. Danny doesn't seem to notice.

"I've been doing a lot of thinking, Terry," he says, sitting straight up. "I don't understand a lot of things, but I'm gonna give it a try."

"Huh?"

"I guess I'm ready."

"Ready for what?"

"To become a Christian."

"Pardon me?" I try to hide my shock. "Who do you take me for? Ned Baumgartner?"

"No, I'm serious."

"You're kidding."

"No I'm not," says Danny, and suddenly I know he is telling the truth.

"Well, um…can't you wait till church?"

"Why not now?"

"Well, why don't you talk to my dad? He's in the house."

"No, I wanted it to be you."

"You're not kidding?"

"There's stuff I still don't understand. But I believe. There's no way around it. It's making more sense than anything else. I can't turn out some broken-down shadow like my father. I've watched your family. There's something there I can't fight against. It's enough for me."

I'm trying to think of something to say, but I don't know where to start.

"Isn't there a prayer I'm supposed to pray or something?"

I want to speak, but warring emotions are strangling my words. All I can do is hang my head in shame. Danny thinks I'm bowing in prayer, so he folds his hands awkwardly like he's seen the people do in church. "God," he whispers, in a twittery voice which grows bolder with each sentence, "I don't know what You could want with a kid like me, but I'd like to be Your child. You be my Father now." He looks at me. "Is that it?"

"I think you should tell Him you're a sinner."

"He knows that already."

"Then say amen."

"What does that mean anyway?"

"I don't know. It kind of seals the deal, I think."

"Amen."

And here I am. Standing to my feet in a phony embrace. Ashamed and angry. Angry that the one friend I had who was heading my direction has turned tail and run. I'm surrounded by trouble, cornered by Christians. Questioning God more than I ever have before.

—w—

It's half past midnight and I'm still awake, still stewing over the events of the day, still wishing for some things. I wish I'd finished studying for Monday's chemistry exam. I wish I'd kept my big mouth shut with Tony's bogus answers. I wish my brother Ben would come back even if he scares me to death at the window. I wish he'd tap on it now to explain the mysteries. Maybe we could find Danny and talk him out of his decision. I wish my window was on the south side of our house so I could see a little more of Mary Beth tonight. I wish she hadn't talked of leaving.

My thoughts drift toward my mother, as they do so often in the night. Not a day goes by, not one, when I do not think of her as she used to be. But the image is slipping further from my grasp. As I lie alone in the darkness, I search my memory for some small scrap of recollection that has eluded me: a crumb of a conversation, some gesture, some shared experience. When they come, the memories are valuable coins that I turn over and over, hoping the markings haven't faded.

Almost unbelievably, there's a gentle tapping sound at the window, barely audible. Harry lets go a low growl. Could it be?

*Ben.*

I'm almost too terrified to look out, but I walk on wobbly knees and peek over the windowsill. The moon reflects off Danny Brown's forehead, and a pleading look is in his eyes.

"I need a place to stay," he whispers, once I finally push the window up enough. "It's just for tonight. My dad wants me out."

"Huh?"

"I told him what I did. He wants me out of the house."

"What the—" I feel like finishing the sentence but better not. "Uh…come in," I stammer, "you can sleep in Ben's bed."

"You sure? What will your dad say?"

"It's fine. I'll tell him in the morning."

"Funny," says Danny, when he's finally wedged his body through the window. "The best day of my life turned into this." He stands there like the orphan he is, holding a small makeshift bag of some sort. Probably jammed with whatever he could scrape together.

"It's not so bad," I offer, "Come on, try out the bed. A little lumpy but you'll be fine."

Danny smiles. "Thanks," he says, slumping on the bed, clearly exhausted. "Um…do you pray before you go to sleep? It seems like we should."

I can't help grinning at the darkened ceiling as Danny leads us in a faltering prayer. Strange things have happened to me in my short life, but few stranger than the events of this night. Me, an eighteen-year-old party-loving agnostic leading my atheist friend to Christ. Who will buy cigarettes for me now?

# twenty-five

# Direct Line

My father, part-time mechanic, World War II veteran, and the greatest earthly hero a boy can imagine, stands beside my mother's bed while she sleeps. He doesn't look at her so much as he looks about the room, memorizing the nooks and crannies, I suppose, remembering what once was. Lately I have seen him reading books to her, books that she read me in childhood. The covers held a magical world for me, a world where animals talked and laughed and cried, where they loved and were loved. Perhaps it is the only world my mother has left, an imaginary world of what might have been.

My favorite stories were the ones by Thornton W. Burgess. Mom would finish one of his run-on sentences, lay the book aside, and tell me how Mr. Burgess loved Jesus and how a hundred-dollar bill had been found in his Bible when he died back in 1965 at the age of 91. The Gideons place Bibles in hotel rooms, she told me, and wealthy people sometimes put money in them as a reward for those who read them. "It's usually placed near Matthew 7:7, 'Seek, and ye shall find,'" she said. "Never stop seeking, Terry."

My mother was seldom able to resist preaching a good sermon—back when she was able to talk.

I am in the kitchen earlier than usual this Saturday morning, watching my father through the bedroom doorway and wondering how I'll break the news about Danny, whose newfound faith has not yet cured him of snoring.

Dad tilts his head to the right while scanning the titles of books he has enjoyed with her, his fingers marching along the spines. I can't help noticing that he has moved a small cot in there, a cot where he sleeps now, a few feet from the double they once shared. It's awkward to think of your parents in separate beds, not that you dwell on it or volunteer the information to your friends.

In most families it is the father who begins to stoop through the years. He develops a bubble in the middle and a crouch in the posture and the ever-present desire to yank the footrest on an easy chair so he can fall asleep reading the newspaper. As time advances, our fathers age more quickly than our mothers. They lose their hair and their patience, appearing less agile to withstand the passing years. But not in the Anderson household. I have often wished my miracle-working father would heal my mother, but perhaps it is a greater miracle to see him grow stronger as he cares for his invalid wife. And the more he cares for her, the more I care to know where this courage comes from. The truth is, everything about him stands in sharp contrast to the way things should be.

My father's father was a stranger, seldom around. A visiting celebrity in his home, Dad once called him, while we were chucking a tattered baseball around the backyard. We stopped throwing for a minute while he told me that a whiff of cigar smoke on a busy sidewalk, or plaid shirts in a store window, or trout flies in a tackle box brought his father back to life. When we resumed throwing the ball, I didn't notice him staring at me without seeing and the ball struck him hard on the shoulder. I half expected him to fall to the ground or at least start hollering at me. Instead, Dad simply picked it up and chucked it back as if nothing had happened.

Most of my friends' fathers are good for nothing except making money. My dad does a lousy job of that, preferring instead to make memories. He helped me build a go-cart once and showed me how to string a baseball mitt. Though he's forty years my elder, he used to wrestle me on the musty carpet whenever he could. In some ways I've never thought of him as a dad really, more as an old uncle who tries to spoil you a bit when your parents aren't looking. Aside from hoping I would pick up the family business once he dropped it, I've felt little pressure from my dad. Perhaps he is too busy with other things. Or he may have noticed that I can scarcely tell which end of the wrench to turn the nut with. Or is it the bolt?

I have often thought that my father is in the wrong line of work. He should be a faith healer or something. Last summer, after a morning church service, we went out to the parking lot to find that the side mirrors on our old Mercury had been torn from the car and placed on the driver's seat. I was ready to rip the culprit's head off and throw it in with the mirrors should we ever find him. But Dad had other plans. At lunch that day we prayed for the guilty party, and Dad told us he'd be adding whoever it was to his lengthy prayer list. Two weeks later with the mirrors repaired, we parked in the same spot and dutifully sat through the service. Pastor Davis opened a new series on Second Peter that day. His first sermon was called "Be Heart Smart," which Tony anagrammed for me into "breath tamers" and "Beth are smart."

As an opening illustration, a cardiologist from our church stepped forward to give our slightly pudgy pastor a physical, something that thrilled us all to no end. He didn't do a complete physical of course, but we did get to see Pastor Davis submit to a pulse check, a blood pressure exam, and a flashlight probing of the eyeballs. The cardiologist then suggested to our dear pastor that he get more exercise and endure a little less stress. Then he patted his paunch and recommended a little weight loss too.

Perhaps it was the pressure of the moment, but Pastor Davis did something he would regret all summer. He told the congregation he would lose one pound a week for seven weeks. Then, in a moment of further insanity, he told them he would weigh in each week before the message in front of the faithful.

By summer's end he had lost twenty-four pounds, six ounces.

The final message of the summer was on accountability, and surprisingly, Pastor Davis gave an altar call. More surprising still was the fact that thirteen people came forward and knelt at the front. Dad went up to pray with one of them, a young man who couldn't stop crying.

Turned out he was the one who had done the damage to our mirrors.

Without a doubt, my father seems to have a direct line to heaven. But when I ask him why he can't get God's attention about Mother, he just smiles. "Sometimes God says no," is his response.

Other mysteries surround my father, things he won't tell me about even when I ask. Snooping through the attic years ago I pried open a letter he had written that was intended to be read when his last will and testament was opened. The letter hinted at an inheritance, but no amount of questioning has brought me the truth.

From my brothers I have heard whispers of a great deal of money awaiting us upon someone's death—maybe mine. And, not surprisingly, rumors drift through town. I have heard it said that my father once invested in stocks and bonds in his spare time and is now an eccentric millionaire who wouldn't have to work another day unless he wanted to. There has been talk of lottery jackpots, of my grandfather striking it rich at the racetracks, of a lawsuit that was settled with a negligent doctor over my mother's illness. Dad shakes his head at such suggestions. "Ludicrous," he says, his eyes twinkling brightly.

But one thing is sure, there is a mysterious inheritance to be had, and I'd like to know how. Maybe Ben is out there now, trying to ensure that we collect, trying to finish the deal.

Perhaps a clue lies in a story I've often heard my father tell.

When my parents were first married, they found themselves living next door to a bedridden widow lady, four times their age, who had one foot in the grave and the other on a banana peel. She rarely left the house and was as mean as a den of wolverines. "She would sooner bite you than look at you," was the way Dad put it. So he took it as a challenge to coax a smile out of her. He brought her fresh-cut flowers. "Get them out of the house," she hollered. "One whiff of those things and I puff up." He brought her home-grown carrots from Mom's garden. "I can't chew carrots, you idiot," she told him, "What'sa matter wichew?" He tried home-made bread. She said she had celiac disease, whatever that is. He tried chocolates—they made her chunky.

Impervious, Dad found some discarded lodgepole pines, peeled them himself, milled them into boards, and fashioned them into a chair. He perfected the project with mortise and tenon joinery, stained it like it was mahogany, and covered the sanded chair with a shiny veneer. With anticipation, he placed this work of art on her front patio and waited three days for her to notice. Of course she said nothing, so Dad went over and offered to lug her out the door each evening so she could sit on his beautiful creation and watch the world go by.

My mother heard the yelling and thought she'd pay the miserable old lady a visit. Nudging my father aside, Mom cleared her throat and let her have it. "Ma'am," she said, "you're gonna sit in that chair if I have to kill you and plant you there myself."

The poor woman's bottom jaw dropped dangerously low, and for the first time in years she was speechless. For more than a month, Dad carried her outside and placed her in that blanketed pine chair. Twice each day Mother brought her soups and breads and strained carrots. She was slow to eat them at first, perhaps from wondering if Mom would follow through on her threat, but the meals didn't kill her. In fact, they had quite the opposite effect, bringing her to life for a time and coaxing a beautiful smile to her face.

"She went peacefully in her sleep," my father told us. "It was the only funeral I ever conducted. We could find no one else to attend, though we tried to contact her only son. It was just me, your mother, and an undertaker who was wearing a chalk-covered black suit and a crooked red tie with the knot tucked under the collar. He cried like a baby. I still don't know why."

Three weeks after they laid her to rest, a letter arrived. "It was from her son," said Dad. "He was in California or someplace warm like that. Said he'd be coming through town, that he wanted to meet us. I couldn't help wondering if he'd accuse us of killing her with flowers or with yeast. But he never did."

"Wasn't she rich?" I interrupted. "Didn't she leave you something?"

"Nope."

That's all Dad would say. I guess the meeting wasn't important.

# twenty-six

# Chef

"Dad, is it okay if Danny Brown stays the night? And do you think you could buy me a car for graduation?" I've always found two questions can confuse my father into saying yes to the lesser one.

My father steps from the bedroom and quietly closes the door.

"What's that?" he whispers, joining me in the search for some cold cereal.

"Danny Brown?"

"Oh," he says, "sure, no problem."

"The car?"

"I'll fix up the old Merc for you. Maybe even wash it." Then he adds, "You're up early, aren't you? You teenagers are in the prime sleeping years of your life."

I smile. "Yeah, I've got a few things to do."

Beside my foot is a Singer sewing machine, standing in sharp contrast to the plain furniture throughout the rest of the house. Dad proudly proclaims it to be the first ever zigzag machine, the most advanced product of its day, from a company "dedicated to helping people express themselves through sewing." It must have been a gift, something so beautiful.

"Where did we get this?" I ask.

"Oh, it's a long story," says Dad.

He bows his head in prayer, and we sit in silence at the table, the only sound the quiet munching of corn flakes before they turn soggy and lose their crunch.

Dad breaks the silence. "Did I hear something last night? About midnight, maybe later? Sounded like banging."

It would be foolish to disguise a truth that is destined to come out.

"Danny came to the window last night."

"Oh?"

"He's sleeping in my room. His...well, his dad kicked him out."

The crunching stops. "He *what?*"

"Kicked him out. We were talking last night and Danny...well, I led him to Christ." I regret the words the moment they're out. My father's mouth is full and he's trying to process an earful of surprising information too.

He grabs my shoulder too hard. "Terry, I'm so proud of you! That is marvelous news! Praise God! But what will we do?"

"I thought he could stay here with us for now. Is that okay?"

"Of course it is. I just don't know...I guess...well, I guess I'll have to visit Mr. Brown."

Danny staggers into the kitchen, bleary-eyed. He doesn't say a word; he just sits down at the table and looks at us as if he's still in a dream. Dad smiles at him and reaches across the table. "Welcome to the family," he says, grabbing Danny's hand a little too tightly. Then he wrinkles his nose. "Whew. You been smoking already?"

"I...I...didn't smoke in the house, Mr. Anderson, just outside Terry's window. I'm sorry."

Dad laughs. "Smoking won't send you to hell, Danny," he says, "it'll just make you smell like you've been there."

Dad grabs our hands and bows his head, thanking God for our

"new brother," asking for God's hand upon his new life. Then he adds, "and Lord, would you deliver your child from tobacco? You did it for me all those years ago; would you do it again? Amen."

———

Liz is sick in bed and refuses to come and make us lunch. Dad insists we have a "kingdom party" for Danny and threatens to make something himself. Though he's capable of performing some wonders, this is too great a miracle to ask.

I stand at the open fridge door, wishing I could make something wonderful spring to life. When Mom was healthy, Saturday was Waffle Day at the Anderson house. I used to follow her around the kitchen, watching her mix ingredients in a bowl, gazing with fascination as the batter sizzled out the sides of the waffle iron. I can still taste that batter.

Perhaps I could give it a try.

Flipping through a small file box, I discover her recipe and lift it out with reverence, wondering how she was feeling when she last put it here. The waffle iron is on a top shelf, almost camouflaged by a half inch of dust. Danny reaches on tiptoe and pulls it down along with a stainless steel bowl.

It's easy enough to throw a teaspoon of salt, a tablespoon of sugar, two heaping teaspoons of baking powder, and a few cups of flour in a bowl. "Mix it with this," I command, and Danny seems happy to do something useful for the family that's taken him in. "Wait," I tell him, "wash the smoke off your hands first." With a fork I beat the stuffing out of two eggs just like Mother used to do and then slowly pour two cups of milk into Danny's bowl. Four tablespoons of butter melt quickly on the stove, and I pour them in too. The final ingredient Dad had to fetch from Solynka's Grocery along with a bottle of Aunt Jemima's syrup. Waffles are not waffles without golden pecans. I chop up half a cup and dump them in. The last step is a little more delicate. I fold in the eggs, careful to hardly mix them in at all.

We cook the waffles together, Danny and I, leaving them in until they're crisp on the outside yet moist and tender within.

Even Harry is interested.

———

Tony has been typing away at the kitchen table for the last hour. The smell of the waffles has him humming now too. The table is littered with information on the International Society of Krishna Consciousness on Watseka Avenue in Los Angeles, California. He's pecking out a letter to them, whacking the keys extra hard so the carbon copies turn out nice and clear.

He says he'll be using the responses to his letters for a class he's enrolled in next semester called World Religions.

Danny is fascinated with all things religious, and he sits close to Tony, watching him work, interruping often with his questions.

I push the papers aside, set the table, and listen as Dad thanks God for the food. "Not bad," says Tony as he squeezes the syrup onto a steaming waffle and takes a bite. Dad doesn't say anything, but you can tell he agrees. The most satisfied eaters are the quiet ones. I slide the last waffle onto Tony's plate, and when he is done, he pats his belly, picks up a letter, and reads it to us.

Howdy!

I was driving home the other day and I heard George Harrison's song "My Sweet Lord" on the radio just as a dove began flying along right beside me. The dove stayed there (still flying!) during the entire song (over 3 minutes!), even for the chanting of "Hare Krishna" and I just knew this was no coincidence. When I got home I realized I had to join the Hare Krishna movement. The problem is, I've had a very hard time finding you. Are your numbers slipping? I really hope this is your right address or I don't know what I'll do.

I did some research and you guys sound like the real article to me. I like how you stress freeing the spiritual body from the physical body by chanting "Hare Krishna" a lot. I like how you say there is no sin to be saved from (boy, that's a relief!) and that evil is only an illusion (I thought so). I understand that your founder, A.C. Bhaktivedanta Swami Prabhupada, died in 1977. Sorry about that. Do you know if he's still dead? Someone told me that Jesus Christ died but rose from the dead. Do you know if that has happened to your founder yet? That would be quite something, wouldn't it? Let me know if that has happened.

Well, I just want to know how to join up. Do I send in money (how much?) or just start listening to George Harrison albums (can I order them from you?), or do you have a book I can use or what? As George Harrison would say, "I really wanna know you. Hare Krishna!"

Yours truly,
Tony Anderson

---

With the table cleared, Dad is whipping up a protein shake for Mom, and Danny pokes his head in Liz's door to ask what she would like. She tells him to bring her a warm glass of milk—not too warm though—and one piece of toast, medium dark, cut diagonally, lightly buttered, with no jam.

He laughs and gets busy in the kitchen.

We may not see eye to eye on everything, but Danny Brown is without a doubt my very best friend. I guess you could call us inseparable.

# twenty-seven

# The Curse

*I* am sitting in church watching my skinny left hand twitch just below my slender left thumb right where the lines intersect with the palm. The involuntary twitching has arrived with increased regularity lately, but this is the first time I've noticed it wiggling my hand. I was standing before the mirror last night, smiling the kind of smile Mary Beth would undoubtedly find attractive, when I noticed a similar twitch tugging at the corner of my left eye. "You should sleep more," I told myself out loud, and that comforted me for a time. But now it's happening to my hand too.

The spasm is no big deal for a normal person. I didn't tell Danny Brown about it, but it's confirmation of a terrifying threat I've suspected for too many years.

I massage the hand and hope it will go away. If only I'd left that medical book at the library. Then I wouldn't know what to look for.

Danny interrupts my thoughts. "Pray for me," he says as he rises to his feet, shuffles into the aisle, and climbs the steps to the stage. The congregation is curious, of course, as he stands beside Pastor Davis, nervously pulling on a shirt button.

"I've asked Danny to bring you the most exciting news in the world," he says, "something that has set off a little party in heaven."

The congregation has moved from being curious to being certain, and the smiles break out throughout the place.

"I...um...you know me pretty well, I think," begins Danny, who is probably kicking himself for not writing something out. "But you don't know what happened to me Friday night. Friday night...um...I went to youth group for the very first time and afterward—" here he stops and looks directly at me. "Afterward Terry Anderson brought me to Jesus and I prayed."

People behind hoist themselves higher to see me, and the ones in front turn completely around, unashamed to look my way. Some are dabbing their eyes with hankies, others are shaking their heads in disbelief. This is not just any old black sheep. This is the atheist's son. I find myself sliding lower and lower, wishing I could shrink and completely disappear.

"Thanks for praying," says Danny, providing a welcome diversion. "I guess it worked."

Pastor Davis rests a supporting hand on Danny's shoulder and asks a rhetorical question if ever there was one. "Isn't God good?" Many of the faithful are nodding along like they're sitting in rocking chairs. "You know, there are churches in China that welcome new believers by saying, 'Jesus now has a new pair of eyes to see with, new ears to listen with, new hands to help with, and a new heart to love others with.' We like to say that in this little town too. Let's stand to our feet, everyone. We're gonna pray."

During the prayer I look around to find Mary Beth. Her eyes are open too. She see me, clenches her fist and smiles as if our high school football team has just creamed the Minnesota Vikings. Pastor Davis is tactfully praying for Danny's father and then hugging Danny hard as the entire congregation breaks into applause. I am clapping too, of course, and turning to Mary Beth, trying to act as pleased as she is.

—m—

A visiting minister is here this morning, a pretty funny guy. Pastor Davis introduces him as a traveling evangelist, but how do you evangelize with humor? The title of his sermon is "The Fruit of the Spirit Is Not Lemons." I can hardly wait to see Tony's anagram. The message comes complete with a Scripture text from the book of Philippians, something about joy. Danny sits next to me, taking vigorous notes, hanging on every word. The preacher claims that every situation is cause for weeping or rejoicing. That the world is full of poison oak but we don't need to sit in it. That if we have a crummy attitude we won't be a smart cookie. Everyone howls at this, which doesn't happen often at Grace Community, such howling. I can't believe they have let this guy into the building. He stands up there in his dark blue suit, and I'd love to rise to my feet and say, "What do you know about poison oak? You've got your cute little wife in the front seat adoring your every word, and you travel around the country giving this cute little talk about how attitude is everything, and you're probably getting paid a cute little wad for doing it."

A pink encouragement card pokes from a wooden holder in the pew before me. It will have to do. I lift it from the pocket and prepare to fill in the blanks before they take up an offering for him.

Danny leans my way to show me something scrawled on the back of the bulletin. Apparently Tony has been taking notes too. The note has Danny snickering. It's an anagram.

"Good news, Danny Brown."

"Wo! Danny! God's newborn!"

—m—

You'd have to be blindfolded to miss out on the fact that our numbers are swelling at Grace Community Church. I wonder where they're coming from. It makes me uncomfortable, seeing folks I don't even recognize in our very own church. Like the bum two pews in front of me and a little to the left. What's he doing here? His collar is pulled high. His hair is disheveled. Thick sunglasses try to disguise the fact that he's been drinking already this morning. He looks like he just crawled out from under a rock, for goodness' sake.

When I was a kid, there was a church split here, an ugly one. I've tried to find out why, but no one seems eager to talk about it. A few years ago, however, each side voted to forgive the other, and when the hugging and apologizing had subsided, they resolved to merge. I don't know when I've seen my father happier than the day it was announced. He held my mother's hands and tried to dance with her, shuffling across the kitchen like people in a seniors' home, something that would have caused our founder, Francis Frank, to roll over in his grave, except I've heard he isn't dead yet.

Since the faith of our building committee was larger than that of the other church, it was decided that everyone would congregate here. The folks at Grace Baptist insisted on chipping in though, gladly lugging their pews across town and placing them down the center aisle. It's quite a sight, especially when the place is empty. The center benches are Baptist pews, dark oak, probably ordered from a fancy catalog. The ones on the outer edges are plain slivery seats whacked together by our janitor, Murray Nichols, who, though he has little to do, is usually in a hurry to do it.

—◦◦◦—

In attempting to write a note to the visiting speaker, I can't help noticing the blasted twitch in my hand. Last night I stood at the refrigerator door without the slightest recollection of what I was there for—was it the mayo or the Cheese Whiz?—and the feeling returned. Two days ago I failed to recall the name of the guy who packs our groceries, and the previous day I forgot an important assignment. On each occasion my horrible suspicions were more deeply entrenched. Suspicions I have carried with me for several years now.

Simply put, I have *it*.

I am cursed with my mother's ailment: Huntington's disease.

I have mouthed the words to the mirror a dozen times before, hoping it would correct me, hoping that by saying them out loud I would defuse the power this malady holds over me, hoping against hope that I am wrong.

There's a greater sense of urgency that comes with knowing I have what I have. Knowing my friends will outlive me. Knowing I'd better live for today because tomorrow may have a little less life in it. Sometimes it's the dying that makes you feel alive. Perhaps that's why I find myself orbiting around the vices of life a little more lately. Why wouldn't you smoke and drink and do a little dope if two or five or ten years from now you'll be lying in a little room, unable to move your limbs the way you want, unable to remember what whipped vegetables you had for lunch? There are days I'd like to get roaring drunk and drive my father's car with the pedal to the metal without attention to the warning beeps and the fasten seatbelt light, but mostly I'm okay. You deal with it the best you can. You put your pants on and then your shoes. And if you forget your socks, you take your shoes off and start over.

Sometimes emotions overwhelm me, and I struggle with the urge to break into tears, which is not something you're hoping to do in your senior year of high school, not while the entire congregation of Grace Community Church sits around you, laughing at the speaker.

"Don't hold a grudge," he is saying. "While you're holding a grudge, the other guy's out dancing."

Pastor Davis is sitting up front taking notes and chuckling. Until recently, I thought highly of him. Used to be he visited once or twice a week to see how Mom was doing, to bring her some sweets, or just to be there to pray with my parents. That was before the falling out. Before he quit showing up. He hasn't been in her bedroom in more than a year, though he sometimes visits my father. I wonder what was said or done or who was misunderstood. I wonder if he is just plain chicken like most other folks when it comes to facing the truth about my mother.

Directly behind the pastor is Miss Thomas, taking up enough room for two. Funny how I feel sorry for her sitting there all by herself. I wonder where her boyfriend is. Rumors have been swirling since Danny and I misplaced his car. Is the little hypocrite skipping the service? Is he ill? Is he out swimming somewhere?

Yet how can I look at them this way? Here I am, sitting in church, the biggest hypocrite of all. I've been nominated Evangelist of the Day, yet the only reason I'm here at all is in hopes of impressing Mary Beth.

Years ago I was a frightened child, sitting in the backseat of the DeSoto sedan, wondering where we were going. "Are we there yet, God?" I sometimes wondered. Now I've come to the conclusion that if there is a God, He doesn't care, and I guess I'm okay with that. God may have made this place, like they taught us in Sunday school, but He discarded the instruction manual or misplaced it, or He's hiding it behind his back, playing some cosmic joke.

I write a note: "Loved the suit, sir, but you don't know the first thing about poison oak. You should live at the Anderson house."

I don't know why I put our name on it or why I drop it in the offering plate when it comes around.

It's not like I'll ever hear from him. He's as big a hypocrite as me.

# twenty-eight

# Voyeur

wo rows ahead of me, the bum coughs and turns slightly. A frown crosses my face. There is a certain familiarity that's undeniable. The hair seems out of character, but something about the neck is recognizable. A light birthmark the shape of Brazil is poking out from beneath the hairline. Could it be? Impossible. Or is it?

"Fear is the little darkroom where negatives are developed," the preacher is saying, but what could he know about fear? Does he dread some horrible hereditary disease? Does he see a mysterious body in a backseat every time he closes his eyes? Across the aisle sits Michael Swanson, staring at the floor. Speaking of fear, his enormous father sits beside him. He has always struck fear into my heart. I wonder what method of torture or death he has designed for me tonight?

I slip the encouragement card in the offering plate as it passes.

And upon the pronouncement of the benediction, while folks surround Danny Brown and smother him with kindness, I am off to try and talk with the bum before he can escape through the side door.

"Ben," I whisper, when I catch up to him, "is that you?"

It is, of course. His eyes are shifting back and forth like a lizard's behind those dark glasses, and his words are short and staccato-like.

"Terry, you've gotta meet me tonight."

"Where?" I am still whispering as if I'm trying for a supporting role in some gangster film.

"You know where you and that girl were the other night?"

"Mary Beth?"

"Yeah."

"How'd you know about that?"

He grins. "Just meet me there."

---

I feel like an eight-year-old, sitting here before Mr. Swanson, wishing he would just go *poof* and disappear. I'd rather face a cross-eyed javelin thrower than this disciplinarian. I scan the room for the strap Michael says he uses, but I can't lay my eyes on it. Mr. Swanson is the fattest man I have ever met. His stomach pokes out in a shelf before him. You could put books on it, and they would stay there. I've heard his shirts are made by a tent and awning company, and though he has lost a boatload of weight over the years, he keeps finding it. I wonder what it's like to be this man's child. The lines around his eyes and forehead are exaggerated beyond their years. His large upper lip is curtained by a moustache that's too small for the job.

I sit on the diagonal sofa—careful not to slouch—while he settles into his spacious recliner with a grunt. It's a little like being on trial, and I remember stories from Sunday school, terrible threats that I will sit before God on Judgment Day. Is this what it will be like? There are plenty of Bibles around the house, and I wonder if he'll have me place my hand on one and swear to the truth.

"Terry," he begins, and I am already resolved to wear a sincere expression, to appear like I have a good attitude, to pretend I am hearing the man out. "Terry," he begins again, as if I am twins, "I found in Michael's room a tape you have made, and I have listened to most of it, I am ashamed to say. I do not know how this particular tape came into Michael's possession, but I was surprised to find it there, and I am unable to rectify it being in my house." He has not looked at me yet, preferring instead to gaze at pictures on his freshly painted walls. He hoists himself forward and reaches for something. "Here is the tape, Terry." He holds it up and wiggles the inner mechanism, as if it is Exhibit A. "I am grieved, to say the least. After all you've been through, I certainly have come to expect better things."

There is silence, and I am not sure if he wants me to fill it.

"Some of the words on this tape are contemptible, Terry," he shudders. "Others are just plain ungodly. 'I've been searching for the daughter of the devil himself? Jungle love in the surf in the pouring rain?' I won't even finish the sentence. What kind of verbiage is this for a young Christian man? A young man who is about to graduate, I believe. Is that correct?"

I nod my head. So far I have not been informed otherwise.

"How did such material come into your possession? Wherever in God's wide world did you uncover this trash?" He is trying not to raise his voice, but he can't help himself.

It's easy to play dumb when I don't mean to, but it's hard when I try. I attempt to convince him with a simple flash of innocence that I am as surprised as he is. It doesn't work.

"I…uh…I am sorry. I had no idea those were the words. I just listen to the music." Feigned penitence is an art form I am still developing. I know it's unconvincing as soon as I say it, and so does he.

"Where did you find these records?"

How shall I tell him that every good hiding place in his own son's room is stuffed with the originals? That Michael has been hoarding popular albums and stashing some of them at my place?

"I…I got them from my brother Ben."

"Well, we know a little about him now, don't we? Are we following in his footsteps?"

"No, sir, we're not."

His face relaxes for a fleeting moment. Then his mouth opens but must wait for the words to come out. "Terry, I have some concern that you are interested in my daughter."

It would be bad enough to tell him that his basement is full of illegal albums, but to try and explain that the only girl I've ever loved is his only daughter and that the rest of my existence has paled in comparison to those two kisses—that would be the end of me. I try once again to deny it with facial expressions.

"I…uh…"

"We both know what I think of that, don't we?"

"Yes, sir."

"We both know that if I catch you around my daughter ever again, I—" He cuts his threat short, apparently unable to think of anything terrible enough.

With great effort, Mr. Swanson hoists himself to his feet.

"I want you to apologize to Michael for bringing this garbage into his room," he says. "You can do that now. And I will be watching you, Son. Don't forget that."

If I had graduated from high school, I'd have some choice things to say to him, things about his weight and his ancestry and his future. But with things the way they are, I am forced to restrain myself, forced to shake his hand and appear contrite.

—m—

Michael has a wide grin on his face when I push his bedroom door open. His eyes are almost the size of the headphones that envelop his ears. He points to a wire that snakes its way toward a heat duct in the ceiling.

"What's so funny?"

"Come here and listen."

Parting the headphones, he clamps them onto my ears.

*Terry, I have some concern that you are interested in my daughter.*

*I...uh...*

*We both know what I think of that, don't we?*

*Yes, sir.*

The little voyeur has been down here listening to the whole thing. Shock gives way to laughter. "No way, no way."

"Here," he says, popping another tape into the recorder. "That's just a start. Listen to this. I taped it this afternoon. It's from Mary Beth's room. Dad and Mom were having a nap." He parts the headphones and plants them on me. Pressing a button, he adjusts the volume. The voices aren't as clear as you'd like, but they're clear enough.

*Oh Danny, I'm so happy. I've been waiting for this moment for years.*

*Well, I uh...*

*I've been praying for you since eighth grade, you know.*

*Really, I...*

*I'm so proud of you, Danny Brown.*

You don't need visual images to know that they are embracing. The sound of it is clear enough. I peel off the headphones at the sound of their embrace. "I gotta go," I say, retreating abruptly from the room.

My right eye is twitching and I cannot stop it. Once I am out the door, I cannot stop the tears either.

Danny Brown and Mary Beth. How could I have missed it?

# twenty-nine

# Vengeance Is Mine

*I*t's the longest bike ride I've ever taken, though it's only a mile. Through the heart of our boring town I pedal, past the decaying Five and Dime, across the rickety bridge, between colossal potholes, under the barbershop's crooked lamppost, each landmark a minefield of memories. Short days ago I rode this same path, avoiding these same ruts with a boyish grin on my face, dazzled by the sights in all directions, particularly the glorious view of the girl riding with me. Tonight I am painfully alone, aware of a growing bitterness that grips my innards. Michael's recorded conversation plays over and over uninvited while I try my best to yank the plug on it: *I've been praying for you since eighth grade.*

Praying for you, my eye. Loving you is more like it.

Somehow I must think of something else.

Not much is open past eight PM on a Sunday night here, save for the Holy Grill. I speed past the door as it opens. Danny's dad steps out, laughing with some woman I've never seen before. I wonder if Danny knows.

—⟋⟋⟍—

Of all the places to hide, why would Ben pick this one? And why would he ask me to meet him here late at night like I'm James Cagney? Couldn't he just tap on my window and give me another heart attack? It's not like I'd be sleeping anyway, as things have turned out.

The recess in the rock is much the way we left it. As I step past it I spy a sticky sucker on the ground. The half-eaten candy tightens the knot in my stomach. Ah, what might have been. It's creepy being here all alone when the light is fading and you're hoping your brother shows up and hoping he doesn't, all at once. How I wish I'd brought Harry.

I was just a kid when Ben introduced me to the cave, showed me where to find it just past the recess, how to get down on my hands and knees and curse the claustrophobia, how to push myself on my belly through an almost invisible hole. Ben used to hide his cigarettes in this cave, both the legal ones and the other kind, used to sit up here and smoke them with an unending string of girlfriends. That was before he grew bold and started smoking on main street.

I have not entered the tiny cave since last summer, and the musty smell conjures up more memories. Inside, the ceiling heightens quickly, and I'm able to stand with my shoulders hunched. Dim candles flicker on the wall, lighting the room. Save for a few objects against the far wall, the small room is vacant. I move to inspect the objects, stepping past the embers from a dying fire. They look like trays. As I bend to look in them a powerful chemical singes my nostrils. Beside the trays rests a tiny camera, and a larger one is attached to a small bellows and pointed at the floor. From one wall hangs a string with a dozen eight by tens clothespinned to it. They are pictures, mostly out of focus. One is a small list that I squint to read: *Socks, soup, scissors, shotgun.* I don't know if it's an alliterated shopping list or just some silly doodlings. Beside the list is the worn and aging picture clipped from the *Grace Chronicle.* The same picture I studied in the library.

In the dying light the group of men seem an odd assortment

of dimly lit characters. Ben has penciled a circle around the face of the one on the far right. I'm beginning to fit a few of the puzzle pieces together, but it could be revenge that has me drawing these conclusions.

The candles flicker as Ben slithers into the room. "Hey," he grunts. It's part greeting, part warning, I suppose.

I turn from the picture and face him, quickly tucking the envelope I've brought with me behind my back.

The last few weeks have not been kind to my brother. His unshaven face pokes out from under a Cubs hat, and his carbon black eyes are droopy. His cheeks are more pitted and scarred than I remember them, and the very act of breathing seems to take more effort than usual. He is squinting through cigarette smoke, and perhaps that is the reason. Ben's nose looks slightly swollen, and a delicate web of purple lines runs up his cheeks through the undergrowth, something I've seen before whenever he's been drinking.

"You asked me to come." I am not impatient, just uncomfortable with the silence.

"Yeah, I guess I needed to…talk to someone." He pulls two sweaty twenties from a pocket and thrusts them toward me.

"What's that for?"

"It's a graduation gift. It doesn't look like I'll be there."

"Sure you will, we'll get this sorted out."

He looks up at me for the first time and grins. "Not a bad kiss," he says.

"What?"

"The other night. You and that Swanson girl."

"Come on. You didn't. You weren't. You were spying on us?"

"Not much else to do up here."

I shake my head in disbelief. Ben laughs. "She's cute," he whistles.

"How long you been holed up here?"

"Not long."

"Why *here*?"

"Things are a little hot where I was living," is all the explanation he offers.

"Oh," I say.

"Have you heard much?"

"Just that you're in trouble. That they're looking for you."

"Who?"

"The police."

"Oh, them." Ben offers a brave little laugh and squats beside the fire. Is someone else looking for him too?

"Mom's okay." He didn't ask, but I thought he'd want to know. "Allan's good too."

"Thanks. I saw the way you treated him the other night. The girl too. It made me want to come home—seeing Allan." Ben stirs the coals and moves a charred coffeepot closer.

I step toward the fire and offer him the envelope. "Ben Anderson," my brother reads out loud. Thankfully, I had the foresight to tape it back up.

"What's this?"

"I don't know," I lie. "Some guy brought it to the house."

"When?"

"Last Sunday."

I have never seen my brother more surprised. He stares at me for a full minute, then pries the flap of the envelope open, turning the contents to the light. Embarrassed, he promptly stuffs them back.

"What is it?" I ask.

"Oh, nothing. It's okay." There is another long silence. "I need you to know something," he says at last. "I've gotten myself in a little deeper than I'd hoped. Would you tell Dad I'm okay? I wanted to last night. Until I noticed a police car parked on our street. Guess they're watching for sinners like me." He laughs as if there's nothing to worry about, as if the cops are little more than a minor speed bump in his plans.

Ben's words are not the worst ones I've heard today, but I can tell where they're headed. Each one seems to tighten the noose around his neck, driving him further from home. Suddenly I'd rather not ask about the murder. I'd rather not know too much.

Ben is looking at me, but I can't meet his gaze.

I wish I knew why life is jammed with such tragedy. Why my mother is old before her time and my father's eyes are sunken. I wish I knew why my brother is lost forever on this earth and in the next. Why can't life come to us safe and seamless like a Disney movie?

"You need to know that I won't be around for a while."

"But why?"

"I don't know how much to tell you. I'm…involved with some people, with some things, shall we say?" He stares into the flames as they eagerly consume small chunks of wood.

"Who, Ben?"

"I've said enough already."

"Go ahead, you can tell me."

Ben stands to his feet. "When you were just a baby," he says, "Dad brought home a puppy. We called him Jerry, don't ask me why." His face is drawn into a momentary smile as if he can see the pup's face. "That dog was the only thing I cared about really. It slept on my bed like Harry sleeps on yours. It ate from my plate when Mom and Dad weren't looking. It gave me a reason to come home from school. He was a small black terrier, and he liked to surprise people." Ben lets out a soft snicker. "People strolling by our house late at night, out for a walk with their lover, would be gazing upward trying to find certain constellations, and suddenly this black dog would be there. They had no idea how fast they could run until Jerry showed them. He brought out the best in people, that's for sure. Made them yell their loudest, run their fastest, and write the most articulate letters to Dad."

The smile fades as quickly as it arrived. "One Sunday we came home from church and there he was, lying by his dog dish, peacefully asleep. Or so I thought. Only he wasn't sleeping. He was dead. Poisoned, I think.

"All my life the only things I've really wanted have been taken from me, it seems. My birth parents. Your mom. My wife. And now, my freedom, I suppose." He stirs the embers some more without really looking at them. "This should be my last night in this little palace."

In eighteen years I've never hugged my brother, not that I can remember. But I can't help it tonight. The truth is, I know what it's like to lose the things you care the most about. I wish I could tell him so.

Instead, I turn away before he can see my tears. "I'll pray for you," I say, as I lower my skinny frame and crawl through the opening.

It's the only lie I feel like telling tonight.

—⚡—

Why I am standing at the attic window squinting at my watch and sweating is more than I will ever know. I suppose I just have to see Mary Beth, and there is no other way. Maybe I'm here to say goodbye to her, like I've just said goodbye to my brother. Maybe I'm hoping she'll see the moon reflecting off my face and push open her window and tell me she was kidding, that she's loved me all her life, that the kisses were sincere, that I should come and get a few more. The thought offers a small glimmer of false hope.

Her bedroom light is on, casting the broad shadow of a lampshade up against the far wall. There is no movement within, but she is awake, and that is enough.

I hate to tell you, but there is a growing evil in my heart. An evil that had me pedaling faster on the way back to town. How can I look on Danny Brown without thoughts of reprisal? He's staying in my bedroom and he's stolen my girl. Maybe I could arrange for a second murder. That would boost sales of the *Grace Chronicle*, wouldn't it? I chuckle to myself but let my mind wander a little. People would connect the two murders, of course. And what then? They would blame Ben for both of them. But they can't kill my brother twice, can they? Maybe they don't even kill you for murder in this state. I should probably find out. I laugh again at the thought. But there is something else here. Something less violent and more expedient, an opportunity my tiny brain is just a few cells from grasping.

What is it?

*Aha.*

What if I found a way to pin the crime on someone else? Danny's father, for instance. What if he were found guilty of Ben's transgression and thrown in jail? It would accomplish any number of things, all of them favorable for me. Not only would my brother be free, it would halt Danny's romance in its tracks. Surely Mary Beth wouldn't marry the child of a killer. But how can I accomplish it? How do you pin a crime on an innocent man? You plant evidence, that's what you do. You put poison in his cupboard, plant a gun in his car, or wedge an ominous note in a strange place. I can see the caption now: "Murder weapon discovered, suspect hauled away while son stands by brokenhearted."

The shadow changes directions in Mary Beth's room, jolting me from reverie. And standing there in the darkness I am confronted with images too terrible to witness. Danny Brown is in her room, the sneak. How did he get in there past the fat guard dog that is Mr. Swanson? I curse softly and lower my eyes. I cannot watch. Anger builds within me. Years I've spent dreaming of her companionship. Now this.

Quickly I turn from the window, my fists tightening until the nails dig into my palms.

When I was a child of twelve, I stole the greatest treasure a boy could imagine. It lured me. It delighted me. I relished that fortune. And then it tortured me. Six years later, another treasure was within my grasp. Until tonight. The irony is not lost on me now, and I can think of only one thing: the wild justice of revenge. I know not how, but it will come to me if I meditate on it long enough.

I have given Danny Brown so many things over the years.

Food, money, my companionship, my trust. Most recently I have offered him a place to sleep and a place to heal. He has repaid me by robbing the one treasure I want most in this world: Mary Beth.

Normal people would be satisfied to punch him out good or scrawl horrible things on his locker door, but the cold reality of it is this: A far more sinister plot is brewing in my brain. Its icy talons grip my spine as I stand here in the heat of the attic. For the first time in a long while, a wicked smile creases my face, and I turn back to face the amorous scene before me.

What if I could pin the crime on the biggest thief of all, Danny Brown? He's certainly old enough to rot behind bars. That would change things, wouldn't it? It's tough to date a man when he's locked away. Mary Beth's father thought I was bad. I'll look positively angelic visiting this criminal. And she'll dump him like withered broccoli. You can't date a man when he's in jail, can you? Or marry him for that matter.

If Tony were here, he would offer me better advice. Or perhaps an anagram of a word like "desperation" ("a rope ends it"). But Tony calls revenge "a weak pleasure of a small mind." "The sweetest revenge is forgiveness," I've heard him say. What does he know of forgiveness? Has he ever been wronged beyond all sensibility?

We've been reviewing *The Merchant of Venice* for our English lit final, and a delightful passage comes to mind:

> *If I can catch him once upon the hip,*
> *I will feed fat the ancient grudge I bear him.*

My grudge is not so ancient as Shylock's, but it is no less real. Danny's presence in our home has provided me the perfect opportunity. "Go ahead," I say out loud, "steal her from me. Pretty convenient, this becoming a Christian, wasn't it?" As for me, I will take delight in mulling over the endless possibilities of payback. I will bide my time, and then I will strike.

I am cooking up a dish of sweet revenge.

I will serve it cold.

# thirty

# The Visitor

Monday morning, as if to put an exclamation mark on all my troubles, little Allan has gone missing. He was here ten minutes ago, kicking his high chair like a stubborn mule while I fed him a disgusting ball of goop Liz had flung together. But when he began pulling gobs of it from his mouth and hurling them like shrapnel in my direction, I unfastened his seat belt and let him wriggle his way onto the floor. Danny was pestering me with questions at the time, questions about some obscure Bible passage he'd been reading last night, something about forgiveness. I excused myself to the bathroom, where I stood before the mirror, imitating the kinds of faces Danny would make during the satisfying moment when I strangled him.

Emerging from the bathroom, I discovered that Allan was nowhere to be found. If only I could get Danny to disappear as easily.

Last night when the jerk finally came in about midnight, he fell to his knees in prayer and then sat in bed with the light on, reading Scripture—probably something from Song of Solomon. I turned my face to the wall, crammed a pillow over my head, and pretended to be asleep. But the truth is, I was thinking up a headline for the *Chronicle:* "Local Boy Found Bludgeoned to Death with Huge King James Bible."

The doorbell rings, interrupting the search for the missing toddler, and I can't help imagining that someone is dropping off a ransom note, that they are holding the little guy hostage. Stranger things have happened. But what could anyone possibly want for a ransom? All our money? That would be like collecting Bibles at a bingo parlor.

"Take him," I'll say, pointing at Danny. "It's a fair trade."

A lady stands at the door when my father opens it. One look at her and I know she is up to something weird. She is dressed from another time, bedecked in a high-necked and low-hemmed outfit. I'll bet she's done something with my nephew brother. You can tell from twenty feet away that she is nervous. She holds a Bible in one hand and clutches a letter with the other. Is she crazy? It's barely eight o'clock in the morning.

For some reason Harry goes completely bananas at the sound of the doorbell, lunging from the sofa, lurching around the corner, and standing before the woman, the hairs on his neck vertical. Dad moves him back with a gentle foot. "Hello," the lady says sweetly, hesitantly, her voice all atremble. "I was given your a-address. I'm sorry if I'm too early in the day, but we understood you had some q-questions. Do you have a minute?" My father always has a minute when people ask him for one, but not this morning. He orders her into the house immediately to help us look for a little boy about this high and to hurry up about it, this is no time to hopscotch our way through the New World Translation or talk about the Mark of the Beast.

It's the first time in world history that a Jehovah's Witness has been invited into the Anderson home, and it is strange to see her flop about the house like a fish outside its aquarium. Such folk wander into town sometimes and find themselves on our porch, wondering how they ever got themselves into such a mess, but never have they made it past our screen door.

When Mother was well enough to talk to them, they were always in for a surprise. I used to eavesdrop on some conversations that were better than television when Mother was in her prime. Though she loved to contribute what she could to any child's fundraiser, no insurance salesman, Jehovah's Witness, or Mormon ever came here twice. Boldness was my mother's strength. Tact was not.

When I was eight or nine, we were on a summer vacation up in Canada, winding our way through the magnificent Rockies. We set up camp on a Saturday afternoon near Banff at an enormous campsite on Two Jack Lake. The surroundings were every boy's dream, with ample wood to be chopped, fires to be lit, and the occasional bear strolling through to check your dinner menu. Our first night there, we were sound asleep in our family-sized tent, which smelled like it had been through a world war or two, when half a dozen Harley motorbikes turned in at the front gate, their radios on high, their mufflers on low. Of course the only vacancy was right next to us. As the music got louder, I stuck my curious head through the tent flap, and before my brother could pull it back, I'd seen the closest thing I would ever see to one of those Greek parties spoken against in Scripture. I got back to sleep easily, but I was the only one.

The next morning, when finally I awoke and nudged my head through that tent flap, there was Mother right in the midst of them having her devotions from the Gospel of John. The bikers weren't the most alert group of people you'll ever see, but there wasn't a one of them that mocked her for it. She motioned our family over to the neighboring campsite, where we timidly pushed aside enough beer cans to have a church service that Sunday morning. And although the leather-clad hippies didn't know all the words to the hymns, and they seemed a little bored with my father's sermon, no one skipped out on the service. They even bowed their heads for the closing prayer. Ben was out on a "nature hike" while we had church, but he arrived in time for lunch.

Tony must have been paying more attention that day than I was, for he seems eager to practice on his newfound target, which is only right, him being the one whose letter she holds in her hand. Perhaps it was Tony's dream to have her come. He's been studying their beliefs in stuffy old textbooks in Bible college, and the chance to meet a live one is as much an honor as it is a challenge. He doesn't start work until ten, and the questions he's asking should keep things lively until then.

"If I were to die right now, could you tell me I'm going to heaven?" Tony is asking this as he pulls aside pillows and looks under the dining room table.

"Well, uh, no, actually, I couldn't," she stammers. I'm sure she's been in some difficult situations going door to door, but this one's near the top.

"If you were to die right now, where would you go?"

"Well, that's a tricky one. You really need to—"

"But the Bible says that to be absent from the body is to be present with the Lord."

Allan has been absent from our house only once before, when he took off after a bath, stark raving naked, and ran the length of the street before someone brought him home. But I can't believe he made it out the door without us hearing the squeak. He has to be in here somewhere. He is not in the cupboards, where he loves to play hide and seek. He is not in the bathtub or the kitchen sink or even beneath it. Dad tells me and Danny to go ahead and take off for school or we'll be late and that he'll call if he hasn't found the little guy within the hour and remember, tonight's the night we've been looking forward to for weeks.

Tony and the Witness lady are seated at the table, where he is pouring on the questions: "Is it really true you believe there's no hell and no Trinity? That you refuse to vote, salute the flag, serve in the armed forces, or wear pantsuits?"

She seems stunned, as if he knows as much as she does.

I have to drag Danny out the door, so fascinated is he with the conversation.

"Is that really what they believe?" he asks as we plod our way to school.

"I guess so."

Each time a truck comes past I resist the urge to push him in front of it.

"Terry, I didn't realize something until this morning. I completely forgot about the cigarettes. Haven't touched one since Saturday morning."

I hardly hear his words. I am too busy wondering if I can bring myself to water and nurture the delicious germ of a plot that has been planted overnight.

I must and I will.

---

The questions from my classmates have subsided. Most are convinced that I did see a body, but that's the end of the matter. They've either forgotten or arrived at the same conclusion most have, that the stranger was some poor unfortunate drifter. Besides, if there is a mystery, it will never be solved by our police force.

After school, I drop my books off at home, hurriedly grab a handful of unleavened bread, and pinch off a piece of cheese to go with it. Liz will have my head for the bite mark, but she'll get over it. Before I can escape out the door, my father's voice summons me from the bedroom: "Terry?"

He sits on one side of my sleeping mother, a well-worn Bible in his lap. In a chair across from him sits the Watchtower lady, leaning forward, her New World Translation discarded on the bed. Could she have been here all day? "Terry, there's something on the table from that minister who spoke at church yesterday. Oh, and I want you to meet Edna Redding. We've been having a lovely visit. She lost…well, you tell him, Edna."

Edna doesn't seem quite as stilted as she did this morning, but still her speech is halting. "I…lost a husband to this disease four years ago. I know a little of what you're going through."

I just stare at her.

She smiles kindly. "His name was Gordon." Her smile turns to a faraway stare. "I wish I had…well, your father has this hope, this assurance of seeing your mother again, no matter what happens. I would give almost anything…"

I feel like saying, "Listen, I've got some pressing issues to deal with myself, okay?" But instead I listen politely for a few minutes as Dad kindly reminds her of ground they must have already covered. Jesus is God incarnate, not *a* God, as her version claims. He flips around in his Bible, drawing conclusions she can't poke holes in, things about the promise of heaven, the reality of hell, that none of us is disfellowshiped—whatever that means—that God's grace is enough, that He loves us. I wonder why she stays here. She keeps looking at my mother, sound asleep in bed.

It's like Mom is a magnet, and she can't pull herself away.

# thirty-one

# Snitch

iss Hudson looks up with astonishment as I enter the Franklin Library. I haven't frequented her domain in years, so what could I possibly be doing here twice in the space of one week? She is sporting a mint green polyester pantsuit today, one that must have been on special at the Ricochet Clothing Store on Main. She smiles kindly as I walk past her to the archives of the *Grace Chronicle*. There is curiosity in her smile too.

Minutes later I have what I came for. The clipping is hidden away on page ten in the September 25, 1957 edition, a small item pasted a little crookedly under the heading "Ministry Plans No Longer Feasible." The short piece describes the disappointment experienced by several local men, citing differences of opinion on some unnamed issues. The article does quote my father, who is his usual kind and flattering self. Not surprisingly, it lacks the facts a big-city newspaper would contain.

Miss Hudson looks up again as I head for the door.

"Find what you were looking for?" she asks kindly.

"I think so," I say. "Thanks."

The Grace Municipal Police Station is not one of those precincts you see on TV shows where they crack jokes and write up reports while people wait in handcuffs. There's a pleasant lady who bids you wait for a minute when you tell her you'd like to speak with an officer. She sits behind a battered old desk and smiles at you, and you half expect her to pull out a plate of cookies and ask if you'd like milk with them. You'd swear she was your mother, so sweet is she. Turns out her name is Pearl and she's new here, just learning the job, just ironing out some wrinkles, she says. And what is your name?

"Terry Anderson," I tell her, quite sure she was the one I saw last night laughing her way out of the Holy Grill with Mr. Brown.

"Ah yes," she says, "Terry." I hang my head in shame. She can't have heard that name in the best of contexts. But when I look up, I find her gazing at me with a pleasant expression, as if she'd like to tell me something no one else could know.

Pearl has probably reached the mid-forty mark, something that seems like a black hole to a boy of eighteen. Abruptly she turns back to her IBM electric as Officer Hodges strides through his door and lays a file on her desk. He appears overconfident and a little pompous, as if the FBI has just asked his opinion on a matter of international importance.

His office is not something you'd choose to shoot a movie in either. Few pictures line the walls, and the ones that do need straightening. Papers are strewn about the floor, and on his desk is a plaque that he undoubtedly finds hilarious. It says, "What the world needs is more geniuses with humility, there are so few of us left." He motions me to take a chair, and I must step gingerly to get there. I feel almost grown-up until he addresses me like I'm in his fourth-grade Sunday school class. "Now, how can I help you, Son?" He is squinting down at some papers on his desk, wondering whether he should give me his entire attention.

"I'm here about the...uh...murder." I am trying my best to sound casual, as if I'm working on a special project for extra credit.

"Murder?" He looks up as if I've committed one. "You mean the suicide?"

"No, I mean the murder. I've heard some things that make me think I might know the killer. Or at least someone who knows a whole lot about this thing."

I have his undivided attention now.

Suddenly Officer Hodges appears as if he's just been told to pull up a chair and sit all by himself at a buffet table, so anxious is he for more information.

"Just rumors, really, but sometimes they're true. You may want to check it out."

"And his name?"

"How do you know it's a *him?*"

He is not amused with my cockiness.

I have folded my hands in front of me and am looking at them thoughtfully. "I need to know something before I tell you."

"And what is that, Son?"

"I need your assurance that my name will be kept out of this, that no one will know about this conversation."

He frowns. "Alright," he says. "I can do that. What's the name of this suspect?"

"Uh…well, he's a classmate of mine."

"Yes, yes. And where does he live?"

"Well…right now he lives with me. His father kicked him out."

The officer reaches down and opens a squeaky drawer. "You wouldn't happen to know whose head fits into this cap now, would you?"

He pulls out a Chicago Blackhawks hat. The shock cannot help but register on my face. "It's his," I say, hoping to appear more sad than eager. "It's Danny Brown's hat."

—w—

The kidnapping scare was a false alarm, of course. Dad found the little guy sound asleep behind the sofa moments after Danny and I left for school. He was sucking on a piece of Liz's unleavened bread, dead to the cares of the world. I have no idea how he crawled in there, how he got his body through such a tiny space, but I'm surprised at how happy I am to see him. Harry seems glad to see me too. I can't help smiling as he licks my face. One reason Harry is such a comfort when I'm down is that he doesn't try to find out why.

The note from the visiting funny guy preacher is still unopened on the table. I rip the side of it and a letter pops out. "Thanks for the note, Terry," it says. "I am so sorry for what you are going through. I will pray for you. I promise."

"You're not gonna wear that, are you?" asks Liz as she hurries by me, fussing with her hair and smacking me on the arm.

Ah yes, tonight is the night. I'd almost forgotten with all that's been going on.

Liz and Dad have hardly talked about anything else all week. All month, for that matter. Ever since Dad cracked open the newspaper and landed on the ad buried deep within, right across from the obits; ever since he opened the paper at dinnertime and thunked it on the table for all of us to see. Tony dropped his fork, opened his casserole-stuffed mouth, and scrunched his teeth together. "What? You gotta be kidding. That's the loopiest idea I've heard since we took Elizabeth golfing." Liz smacked him hard on two accounts: Disrespect for Dad and mockery of her ability with a golf club.

"It's alright," said Dad. "Just an idea. I'm not so sure myself."

And for a few days he hid the newspaper somewhere, seeming to concur with Tony's prognosis. But he didn't throw it away or relegate it to the lowly task of lining our birdcage. And when at last he pulled it out again and showed the half-page advertisement to Mom, she didn't say anything, of course, for she had not said a word for many months. She did manage to nod her head, though, an almost indiscernible nod, one that seemed to say, "Sure, I'll go. Anything at all beats this."

I poke my head into her room, marveling again at how fast the disease is growing within her. Marveling how quickly it has pulled her downward these last few years. I'm surprised too at my inability to even utter the word out loud: *Huntington's.* I cannot stand here without being reminded that it's hereditary, that more than likely it waits at some poorly marked intersection, ready to bust through a yield sign and steal my future too.

But the newspaper has offered something my dad hasn't had much of lately. A simple ad has given him hope.

I've not dared tell a soul about that ad. They find out, they'll laugh. Or smile behind their hands as I walk by. Besides, they'll learn the truth soon enough in a town like this one where people know which way you're turning before you flip on your blinker.

I am still as skeptical as ever, but the more we discuss it, the more I find myself filling up on hope. And the more hope arrives at my door, the more frightened I am of answering the doorbell. It's like Christmas Eve where you dare not dream the big gift near the back could be yours on account of the disappointment being too much last year when your sister opened the very one you'd been longing for. Hope is a relay egg at the Sunday school picnic. Those who run with it are willing to risk that it could be dashed. Sometimes you're better off sitting on the sidelines, sipping weak lemonade.

Back in my room, Danny is strumming my guitar, and though I'd love to club him to death with it, I've become rather attached to that guitar since Tony gave it to me for Christmas.

"Danny, are you coming with us?"

"Where?" he asks, so I take him to the kitchen, haul out the newspaper and point at the well-wrinkled page: "Monday Night Healing Service. Believe and Receive."

"We're going?" he asks, incredulously.

"Yep."

He studies my face with an understanding gaze.

So tonight is the night.

A month ago we started praying about this. I even considered joining in for a time. But not anymore. This ridiculous charade is about to be played out in public. I wouldn't miss it for the world, but I dare not hold out hope that my mother could be healed.

# thirty-two

# Big City

It pours rain by late afternoon, buckets of it. With Dad tapping his watch and Mom shuffling turtle-like across the floor, Liz herds us outside, where Tony is loading our big Mercury Meteor. Few events are important enough for him to beg off work early, but this is one. "Hurry up," he commands Danny and me, and we hoist the cumbersome wheelchair into the trunk, both of us drenched within seconds.

The rain is a real gutter washer, not your average June shower.

"Who knows," says Tony, looking upward, "maybe God is saying something with it."

Mother is brought from the house in a ceremony the Queen of England would envy, with all of us scrambling around her, tripping over each other, making sure she doesn't fall. Danny and I move furniture to clear a path, while trying to impress Mary Beth, who has agreed to babysit little Allan. Dad lifts a raincoat high. I fight Danny to hold the umbrella for her. The pointy end would make a nice weapon, but I dare not think of that now.

The backseat is littered with newspaper clippings and envelopes Tony says I'll be interested in, things he will read us on the trip to the big city. On the floor are sack lunches Liz has slapped together, and up front are soft blankets and pillows for Mom to rest upon.

My visions of tonight's gathering come mainly from Tony's active imagination. Though he's never been to one, he has read of healing services and delights in painting pictures for us of the evening ahead. The crowded auditorium. The shouting when people are healed. A preacher so powerful people are afraid to touch him on account of the electricity running through his body. I wonder if Pastor Pedro is his real name or a pseudonym. Does he remember sending us the letter promising all those blessings? I can't remember the last time I actually looked forward to a church service, but more than just a small dose of expectancy is fueling my excitement.

"We've been soaking ourselves in Thy Word," my mechanic father prays out loud once the six of us are belted in and relatively silent. "You've promised that if Your Word abides in us and we abide in You, we should ask what we will and it will be done. So we believe Thee for healing tonight. We ask for Thy will. And we bring Ben before Thee too. You know where he is. Please meet him there."

I can't believe my Baptist father is doing this, sounding like a Pentecostal. What's next? Him speaking funny languages? A Bapticostal? This much I know: If anyone on earth deserves healing, my saintly mother does. And if anyone has the right to command it be done, it would be my father. I look down. Without knowing it, I have crossed my fingers on both hands. A drop of moisture glides from my bangs down my nose and onto my lap. It stays a moment and then vanishes.

Dad guides the Mercury Meteor onto the slippery interstate and quickly accelerates to sixty-five. It's a long, lame, yacht of a car, the kind Dad likes best. He bought it from our former pastor, Francis Frank, and didn't realize there was no radio in it—not even AM—until he was halfway home; didn't notice for a month that Pastor Frank had turned the whitewalls on the tires to the inside so as to avoid any sign of worldliness. It was a warm summer day when they shook hands on the deal, and the car smelled fine at the time. But whenever the rain comes, something awful springs to life in the backseat, as if the car was once used to transport animals from a pig farm, and the pigs are back to reminisce.

Tony cracks open one of the many envelopes that have been arriving in our mailbox, testimonials sent by organizers of the grand meeting. "This is from Tom Kodiak in California," he says, reading loudly so Mom and Dad can hear up front. "My daughter can see now without eyeglasses. Pastor Pedro prayed for her and she was healed. I too experienced a lessening of lower back pain. Praise God!"

Dad has slowed down to sixty now, the rain is hitting us that hard.

"This one's from Florida. 'My mother was in a wheelchair and blind.'" Tony's voice picks up volume, and he leans in Mom's direction. "After prayer she rose out of the wheelchair and walked and can now see. Thank God!"

I lean left to see Mom's face in the rearview, but her eyes are closed, her face expressionless.

"After Mr. Pedro prayed for me at the miracle meeting, I was healed of a major crippling disease. I had to wear multiple body braces for twelve years. I had arthritis and heart disease. They're all behind me now. Thank you, thank you."

Dad smiles at Tony and adjusts the rearview. "God's will, that's all we want."

Tony continues. "I was infertile and went to the Miracle Crusade—"

"You were?" I interrupt, surprised by my own joviality.

Tony doesn't find this as funny as the rest of us. He clears his throat and presses on, undaunted. "Within a year I gave birth to a healthy baby boy. We named him Pedro."

Each story can't help but bring me closer to hope. A boy healed of dyslexia is nearing the top of his class. A stuttering teenager is now training for the ministry. People are waving goodbye to crutches, wheelchairs, back braces, and toothaches. The final letter is from a man who has sneezing fits. "I tried home remedies and over-the-counter drugs," he writes. "This may sound funny, but I was on the achoo-choo train, wishing I were not the conductor. The doctor said I had rhinitis, but during your crusade here last month I was healed and have not sneezed since. Not once. Hallelujah. Lately I've been singing a song I wrote, 'He Is the Reason for Me Not Sneezin'.' "

We laugh together, an excited and anticipatory laugh.

And deep down, though I am wary of wishing for too much, and though I can't believe I am doing so, I find myself talking to God once again. Sure, I've voiced too many unanswered prayers in the last few years for me to believe my mother could change directions overnight, but when a drowning man is thrown a rope he doesn't ask who's holding the other end.

"Have faith," says my father, and I can see the desperation in his eyes reflected in the rearview. I've watched the life sucked out of him too. If he can believe, certainly I can.

"God, heal her please," I pray.

Outside, the clouds part and the sun shines through, glaring off the asphalt, bidding Dad to don sunglasses. Just above the distant mountains the clouds melt from the evening sky, leaving nothing but blue as far as the eye can see.

If this isn't a sign I don't know what is.

I've even warmed up to Danny Brown's silent presence beside me. Is it possible to forgive him? Probably not, but if this healing thing is to work, surely I must. I reach across and smack him on the knee.

"Glad you're here," I lie.

Danny is holding his Bible, a Bible my father gave him.

"Thanks," he says, nodding his head. "Wish Dad was too."

Last night he told me just what his father thinks of faith healers. He tried to do so without swearing, but it was a stretch for him.

Liz breaks out the sack lunches. "You'll need energy for tonight," she says, shoving a sandwich in my face. "Here, eat."

It is peanut butter and something that faintly reminds me of jelly. I wonder if she mixed some aging cheese into it somehow. I haven't tasted anything this bad since her last meal. Danny eagerly accepts his. To him, Liz is a bona fide chef.

"We could use these for Frisbees," I say.

Spinning around, Liz reaches over the headrest and belts me good.

The sights and sounds of the big city are easy to take when you've been trapped in a small town all your life and your ears are ringing from your sister's smack. I hope to live here one day, amid the lights and high-rises and concrete. Imagine shopping after six PM or finding a movie theater just down the street—or a corner store with cigarettes and alcohol and no one around who cares what you're buying. But tonight I must vanquish all evil thoughts in hopes that God will have heard my feeble prayer.

# thirty-three

# Miracles

Tony wheels Mother through the jammed parking lot and up to the front door of the sandstone Civic Center just off Central Avenue. There is a grin on her face—or perhaps it is a grimace; I'm not sure which. Liz clears a path for them. "Excuse us, excuse us." Dad holds the door wide. Tony looks like he's covering the event for a newspaper, so intent is he on every detail. Looking lost and a little bit frightened, Danny trails along behind.

Inside, the expectancy is tangible. An usher smiles as we enter, pointing us to an elevator on the left. We join the long line of wheelchairs snaking toward the magical machine that will deliver us to the lower level where hope abounds.

Another usher asks us to fill out a prayer card: name, address, and ailment. Tony grabs a pencil and starts writing.

The meeting is launched with boisterous praise choruses, something we don't hear much of at Grace Community Church. "I've got the joy, joy, joy, joy down in my heart...where?" Two thousand people are tapping whatever they can and moving to the music. They even have drums on the platform, something that caused quite a stir when our youth pastor experimented with it back home. I've not been in a crowd this large in my life, and I am wiggling my toes and nodding my head, barely aware that I am doing so.

A few short testimonies follow the singing, and then the evangelist sweeps on stage, grabbing the microphone and launching his vivacious message.

Pastor Pedro is in his mid-fifties, though you'd never know it looking at his wavy hair or his tanned and leathery face. He is dressed in a gray gabardine suit and buoyed by black cordovan shoes. His handsome face is all straight edges—nose, mouth, eyebrows—and his broad shoulders are carried easily by his muscular frame. He has been preaching the Word since he was fourteen, he tells us, but did not feel the call to a healing ministry until recently. I am mesmerized. Transfixed. Pastor Pedro is effervescent, bubbly, cheerful. I'm almost willing to admit that the hand of God is upon him. If anyone is capable of being a conduit for healing, surely it is this man.

Tony leans toward me. "Door tappers," he says.

"Huh?"

"It's an anagram for Pastor Pedro."

I can barely stifle a laugh.

As the message unfolds, my father nods his head in agreement. God wants you wise, says the healer in a rather confusing southern Spanish accent, and who can argue with that? My mind is wandering. I am looking around, rating girls for prettiness and reminding myself that I should not be doing so. I catch only brief snippets of the lively sermon as it drags on for almost an hour. God wants you wise, happy, healthy, and rich. Is that a frown on my father's face?

"Tonight we are raisin' monah for the work a smugglin' Bables into the Soviet Union," drawls Pastor Pedro. "We will not ba doin' this in the usual way. No suh, we will be tyin' these Bables to hot air balloons, and they will drift behand the Iron Curtain. *Galory.*" Tony snickers, but Liz shushes him. "Please give generously," Pastor Pedro entreats us. "You can't bah healing, but remembah, you sow sparingly, you will reap sparingly. You sow generously, you will reap a blessin'. Your givin' is a down payment on the supah livin' God promises His children."

Tony leans my way again. "Departs poor," is all he says. It's another anagram, I guess.

Dad isn't reaching for his wallet the way he usually does, but Liz is fishing around her tiny purse until she produces an entire dollar. It will return to her a hundredfold, says the faith healer. Perhaps more. I wish I had brought a few bucks—what a chance to earn some interest.

"Ah am sensin' something tonat, somethin' wonderful."

The first offering is over and everyone tilts forward to listen to Pedro. This is what we are here for. Pastor Pedro closes his eyes for a moment. "Ah sense that a man by the name a Bob is heya," he says, "Bob is sufferin' from a stomach ailment."

A shout arises just a few rows behind us, and a balding gentleman slowly stands to his feet.

"This is him! This is Bob!" hollers the lady beside him. She helps Bob forward, though he is stooped in pain. The healer mutters some things I can't make out and smacks Bob on the forehead. He staggers backward, and down he goes.

I let out a gasp as if something horrible has just happened. But to the others it is marvelous. "Glory!" they yell. "Thank you, Jesus!" Others come forward for similar treatment. Their aches begin to disappear in the rearview mirror. All around me, people are expectant, hopeful. They sway from side to side, eyes closed, hands up, many of them teary-eyed. I've never seen anything like it. Depression is being healed, back pain is history.

I am beginning to notice that no one in a wheelchair has been called forward yet, when Reverend Pedro's words jar me: "Ah believe there is, now let me see, yes, a Ruth Anderson here." My heart leaps. How can he know this? He is far from the podium, far from his notes.

"She's from a little town called…uh, Grace. Isn't that sweet?" He is stumbling a little with this one. "Ah believe she has been unable to speak for some time." My father is on his feet. "Come Sistah!" the preacher is saying. "Come find grace tonight."

Tony pushes the wheelchair forward as Dad gently stoops and pats Mom's shoulder. Her hands are folded on her lap, her head is bowed, her eyes closed. I push to the front of my seat, leaning slightly to the left, not willing to miss a thing. In eighteen years of living I have seldom been more interested in a single event.

There is no wheelchair ramp to the platform—something I find a little strange—but Tony and Dad lift Mom easily onto the stage. The healer closes his eyes and places his hands softly on her lips. He invokes the Almighty with words from Scripture. I should have my eyes closed, but I dare not miss a thing.

"I understand that Mrs. Anderson has been unable to speak for almost a year." His eyes are still closed, he is still talking to God. "Lord, unshackle these lips, I pray. If not tonight, please do it soon."

Mother sits stone still in the wheelchair. Then, ever so slowly, she stands to her feet and lifts her hands toward the sky. "I believe—" she says, in a voice loud and steady. My mouth drops wide open and I stare at her. It's as if I have just witnessed heaven itself open, seen the earth below me shift. The gift beneath the tree was mine after all, the egg worth carrying. Oh me of little faith!

"Yes? Yes?" Pastor Pedro is eagerly holding the microphone before her, beckoning her to finish the sentence.

"I believe," my mother continues, though her voice has lost some of its clarity, "I believe that God alone can heal."

"Amen, Sistah," says the reverend. He grabs the microphone and begins to dance around the platform. "She's been healed, she's been healed. Did you hear her speak, mah friends? *Galory!*"

Mother stands there with tears streaming down her face.

Pedro stops dancing and holds the microphone before my father, hoping for words of praise.

Dad pauses for a moment, then speaks in a quavery voice. "For ten years we've been asking that God would heal her of Huntington's disease. That's really what we're here for."

Pastor Pedro is speechless for a few moments. Then he looks down at my mother and places a hand on her forehead. "Your faith has made you well!" he pronounces.

A cheer goes up from the crowd. "Does she take medication?" he asks my father.

Dad nods his head.

"Let me see it," he commands.

Dad reaches into his suit coat and reveals a small assortment of bottles. Taking them from my dad, the reverend hurls the bottles the length of the stage, spilling the contents all over the floor. Many stand to their feet and shout their approval. "She's been delivered tonight, mah friends. Galory!"

How I wish my brother Ben could be here to share in this moment.

Mom and Dad and Tony are whisked off the stage as the lineup of hopefuls lengthens. Tony pushes an empty wheelchair up the aisle. Mother walks behind him, unsteadily at first, hanging tightly to Dad's arm. Then she steps boldly forward, smiling as she walks. The rest of us follow amid pats of congratulation from the onlookers.

—⚬—

The atmosphere in the car is positively festive. Tony is collecting the letters of healing he read on the way. Maybe he'll paste them to his wall as souvenirs of this great night. Liz is scouring the lunch bags, hoping the leftovers have multiplied like the five loaves and two fishes. And why shouldn't they? It's a night of miracles. Dad is noticeably silent, but that doesn't stop the feeling of thanksgiving that wells within me.

"How did he know about Mom?" I ask excitedly.

"I filled out the card," offers Tony.

"But there must have been a thousand cards. How did he read all of them?"

"I don't know. Anyhoo, it doesn't matter. What matters is Mom. Look at her."

In the darkness there is only the sound of the windshield wipers and the rhythmic slapping of the pavement beneath our feet.

Then, something beautiful happens.

My mother starts to sing in a soft voice that's almost lost to the noise of the road:

> There is a fountain filled with blood,
> Drawn from Immanuel's veins.
> And sinners plunged beneath that flood
> Lose all their guilty stains.

Tony and Dad join in, repeating the words over and over: "E'er since, by faith, I saw the stream Thy flowing wounds supply, redeeming love has been my theme, and shall be till I die."

The rain has returned with a vengeance, but no one seems to mind. Traffic on the freeway is lighter now, and so are our burdens. I look at Danny. His head is bowed. I cannot imagine what he thinks of this strange new world.

---

We should be hanging Christmas decorations, the atmosphere is so festive. We have pulled chairs up to the kitchen table as if it were a warm fireplace, and we watch in amazement as Mother goes from fridge to stove, pulling out bread and lettuce and cheese and mayonnaise—anything she can find—and whipping it into a late-night snack. She's a little wobbly still, but that will change, I'm sure. Dad is her shadow on every step, wondering from whence she summons the strength, unable to believe this could be happening, that life could be this good. I can scarcely remember the meals she used to cook, but I know they were wonderful. I cannot wait for more.

She carries the tray unsteadily and sets it before us. Carrots, celery, tomatoes, surrounding a dip topped with dill and oregano. I have no idea where she found the ingredients. Eagerly we dig in, laughing and chattering like third-grade recess.

Dad stops us for a glorious prayer of thanksgiving, the first prayer I have closed my eyes for in a while:

"Lord, in a world where many go hungry, we thank Thee for food. Where many walk alone, we thank Thee for family. Where many long for healing, we thank Thee for hope."

---

Darkness descends on one of the most fascinating days of my life. It finds me stuffing socks in my drawer, whistling happily, and planning to make things right with Danny. I will visit the cops once again, this time with the whole truth, regardless of the cost.

The sound winding its way to meet me is an unfamiliar one.

I follow it down the hall, through the kitchen and into Mom's room.

She is propped up in bed, her shoulders hunched forward, her body shaking. It shakes not from the disease that has imprisoned her these ten long years. The disease that has dashed her hopes, flattened her dreams, and jammed her husband's prayers tight with urgency. No, it shakes this time from pure joy over the unexpected. And relief at the implausible events that have marked the past few hours. It shakes from something unexplainable too. Something divine.

The sound is like a rusty hinge that has finally given way. Like the ice on our creek finally cracking after a long, hard winter.

My mother, you see, is laughing.

I want to linger here, locked in time awhile, for laughter is not something we Andersons are in danger of growing accustomed to. Not in this room at least. Not in a room where my mother has been stretched out flat and wordless for almost a year. We resorted

215

to surprising tactics to encourage her speech—questions, jokes, skits—all without success.

Until tonight.

"Mom, why didn't you talk all that time?"

"I don't really know," she murmurs, and I lean close to make out the words. "I suppose I didn't have much to say." Then she grows serious. "Terry, it's not easy putting a happy face on sorrow. I've been in a dark hole for a while now, trying to construct a future here on earth. I think I let that go tonight. Tonight I told God, 'Whatever You want.' I hadn't done that in a while."

I do not understand her words, but I watch her lips curl upwards at the corner, allowing a soft laugh to escape.

I cannot help smiling myself, for the laughter is part false teeth and part tears, but mostly it is a little girl locked up inside this beautiful woman, longing to come out.

# thirty-four

# Seizure

Tony is downright proud of his latest creation, a stunning and punchy diatribe addressed to the headquarters of the American Atheists via some post office box in Parsippany, New Jersey. He won't let me go to sleep until I read it out loud with him standing in the doorway, holding the envelope. Danny is folding his hands behind his pointy little head, tilting a listening ear my way:

Hail!

I am an atheist and darn proud of it. I have been since I was young and couldn't get anything I asked God for. I mean, couldn't he just give a kid a red bicycle? But no way, I get one of these little banana seat things for Christmas. It was pink. It was my sister's old one. I asked God to help me sleep at night, and I would lie awake until I got so mad I just quit praying. I was six then. I prayed only once in my teen years when I told God I'd start talking to him if he got me another job besides cleaning grain bins, but no way. My uncle was an atheist. The only time he mentioned God was at football games!

I've studied everything Sigmund Freud wrote. As per our creed, I've spent many years learning "to love myself and my fellow man rather than a god." I've worked for heaven on earth, developing "the inner conviction and strength to meet life, to grapple with it, to subdue it and enjoy it." The problem is, it isn't working. I'm fifty-four now, and I've got a bit of a heart condition. Lately (this is embarrassing) I've taken to reading a book called *Mere Christianity* by one of these Christians. Last night when I couldn't sleep I even started reading the Bible, if you can believe it. I was looking for mistakes of course, but now I wonder if I was really looking for peace and hope. In one place it states "the fool hath said in his heart, There is no God," and I got to thinking, what if that's me? You know? What if my atheism is really my desire just to do my own thing? Let's just say that I die and find out that God was really God after all, and I'm accountable and maybe in a truckload of trouble. If I die as a Christian and go to heaven, what have I lost out on besides the drunken parties? But if I go to hell, that's quite a whopping big price to pay.

As you can see, reading this Bible has done a lot of damage. I'm finding stuff all around me now that makes me wonder. Like the stars and the planets and the way my hand works. I hope I don't sound paranoid, but I'm beginning to think I might be losing my doubt. Can you help me get it back? I want to be the best atheist I can be, but I'm losing faith in my lack of faith. How can I be a better atheist? What should I read more of? What should I avoid? I've done everything right but am afraid it isn't working. I'd sure appreciate a quick response from my fellow man.

So long,
Tony Anderson

The letter is funny enough for me, but it is positively hilarious to Danny, who has spent all his life with an atheist.

He is laughing so hard by paragraph two that he's hanging onto the sides of Ben's bed for support. By the time I'm reading about doubting my doubt he's on the floor, rolling around in hysterics.

"That's it," he says, wiping tears from his eyes and pointing at the letter. "You nailed it, man. Dad didn't reject God because he's sure He isn't there. He just doesn't want Him to be. He's mad at Him. And he doesn't want God telling him what to do, that's for sure."

Tony is quiet for a moment. "I've been talking with your dad a lot the last few days, you know."

"You have?" Danny sits up straight, cross-legged on the floor, probably wondering how his own father could kick him out while allowing Tony in.

"Oh yeah. It started out as a little project I thought I could write about when I got back to school. Turned out I've been listening more than talking. Your dad seems to be a piece of granite at first. Turns out he's softer than a peach inside."

"It's something I never saw much of." Danny says this and then brightens. "Did he say anything about me?"

"He just wanted to know how you were doing."

"He did?"

"He's been through a lot, you know. Things have happened to him in this town that would make a preacher swear. I'm surprised he isn't more bitter than he is."

"Things like what?" Danny is eager to know.

"I've said too much already. He told me in confidence. I'm sure he'll tell you one day."

"I saw him with a woman last night," I interrupt, wishing immediately that I hadn't.

"I know," says Danny, "I think they're living together. I think that's partly why Dad wanted me out of there."

Tony takes the letter and punches Danny softly on the shoulder. "Let's keep praying for him," he says. "Anyhoo, I'd better go. Goodnight." Tony stuffs the letter in the envelope and seals it with a lick.

—ᨊ—

Sleep is an illusive thing this night. I wonder when the cops will show up and arrest my roommate. I think of the ring three feet from my bed and kick myself for stealing it. I think of my former friend six feet away, a friend I have alienated and betrayed. Danny rolls over and turns my way.

"Terry? You doing okay?"

"Yeah."

"You sure?"

"Uh-huh."

"Well, I just want you to know that you're my best friend. I've been wondering these last few days where I'd be without you. It's been an amazing week, thanks to you."

"You stole my girlfriend," I'd like to say. Instead, I pretend to be asleep.

—ᨊ—

Tuesday afternoon the final exam dates are assigned, and reprobates like me are threatened that if we do not hand in our overdue papers we will forever remain undergraduates. I briefly consider one more prayer to the Almighty. I'd like to request another miracle, and I'd like Him to explain why Tony got all the brains in our family. It hardly seems fair. For one thing I've lugged this mystery around with me day after day without uncovering a single clue that makes any sense. Furthermore, there's a queasy feeling growing in my stomach that I will be repeating twelfth grade a year from now. Once or twice Mary Beth has mentioned that she'd love a June wedding, and I can see it now, her and Danny walking up the church aisle, holding hands while people clap and toss rice at them. Meanwhile I'm standing to one side, twenty-eight years old, enduring my eleventh year of twelfth grade.

Mom's healing has me carrying a lighter load, of course, but I still don't know what to do with Danny. I sincerely thought it would be easier to forgive him, to offer an olive branch of lasting friendship. I try to talk with him, but our conversation is always hijacked. The words come out wrong or they don't come out at all. It's like I'm talking to the girl he has stolen from me.

—⁓—

Tony is seated at the dinner table with the rest of us, slurping happily at the finest hamburger soup he's tasted in years. Mother's coaching didn't hurt of course, and I used a little creativity of my own. First I sizzled a whole pound of ground beef in her old skillet, shook some garlic salt on the remains, and doused the thing with two cups of fresh vegetables: onions, potatoes, carrots, and cabbage. I turned the burner on low, slid in a large can of tomato soup and enough water to achieve my desired consistency, and let it simmer. It was easier work than I thought it would be, and although I'm falling behind in the lawn-mowing department, I've seldom seen Liz more grateful. I wonder if she'll cut some grass for me if I cook some meals.

Tony is adding some salt and pepper to his soup, which is redundant. The pot is full of seasoning that was waiting in the cupboard, longing to be used.

And there's a new sight at the table tonight. Harry has edged his way over to my chair and is begging for something to eat. Liz can't help but notice. He never showed much interest in her cooking. Still she smiles at me admiringly. "Not bad," she says. "Not bad."

It is the first evening meal in more than a year when we have enjoyed Mother's presence. Although we were all hoping she would cook the food, she was too fatigued. We'll gladly settle for her cheerful face.

Dad sits beside her, cooling each spoonful before he brings it to her lips, turning the whole thing into a bit of a ceremony, complete with a short speech of gratitude to God.

The door flies open, and Danny Brown comes huffing his way through it like he's just run behind a bus all the way from Great Falls. He is holding the Chicago Blackhawks hat in one hand.

"Sorry I'm late but you won't believe it," he gasps. "Someone ratted on me."

"What?" Tony is in the middle of helping himself to a second bowl of soup.

Oh no. I guess I should have said something last night. But how do you call the cops and tell them you were just kidding? How do I tell Danny of my betrayal?

"Some bozo told the police they'd seen me near this dead body or something. I spent the last hour and a half trying to talk my way outa jail. I can't believe it, can you? No way. Unbelievable. If I ever—" I don't recall seeing Danny this worked up since the time we tossed a bowl of flour on him when he emerged from the shower after gym class. He stomps down the hall and into my room, which seems more his room than mine lately.

So, the Danny-Brown-as-murderer story held as much water as a leaky boot. You can hear him banging around looking for something. He is still huffing as he grates his chair up to the table. "Talk about unprofessional. They stick me in this chair, punch on a tape recorder, and grill me like I'm Charlie Manson. Geez. Whoops, sorry for my language. Pass the salt please."

"So, who ratted on you?" I venture.

"They wouldn't say."

"Come on, what'd you learn?"

"I learned they've probably got their man."

I drop my fork so fast I almost pierce my leg with it.

"They *what?*"

"Officer what's-his-name said they think they've figured it out already. That they've found him. Don't know if they've made the arrest or what, but they dropped some pretty strong hints that it wouldn't be long, that it couldn't have been me because there was, how'd they say it, another?"

Liz grabs Danny's bowl. "Who?" she asks.

"I don't know. Don't have a clue. May I have my bowl back?"

"Not until you tell us."

Danny grins at her.

Mother stands unevenly to her feet like she's about to propose a toast.

Suddenly she lets out a gasp and collapses, slumping sideways into Dad's arms. Her eyelids flutter. Her eyes roll backward. Dad slides her rigid body gently to the floor as a strange guttural sound escapes her throat. All of us are horrified, stunned. We try to be of help, yanking chairs back, grabbing pillows, looking to Dad for direction.

He holds her tightly, stroking her whitening hair. "It's a seizure," he manages, cradling her head, trying to keep her from choking.

"Tony," he yells, "call Doc Mason. Tell him to bring more medication too."

I have not witnessed a seizure before, and, God help me, I never want to see one again.

—⁓—

I know I should have stayed around, should have heard the troubling verdict, should have listened to the good doctor launch his massive words and try in his customary medicalese to explain the unexplainable for the thousandth time. Instead I find myself aboard my bicycle, pedaling fast for the edge of town. I must put some distance between myself and these people, between myself and the thoughts pounding around my head. So the whole thing was a fraud. The healing service a charade. This whatever-his-name, Pedro, a charlatan. I can't believe I was duped. Thoughts of forgiving Danny are smothered in the realization that the jealousy and bitterness have flared brighter, fanned by thoughts of his trickery, by thoughts of a future without my mother, without Mary Beth.

If I had my own car, I would head for Great Falls or maybe take a left for Australia. Start a lawn-care business there, learn to speak Australian. There is nothing in this stifling little town that has my allegiance now, nothing that begs me to stay, to set down roots, to unpack. I have a murderer for a brother, a mother who's dying, a girlfriend who's a cheater, a best friend turned worst enemy, and to complicate things, he's sleeping six feet away from me each and every night, just begging me to hold a pillow over his head and put him out of my misery. The only thing remotely worth sticking around for is graduation, and even that seems a vague possibility now.

Hector's Hollow is a welcome reprieve, a guarantee of peace and quiet for my weary mind. I started coming here when I was a kid, usually with a friend but sometimes just to get away. I'll find a stash of Ben's home-rolled doobies in the cave and smoke my way to blissful oblivion. I've done it before. I should be able to find a few somewhere if the batteries in my flashlight hold up.

# thirty-five

# Big Fish

The light of early evening is strong, and I'm glad for it as I crawl like a snake through the tiny hole of the cave. Standing up, I brush myself off. The odor of cigarette smoke is pungent, almost overpowering.

"Terry?" a surprised voice cuts through the darkness.

"Ben! What the—"

"Whew, I thought you were—"

"What are you doing out here?"

Ben strikes a match and a small lantern flickers to life. Timid pools of light bounce off the walls, far enough for him to see my startled face.

"I guess I'm wondering the same thing. What's going on?"

"I'm running too, I guess…" My voice trails off.

"From what?"

"It's Mom," I say, edging closer to him. "She's not so good."

His head jerks upward. "What do you mean?"

"She just had a seizure an hour ago. The doctor is there. I had to get out."

"Sit down," he motions impatiently, patting the dusty ground beside him as if it is a soft sofa. "How is she?"

"I don't know, Ben. It's not good."

He draws his hand down the length of his face, scratching the stubble on his chin.

"I told Dad you were okay," I say. "You know, like you asked."

"Thanks."

"I thought you were gone. What are you doing here?"

"I just came to pick up a few things, remnants from before."

"So you'll be gone again?"

"Not for long."

"Are you hiding from…them?"

"From who?"

"The cops?"

I search his face. He seems fearless. "No. Not anymore."

"You're giving up?"

Ben laughs. "What did Mary Beth say the other night? Shut up and kiss me? Well, seems like you need to shut up and listen, okay?"

He grows quiet as I sit down beside him. Is he weighing the pros and cons of confiding in me? I've only lived eighteen years, but I know of few greater feelings than enjoying an older brother's confidence. As the youngest in the family I sometimes feel like all the useful genes were gone by the time I arrived, and though Ben and I are not blood brothers, I grew up admiring his inherent tenacity, his fiery temper, his ability to defy God and walk his own way. My mind races with the possibilities. Does he have a plan for me to break him from jail? I listen carefully as he fills my ears with more puzzle pieces.

"I think it's time you knew a few more things, Tare."

What? He never calls me Tare. Liz does, but I've rarely thought Ben viewed me as important enough to bequeath a pet name. He slouches against the wall, and as I sit beside him in this dank cave I see for the first time the gun he is rotating slowly between his knees. I avoid saying anything about it, for I am hoping his words will solve greater mysteries than this.

"Did you ever hear of Francis Frank?"

It's hardly the opener I was expecting. "Sort of. Isn't he the guy who was our pastor when I was a kid?"

"Uh-huh."

"We switched churches when I was pretty small. I don't remember much."

"Well, he was a Bible-thumper, for sure. But I'm not sure he was thumping the Bible God wrote. The one he preached from had mostly things about being obedient to Francis Frank in it. We lived in fear that we'd offend him. Lived in mortal terror that he would chastise our parents or expel us from the church. It happened several times, you know. Whatever he said was law."

"I don't remember any of that. I was too young."

"I think I was about ten when he left this place, and I thought he went back to Alabama or wherever the…wherever it was he came from."

"You can cuss around me, Ben. I don't mind."

He laughs. "This Francis Frank took an interest in me when I was younger, a very strange interest, but I never liked him. Gave me the creeps. In fact, he drove me from the church really. I'll go back just as soon as hell freezes over, if you'll pardon me for saying so."

I nod my head. It's my story too. "So what was he like?"

"Well, just before he left here, he pulled a Ponzi."

"A what?"

"You've never heard of him?"

"No."

"Charles Ponzi was the granddaddy of scam artists. He was the son of an Italian fruit vendor, so he found out early that making money was hard work. In the 1920s, he devised a plan to make a fortune the easy way. He bought postal union reply coupons real cheap overseas and sold them in Boston for a fifty percent profit."

"I'm sorry, you're losing me."

"Well, what he was doing was legitimate, but it was too slow for him. Back then the stock market was in a dive and the country was going into a depression, so Ponzi started promising investors a return of fifty percent in two months if they gave him their money. Not bad, huh? People couldn't send him money fast enough. Mail flooded his office. He was stuffing money in drawers, in closets, in wastebaskets. Money talks, but big interest has an echo." Ben laughs at his own clever line. "In the summer of 1920, Ponzi was raking in around two million bucks a day. Trouble is, the funds were never invested at all."

"I don't understand. How did it work then?"

"If the old investors wanted their money back, he returned it by the boatload, but the money he gave them wasn't their money. It was from the new investors. Of course, they went out and told all their buddies how wonderful it was, and their friends lined up to invest. The cops discovered the fraud and sent him to prison. When he was arrested he had two hundred tailored suits, a hundred pairs of shoes, tons of diamond tiepins, and a fortune in jewelry. He died penniless in 1949."

"Wow. Where'd you learn this stuff?"

"Hey, Tony's not the only one who reads."

"So what does this have to do with Francis Frank...and with you?"

"Just shut up and listen," he laughs. "From what I know, Mr. Frank started out with good intentions. He had these grand dreams, but he needed money. He discovered he could raise it by packaging his idea into a glamorous, can't-miss proposition, and I'm sure he fully intended to return the money. People invested with the promise of higher interest than they could get anywhere else, and when they got suspicious, he did what Ponzi did. He paid off the original investors with new money coming in. Doctors and dentists fell for it. And that's not all. Dad told me once that he and Mom trusted the guy so much that they opened their entire savings account to him and lost everything. Dad said he couldn't believe he fell for it, but by then it was too late."

"Unbelievable. So that's why Dad's been scraping to get by all these years."

"I guess so."

"So what happened to this jerk? I heard he was in Alabama, and then I heard he lives near here."

"He ended up like Ponzi did—in prison."

"Serves him right."

"I wish that were the end of the story."

"What do you mean?"

"White collar crime doesn't land you much jail time. Seems Francis Frank is at it again."

"No way."

"He had quite a following here, Frank did, but it was nothing compared to what happened after prison."

"What do you mean?"

"Well, somehow he got himself a few rich friends this time and more money than before, and they started a ministry. They were overseas somewhere holding crusades, and according to the papers, all sorts of miraculous things took place, and suddenly he was traveling full-time, healing people."

"You mean like Pastor Pedro."

"Yeah. Like Pastor Pedro."

"Hey, how do you know this stuff?"

"Oh, I have my sources." He chuckles.

"Ben, I've got some sources too. I've seen the picture, you know."

He stops spinning the pistol. "What picture?"

"The one you came for the other night. Did the others in the picture lose money too?"

"Oh yes."

He turns the revolver in his hands and spins the chamber.

"Is it loaded?"

"Yep."

"Where'd you get it?"

"Oh, it wasn't hard."

"Have you ever...used it?"

He laughs.

"Do you remember how I used to sneak out a lot when we were younger?"

"You kidding? Of course."

"I got into some trouble."

"What kind?"

"You never mind. Suffice it to say that I was arrested and jailed."

"Jailed?"

"Yeah. I didn't think Dad would tell you. It was only a short time. Just a few weeks."

"How'd you get out?"

He pauses here and studies my face, questioning my reliability, I suppose.

"I agreed to rat on some people."

"You what?" He could whack me with a two-by-four, and I wouldn't have been so surprised.

"You heard me. I was a little brook trout and I agreed to be bait, to help the police reel in some whoppers."

I nod my head and smile. A weight has fallen from my shoulders. "But I don't get what that has to do with this pastor what's-his-name?"

"Swear you won't tell?"

"I swear."

"Well, as it turns out, he's the biggest catch of all."

Ben gives the revolver another spin. Small wonder he needs it.

# thirty-six

# Home Free

*I* am standing outside my mother's bedroom, straightening a picture that doesn't need straightening, unable to venture in. At least a dozen others are crammed into her tiny room, most of them from church, most of them looking at their shoes. Tony is there, Liz too. Surprisingly, Danny is in the corner, sitting beside Mary Beth. They aren't holding hands, but their shoulders are touching. I look down at my own shoes and consider running again.

The grief I feel inside is a private thing. I do not wish to share it with these people. Still I shuffle slowly through the doorway, fearful to enter this holy place smelling like smoke, yet more fearful of staying away.

Mother's eyes are shut, her bony hands crossed on her chest. You'd think she had passed away, to look at the faces in here. But a smile as wide as the Jordan River rests on her face. Dad looks up from his shoes and nods a welcoming glance my way. There are no chairs left, so I lean against a wall. The rest of them change positions at my arrival, seemingly grateful for my presence.

I want to lean forward and tell her that I've just seen Ben, that he's okay, that he didn't murder anyone, that he loves her and she'll see him soon.

Pastor Davis and his petite wife, Irene, sit still against the far wall, and the only thing missing is the Hammond organ she usually plays at church. Shamefully I realize that I begrudge their appearance here. Danny, Mary Beth, the lot of them. What could these people possibly know of my mother's pain, of all our pain? Pastor Davis. The one who quit visiting my mother a few years back, neglecting her in her most needy moments. I cannot understand why.

"Why don't we sing a little more," suggests Mrs. Davis, flipping through a tattered old hymnal and landing on something she recognizes. The voices are sweet and soft, like angels must sound: "All the way my Savior leads me, what have I to ask beside? Can I doubt His tender mercy who through life has been my guide?" I know every word, and I mouth them as if I'm singing along. "When my spirit, clothed immortal, wings its flight to realms of day, this my song through endless ages: Jesus led me all the way." It's surprising how many of the songs in the hymnal are about heaven. I hadn't noticed it before.

With the song finished, there is silence, and Pastor Davis begins to speak. "I was just at the bedside of a widower who passed away—I better not tell you who. But his family was around the bed arguing over who got how much from his estate. It was ugly." He pats my mother's hand. "It's a refreshing break...to be here."

Mother's eyes open to look at him. She smiles her way around the room from face to face, ending in mine. The smile gives way to a concerned grimace. "Come," she beckons me.

Reaching for my hand, she whispers in a voice just loud enough for me to hear: "I'd like you to sneak me a chocolate bar, Son. Would you, once they're all gone?"

I can't help but smile. You bet I will.

I can scarcely look at my mother as she says this, for she is a thin wisp of a woman, a picture from a concentration camp. Her fingers are gnarled, her lips cracked.

"What did she say?" whispers Tony, leaning forward like everyone else in here.

"She wants chocolate." Ripples of laughter spread throughout the room.

Mom's chest heaves a little as she struggles for breath. Then her wrinkled forehead softens. She is looking past me at the open door.

Ben is standing there, my big lost brother, dusty and dirty and wreaking of tobacco.

Tears are streaming down his cheeks.

"Come," she says.

He kneels beside the bed and embraces her like he is a child once again.

One by one people depart the room to leave us here alone.

Ben is kneeling and holding Mom's hand. Liz puts an arm on my shoulder as she moves to sit beside me. Dad is quiet, so Tony speaks.

"You're the reason I'm a Christian, Mom. All my life people have come along who have tried to take the faith out of me. You keep coming along and putting it back in. I—" Tony struggles a little, then realizes he can say no more.

Mom smiles at him. Then she is speaking again, loudly enough for all of us to hear.

"Remember when you were small and something was wrong at night? What did I say to you?"

"It'll look better in the morning." Liz brightens at the memory.

"Right," says Mom. "I was saying it for me too. I've been in this bed most of a decade now. All that time I've prayed for healing. I remember standing in the hot sun one day when Terry was just a baby and I knew this disease was coming. I said out loud, 'Jesus, you spit on mud and healed a blind man; can't You touch me too?' But sometimes healing doesn't look like we thought it would. My body wasn't healed, but my spirit was. You see, I've been far more committed to God than if He had said yes. Every day I've been forced to depend on Him for my next breath. Last night I was looking for an escape hatch, but this suffering has been a friendly sheep dog, nipping at my heels, chasing me home. God heals some people, but everyone Jesus healed died one day. It's the peace that won't die. The promise of heaven too."

Ben is clutching her hand, and all of us are scattered around the bed, leaning in close. Taking a deep breath, she continues.

"No matter what comes, I pray you will find that same comfort, each one of you. I pray you will know the Great Physician in a fresh, new way. It doesn't matter if I'm healed down here. I have something far better than healing. I have hope. No disease on earth can steal that from me."

She lets out a soft laugh and a grin pulls at the sides of her mouth.

I will never forget the holiness of her laughter this night. Or those words that foreshadow the joy and the hope and the tragedy that is to come.

"His faithfulness is great," she says. "His mercies are new every morning."

A peace I've not seen before spreads across her face. "I can see," she says.

Those were the last words I ever heard my mother say.

# thirty-seven

# The Hero

*I* suppose I have mourned her death slowly through the years, saying a begrudging goodbye a little more boldly each day. But still the finality of it numbs me now, turning the nights into restless encounters with a new reality, weighing the days down with sad regret. Tony tried to put a brave face on it once. Said that this long goodbye is like watching a child run away on the prairies. You can see him run for days. Dad sits beside me, whispering words of comfort—he, who so needs to grieve, comforting me.

A holy numbness encompasses our house as people graciously help with arrangements I didn't know were needed. And in the midst of it are small mercies. For one thing, no one shows up to arrest anyone. And a note from the principal of Lone Pine Christian informs me that he would very much like it if my friends and I would play our guitars during the graduation exercises just after I receive my diploma.

All I need to do is pull my math grades up a little, and I'll be fine.

I am convinced it is another of my father's miracles, that the decision was made not out of appreciation for my academic prowess but out of sympathy. Mother would have laughed had I told her this. And I suspect she would have agreed with my assessment.

Uncle Roy made the trip from Minneapolis, pulling in late last night, looking for soup and smelling like mothballs. Others began arriving first thing this morning, coming from nearby farms and faraway cities, tapping at our door as if we would know what to do with them. An avalanche of food surges through our kitchen, and I am surprised by the almost festive atmosphere. The house is jammed with people, and many are laughing. Tony is reading some of the letters he has received from prominent leaders, and even my dad is cracking jokes. Two cousins I didn't know I had are in the living room scarfing down turkey on a bun like it's Christmas evening. It's hard to know who's related in a town like this one.

Pastor Davis advises that we change venues and hold the funeral at Independence Arena. Perhaps it's fitting that we say goodbye to her in a dingy place built and used mostly by pagans. Mother once told me that she hoped there'd be plenty of cigarette butts in the parking lot when she died. I didn't know what she meant at the time. Now I do.

Shopkeepers hang up Closed signs at noon, something I've not witnessed before or since on a Friday. I am confused as to the reason but grateful nonetheless.

Backstage the festive atmosphere has vanished as the truth begins to nudge us toward reality: Mother is forever gone. Never again will I hear her shuffle down the hallway or bid me goodnight in that soft angelic voice. Never again will I cling to the feeble hope of healing or the thought that this is all a bad dream and if only I pinch myself it will be over.

Danny will sit with us. He hasn't said much to me since my mother's passing. He just follows me around the house like a lost pup. Maybe he's afraid I'll do something awful.

I peek through a scarlet curtain into the dimly lit audience. Scarcely a chair is vacant; every soul in town seems to be here. Most of their names escape me. The entire Greison family sits near the front—their children, Isaac, Elijah, and Jacob caught in a rare moment of stillness. Blane Wright, Dad's first convert to Christianity, is behind them, sitting with Eunice Archibald, who still speaks in tongues though the closest Pentecostal church is a hundred miles away. I've never seen the owner of the Five and Dime in a suit before. But Anthony Jesperson is there alright, his white socks a glaring contrast to the rest of him. Hilda Wiebe-Evans-Hasborough-Steinburger is clutching her fourth husband, dabbing her eyes already. The two of them never miss a Sunday now, thanks to my father's kindness in fixing her car all those years ago. The Swanson family is down front too. Michael's head is bowed and Mary Beth's blonde hair is drawn tight behind her. A navy blue dress covers her shapely body, and I'm surprised and a little ashamed that I could notice such things at a time like this.

Danny Brown is looking over my shoulder, and I quickly close the curtain.

"I wonder if Dad is here," he says.

Everyone stands as we enter the auditorium, marching slowly behind the casket. A lone piper is off to one side, playing something that could be "Amazing Grace."

All these years later, it still seems as though I am viewing the event through a smoky mirror. I cannot tell you what hymns we sang or who led them, but I remember the front of the bulletin covered in Scotch thistles, the color of the curtains, and the look in Mary Beth's eyes.

And I remember the longings that began to tug at me, longings to see my mother once again, longings for something that cannot be had on this earth.

For though I try to be strong and resolute to hold to the course I have set, a realization is growing in me that I am a fool to walk in any direction but the one she has walked.

Tony climbs the makeshift steps to the platform and unfolds his notes to read a tribute he worked on most of the morning.

"My mother was born in a small farmhouse in upstate New York, the sincere and earnest middle child of pioneering Scottish Presbyterian immigrants. She loved to tell us stories of life there, of the death of two preschool brothers and the declining health of her father. She spoke of the little religious group her parents joined, a group of kind people who denied themselves every earthly pleasure, living in abject poverty and cold houses and complete misery, thinking only of the joyous life to come. They were called the Upper Creek Brethren, and Mother always insisted that she'd probably be their president if Dad had not rescued her and set her straight."

His tribute sounds more like a Bible college paper, but people don't mind the length of it, me included.

Tony tells of Mom's childhood on the farm, and you feel like you are there yourself, watching cows milked and corn shucked, gazing into the faces of my grandparents, those courageous and hard-headed pioneers. "To some it may have been boring drudgery, but to Mother farm work was her lot in life, and she accepted it with a gracious and glowing countenance. She met our father when they were in their late teens and insisted that she married him not so much for romantic reasons but because she felt she could be of some assistance to him."

Grins and small ripples of laughter spread through the audience, and Tony continues.

"Mother's decision to follow her husband to Grace could not have been arrived at easily. She was a fiercely independent woman who loved the ways of the East, but she always told us she came West out of simple obedience to God's call on her life. Mom and Dad shared common values but almost nothing else. To say they balanced each other out would be a stretch, because neither ever moved from their stubborn and long-held positions. Yet the romance blossomed into a comfortable marriage devoid of self-seeking, one that created a home for us where love was readily available to heal wounds, cover wrongs, and offer hope.

"In addition to the onset of her illness, many things seemed to confuse my mother and render her literally speechless for a time. She wondered how grown-ups could teach younger people that tolerance is the greatest virtue while truth is relative. She watched this generation embrace self-actualization, and it left her profoundly bewildered. 'It's not about you,' she often told us. 'It's about Him. It's about others.' To her, people had things backward, as if they were running the bases from third to first, as if they took a bath and then filled the tub with water.

"Before her illness, Mother was not just strong, she was strong-willed. If you didn't hang up your coat, she threw it outside—especially in the wintertime. If you couldn't decide how you wanted your eggs done, she would scramble them right on your plate. Or on your head. She sometimes got her words mixed up, which brought laughter into our home. A few years ago she asked if I would put on an opera album by her favorite tenor, 'that Paparazzi guy.' Once she asked if I would read her a delusional. 'You mean a devotional?' I said. 'That would be fine too,' she replied.

"Mom was ferociously frugal. She rarely discarded a teabag but chose to believe there was still some good in it and that given the chance she could wring its neck and prove her point. She wasn't big on home decoration. I don't ever remember her putting up wallpaper or painting. She just kept piling books on bookshelves. I think my head will always tilt a little to the right because I was constantly examining the spines of old classics that stretched from floor to ceiling. We never had quite enough to eat, but we were allowed to feast on the great Puritan writers, the complete works of Charles Spurgeon, or westerns some would have found scandalous. She didn't separate these books by category. When she tired of reading them she would pull something from the sea of recordings, turn on the record player, stand uneasily to her feet and start to dance. How we loved to—"

Tony stops for a moment, but no tears come to his eyes. I'm sure there are people around us who are frowning at the thought of a Christian dancing, but I can't find any. People are smiling and wiping tears.

I don't know that I have ever admired my brother more. Haltingly he continues.

"She taught us to respect grown-ups, though we didn't always do it. She showed us how to give others the benefit of the doubt, to look for the best in them, and not be too surprised when we found it. When sin manifested itself in my life, she seemed shocked, as if she thought me incapable of anything but resolute honesty and good will. My mother's trust made me fearful of disappointing or displeasing her, not because she was ill but because I knew that to disappoint my mom would be akin to disappointing God.

"What I saw in her extended far beyond morality, frugality, self-discipline, or competence, though she demonstrated all of these. No, it was something bigger. She was a loud woman sometimes, bold in her witness, but more often she was quiet about her faith. A younger lady once stood by her bedside and asked if my mother would be her mentor. Mom was confused by the question. She did not have a schedule for mentoring. Her faith was not something she did, it was something she was.

"She was so devoted to Christ and His kingdom that to think any of us could have another focus was impossible for her to comprehend. 'Why would you look for joy outside of the one who created it?' she liked to say. She found her joy in serving Christ, in knowing Him, in loving Him. No other way was thinkable.

"Mom lay on her back and prayed for just about everyone here. I know this. I heard her. She believed the best for you, she hoped that you in your health could know as great a joy as she did in her sickness. Mother was a lady of the Bible. It coursed through her veins. The psalmist wrote that God's Word was a light to his path, that God's voice warned him where to turn and where not to turn. My mother did that too. We saw Christ when we looked at her, felt Him nearby when she sat by our beds, heard His voice whenever she spoke. There is no more supreme compliment I can pay her. As long as I live I will hear her quiet, persistent, enduring call to live a holy life completely devoted to serving Christ and others."

For the first time, Tony looks up from his notes. He is smiling.

"I counted thirty-four plaques hanging beside her bed the night she died. There were Bible verses and pictures of her children and the husband she loved so much. This poem was taped to the back of one of those pictures. I'm not sure why. It was hand-written by my mother, and I'll conclude by reading it:

"Bury me on Friday, with a candle and some chips.
It's dark down there, and I'll be craving food upon my lips.
Bury me on Friday, as the Master was that day.
Print the headlines just like His: 'The stone was rolled away.'

"I've been counting ceiling tiles for way too many years.
Locked inside this little room, battling my fears.
Though grief was there to block my path, I'll not give in to
     sorrow.
For hope came too that Easter day, hope for my tomorrow.

"So bury me on Friday, with a tear and no regret.
I've gone ahead to cheer you on, I'm waiting, don't forget.
Sing when you remember me, sing praises without end.
Bury me on Friday, Sunday's just around the bend."

Everywhere people are wiping tears and nodding their heads. A few are sobbing outright. Before sitting down, Tony stops at the casket and places a hand on it. I still cannot see tears in his eyes.

Next up is Dad, who thanks everyone for coming. "Ruth asked me to sing to you today," he says in a trembly voice. "I've seen a few miracles in my time. If I can get through this, it will be another one."

He clears his throat. "This song was her favorite."

And, taking a deep breath, my father begins to sing in that rich tenor voice of his:

> He giveth more grace when the burdens grow greater,
> He sendeth more strength when the labors increase;
> To added affliction He addeth His mercy,
> To multiplied trials His multiplied peace.

Throughout the building, people are sniffling and blowing their noses. I cannot afford to let my thoughts dwell on my mother, or I will need a beach towel. I bite my lip and wiggle my foot. My stoic Scottish grandfather would have been proud.

How Dad is able to muster the strength or the resolve to keep putting one word after another, I will never know. His head is back and his eyes are closed. He brought no hymnal with him. He doesn't need the words.

> When we have exhausted our store of endurance,
> When our strength has failed ere the day is half done,
> When we reach the end of our hoarded resources
> Our Father's full giving is only begun.
>
> His love has no limit, His grace has no measure,
> His power has no boundary known unto men;
> For out of His infinite riches in Jesus
> He giveth, and giveth, and giveth again.

I'm not sure how or even why Pastor Davis is getting up after this. His message is the shortest he's ever given us, and it is mostly lost on me, save for a most remarkable admission that becomes his conclusion:

"One wintry day just a few years ago, I was instructed by Ruth Anderson not to visit her again."

The sniffling stops as people lean forward quizzically.

"She told me she was dying, and she had no doubt about where she was going. 'I want you to promise me something, Nathaniel'—she was the only one in this church who used my first name, you know. But she had me lean in a little closer, and then she commanded me in that strong voice of hers, 'Pastor, I want you to spend your time on the living. Spend your energy on those who are in danger of going to hell. I won't let you go until you promise me that.'

"I just stood there, not knowing what to say. But how could I refuse her? How could I say no to that sweet face, that compelling grin? So, foolishly I agreed. Well, those of you who know Ruthie Anderson are aware that she had a way of being fiercely blunt and soft all at once. Listening to her preach at you was like being force-fed chocolate. It was sure enjoyable, but you knew you'd pay for it somehow.

"She said, 'Here's what I want you to promise me, Nathaniel. You've been visiting once a week, so I want you to take that time now and call on one person a week across the creek. One person who doesn't know Jesus. I want you to tell them that Ruth Anderson asked you to come and deliver a message. Be nice about it. Don't go if they don't want you.'

"That's what I've been doing all this time. I've been telling people the truth. That Ruthie would love to see you herself, but she's flat on her back. That she wants you to know the best news in all the world—that Jesus loves you. That Jesus gives you hope. Ruthie said she can't wait to see you on the other side, and she hopes you'll be there.

"Well, I'm here today to tell you that barely a handful didn't invite me in. And that without Mrs. Anderson's influence in this community, our church would be a whole lot smaller. Without her sweet spirit and her godly testimony, we wouldn't have had to bring in extra chairs for this funeral. I would like all the people I've visited over the past two years, all the people who have placed their faith in Christ because of Ruthie Anderson, to stand to your feet."

Seismologists will tell you that there was no activity recorded in the whole state that day, that no fault line developed in the rocks beneath, but I can tell you that the earth moved inside that place. All around me, chairs are pushed back as one after another people begin to stand. A few brave ones at first and then dozens upon dozens.

And deep within my own hardened soul, something begins to crack and thaw too. Something whispers that change is on the way, that death will give way to life, that with a mother like this one, my stubborn resolve doesn't stand a chance.

Danny nudges me hard and nods his head toward the back. His father is sitting there, stone-faced and unbudging. "He's here," says Danny, clenching his fist.

Tony leans over and presents me with the most beautiful anagram he has ever written in his entire life. It leaps out at me from the back of the bulletin beneath Scotch thistles that wrap around from the front. The anagram works out perfectly. You can try it for yourself:

*Mom is the hero!*
*Mother is Home!*

# thirty-eight

# Francis Frank

We lay her to rest in a shady spot overlooking Franklin's Creek. Pastor Davis offers a final prayer of committal as they lower the pine casket slowly into the ground. I hope no one notices that I cannot watch, that I am following the muddy water of Franklin's Creek as it snakes its way northeast toward the Musselshell River and beyond.

They say the rivers of this state lead to four different oceans. My mother's life has led her along a slow and winding path to the one place she's longed for every day these past ten years.

Home.

I picture her making breakfast for someone up there. Don't ask me why. She always seemed happiest in the kitchen, slamming eggs against a fry pan, serving heaping helpings when the times were good. I wonder if she's cooking for the disciples—maybe lamb chops or fish like they hooked when they were catching their limit along the shores of Galilee. She'll be dicing onions and crushing dried bread and grinding pepper, no doubt. There will be abundant laughter, unlimited butter, and generous spoonfuls of oregano. Ah, she'll love that. I wonder if she's ordering the disciples around, telling them to eat up and that if they don't they'll get leftovers tomorrow. One thing's for sure, the smile I've always loved will be tugging at the corners of her mouth once again. Forgive me if my vision sounds irreverent, but such thoughts are a comfort to me as I stand beside her grave.

Mary Beth is in the crowd of mourners to my right. I wonder if she notices the smile visiting my face as I think about my mother scrambling eggs. I've caught her eye a few times, only to have her look away. It's surprising how much grief she is experiencing for someone she scarcely knew. Danny stands beside her, causing me a mixture of anger and self-pity and numbness. Do they have to flaunt it here?

Stepping forward, Dad turns his eyes heavenward, and it's like he can see right through the portals of heaven. "She's with Jesus now." He lowers his eyes and speaks to us in a soothing voice we must strain to hear. "No one has ever seen God's face and lived to tell about it. Exodus tells us that Moses wanted to, but God wouldn't let him." There are no tears in his eyes as he speaks; his face seems radiant, expectant. "The last words she spoke to us were these: 'I can see.' Ruthie is seeing Him right now. She didn't really live until she saw Jesus. And now that she's seen Him, she will never die."

I have never witnessed a committal service before, and the finality of it startles me. My father once advised me to make important decisions in a cemetery. Until today I didn't understand what he meant. The perspective from here is different than from anywhere else.

The only other time I can remember being in this graveyard was three or four years ago on some macabre youth group outing. Noah Corzini, our youth pastor, dragged us here just before midnight after one of his evening pizza and prayer fests. I suppose he brought us here partly to make his lame ghost stories come alive, but also to point with his flashlight at headstone after headstone and say things we would ignore were we not scared half to death. Noah read the names out loud and the dates as well. Some had died as infants, like little Melvin Schwartz, 1963 to 1964. Others had lived well past ninety, like Matthew Jenning's aunts, both of them spinsters, who according to Matthew had vowed to their father on his deathbed that they would never marry, much to the chagrin of a dozen bachelors.

"What is the one thing you see on every one of these gravestones?" Noah asked. We stammered around a little, suggesting things like dates and granite and crosses. "No," he corrected, aiming the flashlight at a charcoal colored stone in front of us, "each and every one of them has a dash between the dates. A very short dash."

Of course we didn't know what he was getting at, all we wanted was to go home—or at least anywhere else but a graveyard. "Your life seems like it will stretch on forever," said Noah, "but it won't. The Bible says our days are like the evening shadow, that we wither away like grass. We are like a flower in the field, you guys; the wind blows over it and it's gone." All in all, it was pretty depressing stuff. Until he uttered something uncharacteristically profound: "Here's what I want you to ask yourself: What am I doing with that dash?"

His words come back to me now as if the preacher is expressing them for the first time. I will never be able to visit my mother's grave without noticing that dash, without knowing that if anyone on earth made the most of it, Ruth Anderson did.

—⁓—

Grace Community is packed for the fellowship time. The pews have been tugged to the sides of the sanctuary, making space for two neat rows of tables overflowing with good things. Ben is outside, smoking up a storm with a few dozen others. I'd love a cigarette right now; I haven't had one for days.

Inside, folks saunter to the tables, trying not to look too eager. The ladies of the church scurry about, replacing empty trays with fresh heaping platters of grapes and honeydew and watermelon. Others carry plates laden with veggies and dip and cookies and squares. I will never understand why we must eat so much at funerals, but here I am loading my own plate, hoping my appetite will return.

Everyone is far too kind to me. People I thought did not know I existed call me by name and tell me what my mother meant to them. They do this with stories and with tears. Others shrink back, unable to make eye contact, uncertain of what to say.

Mr. Brown brushes past me with an embarrassed nod. I've seen him in church only once before. He scarcely notices the crackers topped with assorted meats and cheeses and pickles. He has only one target in mind.

On the far side of the room stands his son, stuffing grapes in his impatient mouth. Mr. Brown walks toward him, pauses momentarily, then opens his arms wide, awkwardly embracing his only child. The two of them stand there, heads on each other's shoulders, weeping.

The crowd eases back to give them space. Not a person in the room has to ask what is happening, or who these people are. Instead the tears are flowing once again. People are surprised to find they have any left.

I study the grapes on my plate and notice I haven't eaten a one. Setting the plate down, I join Danny and his father. I can hold out no longer. I will tell him everything. I will tell him I'm sorry.

—⟋⟍—

Tonight the power goes out just after dark, and I sit with my father in the living room staring at emergency candles and wondering what to say. It's just the two of us, and though I admire him so much, I find myself wishing the others were here. "Terry," he says, pushing wax around the base of a candle, "it's time I tell you something, I don't know why I waited so long. Other things were more important, I guess."

I cannot imagine what it could be, and I lean forward, my heart pounding a little faster.

There is silence for one very long minute. "Dad, what is it?"

As his story unfolds, some mysteries are clearer and others are deepened.

Short days before my parents' first anniversary, something wonderful arose in the form of a knock at their front door. It came courtesy of the widow's son, the elderly widow who lived next door until she passed away. The man stood on their threshold in a sharp three-piece suit, tipping his hat and surveying the room. He seemed surprised to realize that the couple who had been so kind to his mother, the couple she had raved about in her letters, were poor as flies in an orphanage. Yet somehow one had found the resources to build his mother a beautiful pine chair, and the other had warmed her final days with home cooking.

The son, who was old enough to be Mom and Dad's parents, wanted to visit his mother's grave, and once Dad had taken him there, he was bold enough to ask if Mom would mind making him dinner. He even had a special request: soup, fresh bread, and strained carrots. The three of them enjoyed each other's company, and the widow's son listened carefully as Dad spun stories of the widow next door, of her stubborn spirit, which finally gave way to a beautiful smile. "I would like you to have that chair," said my father.

It turned out that their guest had a few surprises of his own.

"Back in the early 1940s," he began, "the U.S. War Production Board was looking for an inexpensive substitute for synthetic rubber. It was to be used in the production of jeep and airplane tires, gas masks, and a wide variety of military equipment."

My mother had completely tuned him out by this point, but she would find the signal before long.

"The board approached General Electric and gave one of their engineers the assignment of investigating the possibility of chemically synthesizing a cheap, all-purpose rubber. He toyed with various materials, finally settling on boric acid and silicone oil, from which he created a rubber-like compound with highly unusual properties. The pliant goo stretched farther than rubber. In fact, it rebounded twenty-five percent more than the bounciest rubber ball. It withstood a wide range of temperatures without decomposing and was resistant to molds and decay. The trouble was, it had no industrial advantage over rubber. In other words, it was useless. The engineer had failed. People at the laboratory in New Haven, Connecticut, found it a curiosity though, and in 1945, the company mailed samples to several of the world's leading engineers, challenging them to devise some practical use for this strange substance. But no one succeeded.

"I operated a small toy store at the time and had the good fortune to be at a party where a big wad of this stuff was demonstrated. You should have heard the laughter. It kept a group of adults amused for hours, and that's not easy. I wrote the folks at General Electric and entered into an agreement with them. I bought a giant hunk of the goo for about a hundred and fifty dollars and then hired a college student to separate it into one-ounce balls. We popped them inside colored plastic eggs and tried to market them. Things were slow until the *New Yorker* ran a story in its 'Talk of the Town' section. Soon it was outselling every other item in toy stores. In fact, during the fifties and sixties, these little eggs racked up sales of six million dollars a year. People wrote us letters. They were using it to collect cat fur and lint. They were cleaning ink and ribbon fiber from typewriter keys, stabilizing furniture with it, and using it to lift dirt from car seats and ink from comic books. The Apollo 8 astronauts took it to the moon to keep their tools in place. And we found out that women were clutching it during childbirth. It gave them something to squeeze besides their husbands' necks!

"I don't think I need to tell you that Silly Putty has made me a wealthy man."

Leaning across the table, he said, "I would like it very much if you had a share in that."

Well, as you might understand, my father was not thinking about finishing his strained carrots right about then. In fact, as he tells it, his mouth fell open and some carrot dropped into his steaming soup. Both of my parents came from humble roots, and to think of vast wads of money floating about the house was almost too much for them.

Once my father rediscovered his vocal chords, he thanked the visitor and then began to dream out loud.

"I have only one wish," he said. "I would like you to place 10,000 Gideon Bibles in hotel rooms back in California. That's it. That's all I want. Oh, and put a twenty-dollar bill in each of them right in the Gospel of John."

Mother just sat there, stunned.

But the millionaire grinned and scratched some notes on a pad. "Gideons," he said slowly, spelling it out.

Then he turned to Mom. "And what would you like, ma'am?"

"I would like time to think about it," she said, adding almost timidly, "Holy smokes."

She poured the man some tea, and finally she spoke. "I would like one of those new-fangled sewing machines. The ones with the zigzag feature. From that...whatsit company—you know—Singer."

The millionaire only smiled. "Is that it?" he asked. "You can do better."

And before the man left, Mother did do better. She asked for some things my father would not disclose to me, though I begged and pleaded.

"Why did you tell me this in the first place?" I ask.

"I don't know," says my father. "I just wanted to talk about her, I guess."

Tears are in his eyes as he says this.

"She was the best," I say, which sounds dumb, I know.

"Yes, she was, Son. Yes, she was."

—⁓—

My mother's body is in the ground less than a week when a phone call comes. I suppose someone figured we'd grieved enough.

"Sherwood Forest, Robin Hood speaking." Tony is the one who taught me this.

The reply is polite but businesslike. "Is Mr. Anderson home, please?"

I hand the phone to Dad. He listens for a minute or two, scratching notes on a sheet of paper. I don't hear all he says, but a few sentences come through.

"What could we possibly gain from that, sir?"

Dad never calls anyone sir.

"You're coming *when?*"

"I'm sorry, you'll have to repeat that. Are you sure?"

Dad's face is ashen white, his shoulders slumped. What could be bad enough to make matters worse for him?

After hanging up, he retreats to his bedroom and hastily shuts the door. I am flipping through a recipe folder, wondering how Mom made a lemon meringue pie and just how difficult it can be. I can hear the floorboards squeak as Dad paces back and forth.

Finally he emerges to use the phone.

"Yes, Pastor, it's John. Would you be able to come over? We're having a little family conference, and I'm needing some advice. Some counsel, I suppose."

—⁓—

From our kitchen table you can see the setting sun, and as we wait for Pastor Davis, the memories in this room threaten to smother me. Each plaque on the wall, every bent fork holds some memory of her. From where I sit, I can see a pair of her shoes inside the bedroom door. I bite my lip.

Ben has stopped by. He comes and goes without warning, always avoiding the cops who sometimes sit a few houses down when they're not off solving other crimes. Liz and Tony are here too.

Pastor Davis is welcomed by my father and they sit down together, Dad clutching a sheet of paper and squinting in a thoughtful way.

"I don't know how to handle this other than to tell you all that I just had a phone call with some rather...well, bizarre revelations. I wanted to tell you about them and see what you think."

We sit in silence, waiting for more. He has done this throughout the years. I don't know if he enjoys the suspense or forgets where he's going.

"First off, someone is launching a lawsuit against Pastor Pedro." There is more silence.

"Over what?" says Tony at last.

Dad glances at our pastor, as if he should tell us something he can't possibly know.

"A lawyer by the name of Gregory Blanton from Great Falls called a little bit ago," says Dad, glancing at the sheet of paper in his hand. "He is asking me to testify in a court of law against this faith healer. He says Pastor Pedro is liable for my wife's death and the death of a dozen others. Says he has two other witnesses in this state alone who are willing to come forward. People who have lost loved ones in a similar way. He would like to hold a trial in our little town, something that would play in his favor if permission is granted."

Pastor Davis leans forward. "I'm sorry, John, but you'll have to explain this to me."

"I mentioned to you that we went to this healing crusade. This Pedro character pronounced Ruthie healed and threw out her medication. He's done the same thing with dozens of others. Ordered them to stop their prescriptions, to stop seeing doctors, to trust God."

"He's a snake oil salesman," interjects Ben.

"Why did you go see him?" the pastor asks.

"I don't know. Desperate times, I suppose. Ruthie wanted it."

Pastor Davis pats Dad's knee and nods as if he understands.

"What could you possibly gain from such a lawsuit, John?"

Ben interrupts again. "Money, for one thing."

"I don't know," says my father. "I've been thinking about false hope. I can still see the looks in people's eyes that night. They haunt me. The wheelchairs that will never make it to the platform because there's no ramp. The people who follow this guy around the country, living for the next meeting, hoping for something they cannot have. I'd like to stop that, I suppose. But I'm not interested in reliving this thing in court. The last thing we need is a circus coming to town. I don't want Ruthie to be remembered that way."

Ben looks disappointed, but Tony nods his head in agreement. Liz is uncharacteristically silent.

"The other bit of news is just as disturbing. Maybe more so," says Dad, frowning at the sheet in his hand. "This Blanton character informs me that Pastor Pedro used to live around here. I think he's crazy, but he claims Pedro goes by this name to cover up his real one."

Once again Dad lapses into silence.

"Yes?" says Tony. "Continue."

"His real name is Francis Frank."

The only eyes that don't bug out belong to Ben.

"Come on," says Tony. "No way."

Ben clears his throat and leans forward. "I've known this awhile," he says, as if he is here in some official capacity. "Almost a year now. Dad, I think it's time we called them together."

"Who?"

Ben smiles. "You know who."

# thirty-nine

# The Stranger

Most of what I have learned in life I have learned from books or from hiding behind doorways, listening to conversations not intended for my ears. You have to move quietly if you are going to learn this way. You discover which doorknobs squeak and which floorboards yelp. You learn how to mute the click of a door handle and which brand of shoes travels quietest.

Tonight, as midnight approaches, I am at it again, sitting on my bed, listening carefully. In the living room, someone has flipped on a light, and a crack in my partially open door allows a sliver of it to filter through. The bed beside mine is empty now. Danny's pillow and knapsack are gone. I entertain a sense of sadness staring at the unrumpled covers. Liz is asleep, but the rest of us are wide awake.

For the past few minutes the men have been arriving, and though I'm a little upset at not being invited, you couldn't pay me to miss this. I should have asked Michael to bug the living room. It would have made things easier.

One by one they are helping themselves to generous slices of lemon meringue pie. I can tell by the clanging of knives and forks. When they have filled their plates, Pastor Davis welcomes them into the living room like he's standing at the back of a church. The reviews of my pie are glowing. "Not bad at all," says some official-looking cop Ben has brought along. "Who made it?"

Tony answers proudly, "My little brother, Terry. He cooks around here. My sister just about killed us."

Mr. Brown shakes hands with the pastor and nods a formal greeting to Mr. Swanson and my dad. As he squats on the sofa between them he keeps one suspicious eye on the thick wedge of pie, as if it is a promise that might not be kept. His hair is slicked back, and he is wearing his funeral suit. I smile to see the three of them together, recalling the picture Ben and I have found so intriguing. It's hard to believe they were friends all those years ago. They seem so formal now.

I congratulate myself on the vantage point. From here I can see every facial expression and hear every word.

The back door opens, and I strain for clues of who it could be. Whoever it is, he's getting a nasty welcome from Harry. The dog is snarling a low snarl that won't quit. "Hey," yells Ben, "cut it out." Grabbing the hound by the collar he pulls him across the linoleum, pushes him through my door and shuts it tightly. "Quiet, boy." I slowly push the door back open in time to hear a nasally voice I'd know anywhere.

"Hello, sorry I'm late…so uh—" It is Mr. Sprier, the world's slimmest skinny-dipper. What's he doing here? Is he here to rat on me? Apparently not, for I hear him sawing himself a piece of pie, and soon he is shaking hands too.

They sit in silence on sofas and chairs, munching happily at my handiwork. The grin on my face is part gratification from watching them eat, but more than that, it comes from the feeling you get when the cast is assembled for the last chapter in an Agatha Christie novel.

"I'd like to offer my condolences, Mr. Anderson." Mr. Sprier's twangy voice breaks the awkward silence. "She certainly was a fine woman, and—" Others join in, and Dad bows his head shyly as they speak of my mother's life. Though they are kind, the courteous words lack the warmth you'd expect from old friends.

With everyone quiet at last, Ben thanks them for coming and introduces the cop. He then explains what our family already learned at the dinner table. That Francis Frank may have a new identity. His audience is as surprised as we were and just as unconvinced. But the very mention of his name causes them to lean forward with interest. Perhaps it is the one thing that unites them, their hatred of this man.

Ben opens a folder and without saying a word passes some photos to my father.

Dad squints at them, and the others gather around him to gawk.

"It's quite a stretch," says Dad. "The looks have changed. He has hair now."

"Try this one then."

They stare at the next photo with incredulity. How I wish I could see it too.

"What I wouldn't give to get my hands on him—" Mr. Brown is angry, but what else is new? "That's him alright. Where'd you get this?"

"Not far from here," says Ben, grinning proudly, and I can't help recalling the camera gear and the makeshift photo studio in the cave. "You just have to hang out in the right places."

He gives all of them a chance to look at the photos, Tony included, before continuing. "As you know, all of you were taken in by Mr. Frank's little scheme many years ago. He got away with it for a while but was eventually sentenced. Twenty years, I believe it was. At the original trial he was ordered to pay back several million, but a few years ago a judge dismissed that. With model behavior he served just over six. Then, after his parole, he pretty much dropped off the map."

"And surfaced here." Mr. Brown curses and then quickly apologizes. He is furious. The others struggle to process the news as well.

"He's done his time," says Dad, shaking his head. "Last I checked there's no law against changing your name. No law against starting over."

From my limited vantage point, I can barely see Mr. Swanson's pudgy face, but his voice carries well through the crack in the door. "There should be laws against cheating your friends, though. We were so close once. We were inseparable, all of us, remember?"

Mr. Sprier has yet to say anything, but he is nodding along in agreement, his Adam's apple bobbing for air.

Dad looks about the room at the somber faces. "He started out with the best of intentions. I believe that. Money is a useful thing. But it can turn men's hearts black. Good men. Godly men. I've seen it happen. We've all seen it happen. Speaking of being close, I stood on the stage just inches from him the other night." He laughs softly, but no one else finds humor in it. "You'd think I would have known."

"I had no idea either when I started out on this," says Ben. "It's hard for any of us to believe. Our good old pastor from the south, the one with the thick rulebook. He's Pastor Pedro. One and the same. The Spanish accent could use some work though, don't you think?"

Dad frowns. "How do you know?"

"I've followed him through four states, watching these healing services. I've seen more than you care to know. He was a little slippery though, until last week."

It's another on a long list of surprises for my dad. "Ben, tell them your role in this thing."

"Some of you may have heard I had a little run-in with the police in Seattle."

Dad fidgets a little. "How could I forget?" he mumbles.

"When they discovered where I grew up, the Fraud Commission talked me into gathering information on this Pastor Pedro and his self-appointed board of directors. It was a no-brainer for me. Find out something about some preacher man, and they promised they'd wipe the drugs from my record."

Dad looks at Ben with a mixture of admiration and regret.

"A few years ago his ministry went global. Then the allegations of financial abuse started. We were given a tip that he was Francis Frank, and once we established that, we started poking around his past. We had to snoop a bit, but it didn't take long to find people who were willing to talk. There are some rather strong feelings in this town, to say the least. People were taken for a lot of money. And that wasn't all. I discovered that he fathered at least two children here, both of whose mothers have disappeared."

My mouth has been open for the entire conversation, but it drops a little more at this. The information doesn't seem to startle Ben's other listeners though.

Clearing his throat, the cop enters the discussion in a monotonous drone. "For what it's worth, we started doing a little surveillance on this mansion he's holed up in. It's not far from here. Under our tax laws his ministry isn't legally obligated to make its finances public because it's a religious organization. Most churches and ministries release financial information voluntarily, but he has never submitted to any form of accountability. And there are no public records for how much the ministry makes or how the money is spent. Of course, Pastor Pedro insists that every penny is spent on the Lord's work. But the confidential financial records we've uncovered from inside this ministry tell another tale. For instance, here's a small sampling from his latest trip."

He hauls out an envelope and everyone gathers around. The envelope is a familiar one. I've held it in my hands. I've seen its contents up close. Thankfully he doesn't bring out the pictures, just the financial papers.

"He was in Leningrad, Russia, for a week of meetings in the spring. Then on a four-day trip to Amsterdam. Here, you can see for yourself. Each hotel room was two thousand bucks a night. The rooms had waterfalls. Room service was fifteen hundred and chauffeur services exceeded that. He handed out tips to the staff at the Victoria Hotel, and the smallest was a hundred-dollar bill.

Here are notes proving that he is routinely given five thousand bucks to spend for no apparent reason. Petty cash, I guess."

"But what about *our* money?" For the first time Mr. Swanson is in full view, pacing the room, clenching and unclenching his fat little fists. "I invested everything I had in this scam artist, and I've been paying ever since. What about the lawsuit? That'll help us get it back, won't it?"

"It's gone," shrugs Mr. Brown. "Nothing we can do. All of us got taken. We'll never see it again."

Mr. Sprier still has not said a word. He wriggles his nostrils in a nervous little gesture as Mr. Swanson sits down again. Finally he speaks. "So, if we can't do anything about it, what's this meeting about then, because—?"

The cop adjusts his glasses and glances at Ben, choosing his words carefully. "A few months ago someone inside the organization wanted Francis exposed. He...contacted us."

"Who was it?" asks Dad. "Anyone we know?"

The cop nods to Ben and my brother stands to his feet. "That's why we wanted you together," he says. "We're not sure who he is. He never gave us a name; he just told us he had worked with Pastor Pedro for a lot of years. He had more than just these financial records. He had pictures this Pedro wouldn't want public. We figured you could at least help us find out who he is."

Ben holds up a familiar photo. The one from the *Chronicle*.

No one moves. Mr. Sprier's Adam's apple even stops bouncing.

"Would any of you happen to know this man?" Ben asks, pointing at the face he's already circled in pencil. The face of the stranger at our door.

My dad exhales loudly. "That's Clive, isn't it? Clive Barker?"

Ben turns the photo a little and squints at it before laying it on the coffee table in plain view. "Clive was our informant," he says. "It's been two weeks since the police pulled his body from the back of that green Charger."

# forty

# The Sixth Man

The single shot that killed Clive Barker came not from the pistol my brother Ben was packing but from a Desert Eagle .357 Magnum with a revolving bolt. It is the least of the surprises awaiting us as the cop reviews select details from the police report. Though the clock has just passed midnight, no one, including me, is in danger of nodding off.

I am sitting cross-legged on the floor, wondering if the guilty party could be here in our very own living room. The truth of it is, everyone looks guilty. Even Tony, who's been sitting there speechless.

As the report is read, each one listens intently. My heart is pounding inside me at each new revelation, and my chin is dropping lower than ever I thought it could.

According to the coroner, the bullet entered Clive's chest between his third and fourth ribs sometime Sunday afternoon about the time I was climbing our poplar tree. Few clues existed, though the empty shell was located along a gravel road leading past Mr. Racher's cornfield. Apparently the killer had driven the green Charger from the crime scene to Three Tree Gap where the body was abandoned in the backseat, its hand curled around the Magnum.

After a few phone calls, local police determined that the car was registered to a Clive Barker in Great Falls, but the address was as phony as a three-dollar bill, and the death was labeled a suicide. Though a few local youth came forward with evidence, their stories made no sense, and the sheriff chalked it up to either mischief or personal vendettas.

What our fledgling police force could not know is that two weeks earlier, Mr. Barker had made contact with the Fraud Commission, promising to hand them some rather unflattering information about Pedro, the now infamous healer. Requesting nothing in return, the informant said he wanted only to clear his conscience.

The cop lowers his glasses and looks up from the documents as if he needs someone's permission to continue. "He only made contact with us twice. The best we can figure is that the killer wanted something this Barker had and was willing to murder him for it. We now know what that something is."

Everyone in the room sucks in breath as if they were rehearsing it. Tony seems to be in shock. They don't prepare you for this in Bible college.

"There wasn't much to go on at first," continues the cop, pacing back and forth, holding a thick envelope behind his back. "We found a ring on the fourth finger of his right hand, but that wasn't much of a help."

He continues, but his words have me gasping aloud.

*What? That's impossible!*

"I've got the ring," I whisper to Harry. "It's in my drawer. You mean he had two?"

Harry looks up at me and cocks his head. "Humans," he must be thinking. "I sure wish he'd get me a waffle."

"What did it look like?" My father's words jar me back from this new reality.

"You mean the ring?"

"Yes."

"I don't remember exactly. It was gold, I think. Had some small diamonds and a blue stone."

"You mean a sapphire. Like this one?" Mr. Brown stands to his feet and lifts a gold chain from his neck. On it is a heavy ring, which he removes and hands to the startled officer.

"Where'd you get it?" asks the cop.

"We all had them. All six of us."

"You've kept yours all these years?" Dad smiles.

"Yep. Looks like Clive did too."

The cop turns Mr. Brown's ring over and over in his hand. "Tell me more about this Clive Barker."

No one answers, so Mr. Swanson speaks for them. "Clive was the only one that stayed on with Pastor Frank after the rest of us called it quits. You can see him in the picture. He was the tallest of us, always wore that Stetson hat. We had a nasty falling out, but for some reason Clive believed in this charlatan when the rest of us were ready to hang him, if you'll pardon me."

He looks at the others, none of whom will deny they've wanted to lynch him at one time or another.

"Clive held to this belief that they were embarking on some noble cause that would change the world," adds my dad. "I talked to him often many years ago. Tried to straighten him out. But there was no listening. There never was—" His voice trails off.

Dad turns his attention to the coffee table, lifts the photo from it, and smiles. "If you look closely, you can actually see one of those rings on my finger—here," he says, pointing. Everyone leans forward again. "Boy, I've put on weight." Dad pats his belly. "Francis bought these expensive rings for us and had a symbol stamped inside," he explains. "'The Circle of Six,' he called us. Mine is in a drawer somewhere."

"I haven't worn mine in years," Mr. Swanson chuckles. "Can't get it on my finger."

My dad turns to Mr. Sprier. "Sorry you got cut out of the

picture, Norm. You're a little blurry there in the background. All we can see is part of your smile."

"I got cut out of a lot of things in those days, so—" he says regretfully. It's the first time I've heard his raspy voice in a while.

"You're right," says Dad. "I'm sorry. If it's any consolation, you're the only one of us that actually lost weight since this picture."

The cop removes his glasses and slides them into his shirt pocket. He opens the brown envelope with Ben's name on the front and tosses the graphic pictures on the coffee table.

No one makes a move toward them. They can tell the nature of the photos from where they are seated. They know why someone would go to any lengths to make sure they didn't surface. And they know that someone is Pastor Pedro.

—⁓—

Never in a million years did I think I would solve a murder mystery. Though I often lay awake dreaming of it, not once in my short lifetime did I presume upon my tiny brain to put together a puzzle this large. But the pieces are clicking into place tonight.

As the cop tosses the envelope down beside the pictures, I flinch the kind of involuntary flinch you experience when you're dropping off to sleep and your limbs start to relax. Harry is as startled by it as I am.

It's not the graphic photos in the envelope or the fact that one of the men is sweating profusely. It's not the realization that the evidence was out there all along, just waiting for me to bump into it. But suddenly the truth whacks me dead on the forehead with all the force of a well-aimed tomato.

The proof has been lurking in my dresser drawer for nigh unto two weeks.

Harry hops down as I jump up from the bed, trembling. Opening the drawer, I fish around a little until I have it in my hand. For once in my life I've figured something out before everyone else on the block has. For once in my life a light comes on, and it's not the headlights of an oncoming truck. Pushing the door open, I stride boldly into the living room, restraining Harry with one hand, clutching Exhibit A with the other.

Everyone is startled to see me. Tony lifts his head and gapes at me like I'm sleepwalking. The rest seem plain annoyed. They've had enough surprises for one night. "Did you…want something, Son?" asks Dad.

I am careful to keep my eyes from the coffee table as I hold my clenched fist in front of me and address the only one in the room who has not finished a piece of my lemon meringue pie.

"Do you have your ring, Mr. Sprier?" I am not trying to sound arrogant or proud or disrespectful. The truth is, I'm a little nervous.

"What?" Mr. Sprier's Adam's apple won't behave, and he looks fearfully about him, his eyes roving desperately from his former friends to the cop and back to me again. "Yes, I'm sure I—" he stammers for the words.

"No, I don't think so," I say, opening my fist and holding the gold ring in front of him. "I've got it here. I doubt anyone else can fit this ring. Their fingers are too…well, too fat."

"Where did you—?" It's one more sentence he will never finish.

"I found it on the floor of a green Charger, sir. Just below the body you left there. I know I shouldn't have taken it. Stolen it, really. I—I'm sorry. Here, it's yours."

Mr. Sprier extends his hand and takes the telltale ring. How he was careless enough to drop it on the floor of the Charger I will never know. But he knows what everyone else in the room knows. Sometimes denial is as useful as pulling in your stomach when you step on the weigh scales.

# forty-one

# Graduation Day

It wasn't easy taking the nondescript interior of Grace Community Hall and turning it into an Arabian castle, but the graduation planning committee has done a stunning job. Giant sheets mask a decaying ceiling, and watercolor poster board is curled into ancient columns ten feet high. Dark curtains cover the windows too, and a desert backdrop brightens the stage. If you stand back a ways and squint real hard, you'd half expect Lawrence of Arabia to come galloping over a sand dune and challenge someone to a duel.

After a dozen years in the classroom, a thousand practical jokes, and a million late assignments, the graduating class has finally donned its caps and gowns in nervous anticipation of the commencement exercises.

Everyone in the audience seems to be holding a camera. I guess we've never looked better.

I survey the audience to see who's there. My family is, every one of them. Mom is up in heaven pointing me out to the disciples. I just know it. Mr. Sprier is noticeably absent, but Miss Thomas sits erect and sober, ready to lead the choir when the time comes. No one has told me what I got on my final math exam. I guess it doesn't matter anymore.

It's been a week since the arrest was made. Since a blubbering math teacher watched in horror as I figured out an equation he never thought I'd solve. He couldn't stop talking there in our living room when he knew the gig was up. Couldn't stop kicking himself for wearing that loose ring, for abandoning the body where he did, for being so cotton-pickin' careless. I guess he'd waited all evening to say something, and once he had his ring back he was ready to talk. Perhaps it was the lemon meringue pie that loosened his lips, I do not know.

There were few surprises in Mr. Sprier's confession, and strangely I found myself feeling sorry for the poor man as he weaved his way through the sordid details of the crime. I think I glimpsed a little bit of myself in him when he blubbered his confession, for I knew if I did not mend my ways that could be me one day, standing before a jury, confessing some crimes of my own.

It's funny how an eighteen-year-old is surprised to discover that his parents had lives and friends and hopes and dreams long before he entered the world. For my dad, those friends were a group called the Circle of Six, young men eager to serve God—until they were sidelined by a swindler. Down through the years Mr. Francis Frank, alias Pastor Pedro, tried to fill the void in his life with broken commandments. And whenever they were in danger of being uncovered, he paid the sixth man in the photograph quite handsomely to keep things secret.

Mr. Sprier was the perfect man for the job. Single and a loner, he was teased incessantly as a child and would gladly blur the edges to be included, to gain someone's approval. It was harmless enough at first. But you open the door to one vice and a greater one will follow.

Whenever Mr. Sprier tried to back out, Pedro threatened to expose some of his own sins and addictions, the least of which was skinny-dipping with Miss Thomas. And when Pastor Pedro learned Clive Barker was about to go public with information that would undoubtedly bring his international charade to an end, Mr. Sprier was handed a pistol and called on for one final favor. A favor he'll be paying for the rest of his life.

As I stood there listening to his painful confession, I noticed tears rolling down my father's face, and I remembered his words to me when I was young. "If you hold sin close enough you won't see its ugly face." It's a lot like encountering piranhas in a muddy creek, I suppose. They have a way of biting you in the end.

And so that very night, after the arrest had been made and the goodnights said, after my brother Tony had patted my back and Ben and I had shared the last piece of pie in the pan, I knelt in my room and prayed a sincere prayer, asking for forgiveness and the strength to change.

It wasn't an ending; it was a start.

Last Sunday I sat in church beside Tony, listening carefully for the first time in a while. Danny Brown was with me, and Tony was doodling pictures of Mr. Sprier and Francis Frank behind bars. I told him to pay attention to the sermon, to act a little mature for a change, but he kept handing me things. He drew the number thirteen hundred and twelve on the bulletin and pushed it in front of me.

I was curious, so I whispered, "What's that?"

"Thirteen people I'm writing letters to. One has become a Christian, and two are on the way. I can hardly keep up with it all."

"Think you'll get a book published?"

"Oh yeah."

"Ssshh," said my brother Ben.

Tony stopped talking and scribbled something on the paper. I grabbed it from him. It said, "Mr. Prisoner."

I took his pencil and wrote, "What's that?"

He whispered, "Anagram for 'Norm Sprier.'"

I shook my head.

"With a name like that you should have known he was guilty all along."

I told him to be quiet. I'm a successful detective now. I could have his room bugged and his phone tapped.

The class of '82 walks the aisle to the vigorous poundings of an out-of-tune piano, courtesy of Pastor Davis' bubbly wife, Irene. With everyone seated, our little three-piece band takes nervously to the stage.

Dave Hofer and Michael and I have been practicing almost every night since we learned we were playing, and though this is not Carnegie Hall, it's a close second. We've chosen an old southern gospel song, a style people love in this part of the world. We took a vote on who should sing, and I was elected two to one.

My voice is only slightly lower than the one Mr. Sprier is known for, but I close my eyes and sing directly into the microphone: "And I know, yes I know, Jesus' blood can make the vilest sinner clean." Dave thunks an acoustic bass, and Michael squints at sheet music as if he were playing a keyboard for the very first time. No one turns down the volume as we play, though there are moments I wish they would.

When I rise to receive my diploma, my brother Ben, who is holding a wriggly little Allan, stands to his feet too. Tony joins him and then Liz and Dad. I'm a little embarrassed, to be sure, and when I notice that a ripple effect has begun—that the rest of the crowd is joining them—I hang my head, not knowing what to do. I guess it's everyone's way of saying they are cheering for us Andersons. And more than that, it's their way of honoring my mother.

As our class scrunches together on the risers to be blinded by flash cameras, I can't help smiling at Danny Brown and Mary Beth Swanson. They are sitting side by side in the very front row. Danny is making faces at me as if we're back in eighth grade. He will walk the aisle in a week, graduating from the Grace Public School on the other side of the creek. I won't miss it.

The night of my mother's funeral, Danny showed up at the house to pack his belongings. I sat on my bed, watching him straighten the covers on his little cot and shove some clothes and a pillow in a backpack. I cleared my throat and muttered that I had something to tell him.

The words wouldn't come out quite right, as if I were speaking to Mary Beth. But finally I managed to tell him about the Blackhawks cap, how it got where it did, and how I ratted on him to the police. "I'm so sorry," I said, "I can't believe I did it." And I lowered my head, thinking he would be less likely to kill me if he couldn't see my guilty face.

He paused for a minute while the shock wore off. Then, instead of smacking me like I thought he would, he said, "Terry, I know I'm supposed to forgive you because I was reading that I'm supposed to in the Bible somewhere. I don't feel like it at all. In fact I feel like braining you, but I'm gonna give this forgiveness thing a try and see what happens."

I winced a little because I had one more favor to ask of him.

I said, "Danny, while I'm at it, I need you to forgive me for one more thing." He gave me a look that let me know that I'd already pushed things far enough, but I pressed onward.

"Danny," I said, "for one very long week I have hated you for stealing my girl."

He didn't move for a full ten seconds. Then he started to laugh. And he couldn't stop himself. In fact, he fell completely off the bed smacking both elbows on the metal bed frame, and still it was funny to him.

It took him a minute longer to regain his breath, but when he tried to speak, he started laughing again. Finally, he inhaled deeply and said, "Mary Beth is a great girl, don't get me wrong. But you can have her. She's my second cousin. I can't believe you didn't know that."

I can't believe it either. Seems half this town is related.

—◆—

The night before graduation I finally got the nerve to ask Mary Beth to go out with me. I knew she'd probably said yes already to someone better looking or smarter or possibly even her height. But I couldn't have lived in the same room with myself if I didn't ask.

I hopped the fence and stood boldly in her yard, tossing pebbles at her second-story window. I had momentary visions of Mr. Swanson opening it and pouring hot oil on me and maybe some chicken feathers, but when the window groaned upward the most gorgeous face I've ever seen smiled down at me.

"Um," I said, "tomorrow I graduate." And my mind went completely blank.

The smile on her face grew even wider. "I know," she said, "May I come watch?"

I said, "I'd like you to go to Great Falls with me after the ceremony. I don't know exactly what we'll do when we get there, but I've saved up a little money." I said this as clearly as people you hear on the radio.

She said, "How will we get there? By bus?"

I said, "No, your cousin Danny has a car, and it's not anything special, but it runs because Liz fixed it. Some mice built a nest in the air cleaner, but she found them and cleaned it out. It's as good as new."

Mary Beth couldn't help but laugh.

"She's showing mechanical abilities, you know, my sister. My dad is real proud."

"So it will be the three of us then?"

It was my turn to smile. "No, Liz told Danny he was taking her to Great Falls too. He had no choice. How does four sound?"

"I'd like that very much."

"You sure your dad won't kill me?"

"Nah. He's been telling me about you. Seems you made quite an impression on him the other night."

She flicked her hair a little and blew the blond bangs away from her forehead. "What would you like me to wear?" she asked.

I didn't even have to think about it. "Those jean pullovers," I said, "if you don't mind."

# forty-two

# Will

In the summer of my eighteenth year I got my girl back. My faith too. I wish it had happened another way. But it didn't. I wish I had learned enough lessons to last me a lifetime. But greater ones lay ahead.

One thing I've learned is this: You'll find grace in the most unlikely places if you don't mind looking for it. That summer of my youth I found it where I never dreamed I would: In the way an atheist forgave his wayward wife, for one thing. You see, the same day I said goodbye to my mother for the last time, Danny Brown said hello to his.

All his life he'd been informed by an unkind and insensitive father that his mother was dead, but she'd been alive all these years.

Danny didn't formally meet her until the night of my mother's funeral, when he packed up his little knapsack and pillow and headed for home. That's when he discovered that the woman his father had been living with the last few weeks had a wedding ring on her finger and was none other than Pearl Brown, the mother he had never known.

They sat him down on the sofa that very night and fumbled around awhile and then told him the plain truth. Many years ago Francis Frank had needed a secretary, and Pearl seemed the ideal choice. She could type 80 words a minute and make a fabulous cup of coffee, and she was awfully pretty too. Those were precisely the credentials Mr. Frank was looking for. Danny's father disagreed rather vehemently with her accepting the appointment, of course, for it meant she would leave town immediately with the reverend, who was being chased by people who had been swindled, folks with loaded shotguns in the back windows of their pickups.

That's pretty much all they said about it, but Danny isn't dumb.

He knows more than you think.

He knew enough to ask a few more questions and then put his arms around them both and cry like a baby. He knew enough to tell them he'd been forgiven too, that he knew what it felt like, that he was qualified to offer some himself. They were more than a little surprised at this, as you might expect, but they come to church now, reeking of smoke and not entirely enjoying every aspect of the service. Danny just keeps praying it will be another link in a long chain of grace pulling Mr. and Mrs. Brown into the light.

My father and Mr. Brown have much in common when they meet for coffee once a week. They both had their wives stolen, in a sense, and they were both scammed out of their life savings.

Yet what I see each time I look in my father's face is nothing short of the greatest wonder ever. Joy.

Tonight I ask him how he can find wonder in a world where tragedy happens and disappointments abound. A world where your wife gets taken before her time, where your future is uncertain and your children don't always behave themselves. He smiles at the question but has to think about it for a while.

"Terry," he says, "I'm a simple man. You wanna know how simple? Did you know that every day I set the alarm clock a half hour early?"

I didn't know this, of course. If I had a choice, I'd set mine two hours late.

"It's because I like to wake up and think that I've got another half hour to sleep in. It's crazy, I know. I hit the snooze button three times a day."

"I don't know what that has to do with my question," I say.

"Me neither." Dad laughs for a full ten seconds before continuing.

"When your mother and I first set foot in this town, we prayed we'd change the world. I thought this ministry would be just the thing. But the dream fell through. I guess my dreams have always been too small. God used your mother's illness to bring about things I could never have imagined."

I want to ask him again how he could smile when things have been so awful, but he's already ahead of me.

"After all these years and all the things I've seen, I still find each day too short for all the prayers I want to pray, all the books I want to read, and all the friends I want to see. The longer I live, the more I'm coming to love God. And the more I love Him, the more I find to be thankful for. When I was cheated out of my life savings, I had a choice: get even or get going. I decided to paddle around an island called Grace. The sins of others aren't as big as your own on that island, Terry. And the shoreline is always full of wonders.

"If I ever get to heaven, the wonders there will never cease. But I think I'll find three right away. First I'll meet some people I didn't expect to see. Second, I'll be surprised at who is missing. But the greatest wonder of all will be to find myself there. I can't stop smiling when I think about that."

—⁓—

I sometimes have a dream in which I see my mother walking hand in hand with Jesus, along dazzling streets I cannot describe. She peeks over a fluffy white cloud, points directly to me, and says proudly, "That's my boy. Take care of him will You? You know what's down the road." And Jesus replies, "Ah yes, I do. But don't worry, Ruthie, I'll be down that road too. I always have been."

I will never forget the words Mom said to me the night she left for Home. They're tucked away in the ancient book of Lamentations in the Old Testament. They are underlined and circled now in a worn-out Bible my mother left me. A Bible I read whenever I remember to. A time or two I've even read it out loud to Mary Beth during long talks we have:

> I remember my affliction and my wandering...my soul is downcast within me. Yet this I call to mind and therefore I have hope: Because of the Lord's great love we are not consumed, for his compassions never fail. They are new every morning; great is your faithfulness.

---

It was a Friday evening when the news came.

With graduation a distant memory and my lawn care business in full bloom, the timing was right, I suppose.

I remember the fields that hot summer night, woven into a patchwork masterpiece, all golden and yellow and green. I remember walking slowly westward into the setting sun. The air was hazy that night, and we gazed across those fields together at the amber glint of our creek as it wound its way from the mighty Missouri and to the Musselshell in a lazy circle. Thick clouds had blocked the sun, but when Mary Beth reached over and took my hand I almost needed sunglasses, so bright was my world.

A car sped up behind us quickly, startling us from conversation. It was Danny's Pinto, and Tony was at the wheel. He rolled down the passenger side window, breathless as a gerbil on a treadmill.

"Hurry up," he said, "something's happened."

My mind was swirling with possibilities as we climbed in—

none of them good. The only consolation was the tightness of the seating arrangements there in the Pinto.

"What's going on?" I asked, still inebriated by Mary Beth's perfume.

"Where were you?" he said. "I've been looking everywhere."

"What's wrong," I asked. "Who is it?"

"It's Dad. He wanted me to find you. Said he has some urgent news."

I bid Mary Beth a hasty goodnight and promised I would say a better one later. Then I walked into our living room, the sight of some startling revelations already this summer.

The rest of the family was seated there, waiting impatiently. Dad looked happy to see me, but he wore his puzzled frown too.

"You live all your life without hearing from a lawyer, and you're fine," he said as I sat down. "This summer I've heard from two."

There was silence. Way too much of it.

"Come on, Dad," said Liz. "What is it? We don't have all night."

"I don't know how else to say this, except to tell you that Monday morning a big-city lawyer is coming out to see us. He called this afternoon, claiming he has the last will and testament of Ruth Anderson."

We tried to catch our breath, all of us.

"She...had a will?" said Ben, his mouth hanging wide.

"Seems your mother left behind a few surprises for you."

"That's it?" Tony asked. "You don't know any more?"

"I'm sorry," said Dad, "I just need you to be here at ten o'clock. I don't know if this guy is the genuine article or what, but you need to be here. Take an hour off work at least."

"You can't leave it there, Dad," I said, knowing I was speaking for the others.

"I'm sorry, you'll just have to wait. So do I."

He smiled and chuckled, and then he shook his head rather vigorously and broke out in a full-fledged laugh. "She was always full of surprises, my Ruthie. She's left a legacy behind for all of us. It would appear she's left a few other things as well."

# The Edge of the World

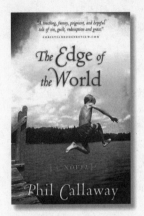

*"You're not much good until
you find out how bad you are."*

—⁊⁊⁊—

**Y**oung Terry Anderson lives in the small town of Grace. He asks honest questions—"If God wants me happy, why do I have to sit through church?"—and notices what adults sometimes miss—"Arthur Tucker, the local barber, never looks you in the eye. He looks you straight in the hair, sizing you up, wondering if you shouldn't have just a little more off the top."

When Terry stumbles onto a startling secret that promises to right all wrongs, his life suddenly comes to a crossroads. Rather than taking his discovery to the proper authorities, Terry tries to use it to his own advantage and becomes entangled in a web of unexpected consequences and inner turmoil.

Inspired by the godly example of an older brother and impassioned by his secret admiration for the prettiest girl in town, Terry knows the right thing to do. He just can't bring himself to do it.

*A tender coming-of-age novel that probes the deep issues of life and faith through the unguarded honesty of youth.*

"Deftly written…sentimental and nostalgic."
—*CBA Marketplace*

$\mathcal{P}$hil Callaway is editor of Prairie Bible Institute's *Servant* magazine and author of fifteen books, including *I Used to Have Answers, Now I Have Kids; Making Life Rich Without Any Money; With God on the Golf Course;* and *Who Put My Life on Fast Forward?* Most weekends find him taking a message of laughter, hope, and joy to conferences, churches, marriage retreats, and events like Promise Keepers. A frequent guest on national radio and television, Phil partners with Compassion, an international Christian child-development agency. His writings have won more than a dozen international awards and have been translated into Spanish, Chinese, Portuguese, Dutch, Polish, and English (one of which he speaks fluently). His five-part video series "The Big Picture" is being viewed in 80,000 churches worldwide. To find out about Phil's other books or tapes, check out his website at www.philcallaway.com. To request a complimentary one-year subscription to *Servant,* write

Servant Magazine
PO Box 4000
Three Hills, Alberta Canada
T0M 2N0

# Also by
## Phil Callaway

**THE EDGE OF THE WORLD**
When young Terry Anderson stumbles onto a hidden stash of money, his life suddenly comes to a crossroads. The mystery leads him to even more amazing discoveries in a town called Grace.

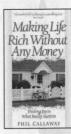

**MAKING LIFE RICH WITHOUT ANY MONEY**
Find joy in what really matters! Columnist and speaker Phil Callaway identifies six characteristics of rich people—characteristics that have nothing to do with money and everything to do with wealth. Convenient mass-market size.

**WHO PUT MY LIFE ON FAST-FORWARD?**
Callaway's personal stories and those gleaned from millionaires, CEOs, and "regular folks so tired they can hardly lace their Velcro tennis shoes" show how God can help us live deliberately in a high-speed culture.

**WITH GOD ON THE GOLF COURSE**
Although Callaway offers no guarantee for a lower golf score, he does provide 40 short devotionals full of wisdom, grace, humor, and enjoyable reflections on the sport Mark Twain called "a good walk ruined."

HARVEST HOUSE
PUBLISHERS